A (VERY) PUBLIC
SCHOOL
AΠ ABBOT PETER MYSTERY
MURDER

SIMON PARKE

Marylebone House

First published in Great Britain in 2016

Marylebone House
36 Causton Street
London SW1P 4ST
www.marylebonehousebooks.co.uk

British Library Cataloguing-in-Publication Data
A catalogue record for this book is available from the British Library

ISBN 978–1–910674–34–5
ISBN 978–1–910674–35–2

Typeset by Graphicraft Limited, Hong Kong
First printed in Great Britain by Ashford Colour Press
Subsequently digitally printed in Great Britain

eBook by Graphicraft Limited, Hong Kong

Produced on paper from sustainable forests

Acknowledgements

My thanks to Shellie Wright, Rebecca Parke and Elizabeth Spradbery for bringing their keen eyes to the fourth draft of the manuscript; they made it better. I am also indebted to Karl French, for his encouragement and insightful edit of the sixth draft. And finally, to Alison Barr who was there at the beginning of the Abbot Peter story; and who thought it would be a good idea if he was let loose for another adventure now. Here's to many more.

Author's note

Stormhaven Towers is a creation of fiction, as are the characters who people the place. But Stormhaven is less fictional – a thinly disguised version of Seaford, set between Newhaven and Eastbourne on the Sussex coast. Any geography or history on display in this story is probably true.

It was their last exchange,

after fourteen years of relatively happy marriage, her words; and she's awkward when remembering that unhappy conversation . . .

'An issue has arisen, a serious one,' says Jamie, head of Stormhaven Towers public school.

'Oh?'

'A serious issue.'

Jamie's been here for just eighteen months and is still making his mark. It takes time. You can't get rid of the staff you don't want, not immediately at any rate. It takes time to winkle them out from their crevices. And then sometimes events loom up from nowhere, dangerous events that can scupper everything . . . like this one.

'What issue?' says Cressida, in her direct doctorly manner, as if it was probably unimportant, a crying over spilt milk. She has short boyish hair, brown with a fleck of grey, aluminium-framed glasses for reading and is working at home today, sitting on the sofa with a computer on her lap.

'At the review weekend,' he says, not answering her question. The issue is too raw, he doesn't really want to speak about it – or not with Cressida at least. It's every head's nightmare, frankly, and has gatecrashed end-of-term proceedings with brutal force.

The review weekend, at the end of the academic year, is Jamie's idea – a get-together with selected members of staff. What he gains from them, Cressida isn't sure . . . she isn't one for navel-gazing.

'But isn't that what these weekends are for?' she asks, attempting some perspective. 'For issues to arise?'

'Of course, of course,' he replies impatiently. He knows very well that this is precisely what these weekends are for – but surely she could be a bit more sympathetic? No wonder he doesn't tell her anything! 'But this one is serious – really very serious. I don't see a solution.'

And each time he thinks of it, the scene darkens still further. If the news gets out, there'll be dire implications for the school finances, no question. The Japanese will pull out of the summer school project, for a start — and that'll be 'goodbye' to a gold mine the school can ill afford to lose. The Japanese takeover of the school the following summer holidays is funding the new dance and drama wing as well as the new science labs.

But how can the news *not* get out? There's no way Jamie can keep a lid on it. Secrets have a habit of reaching the light eventually; and if cries of 'cover-up!' follow — well, that's the end for the leadership . . . certainly the head. No, he'd have to go public on this one, take the hit — but stay afloat, stay honest and build slowly . . . literally.

'You wouldn't believe what Ferdinand has been up to,' he says.

Though he won't tell her.

'Apart from being clinically dull?' comes the reply. Ferdinand is the school chaplain and Cressida is not interested. She doesn't look up as she speaks, continuing with her work.

Jamie paces around their large drawing room in the headmaster's house, a short walk away from the main school buildings . . . with a walled garden for privacy. He wants her attention; he wants her to ask again what the issue is, so he can say, 'I'm afraid I can't say.' Cressida says he's like a little boy sometimes — well, which man isn't? — and she's been down this path before. His life is spent trying to keep some sort of balance, at least avoiding unmanageable *im*balance and some terrible outbreak of excess.

'Why don't you just explode, Jamie, scream what you feel?' she'd occasionally say to him.

'Oh, I don't think me losing my temper is going to help anyone, Cressida. What's the point in losing my temper?'

'It might help you — and postpone your heart attack by a few years.'

'And anyway, there's nothing I can't handle here.' That would just have to be true. 'Balance is always the better path. No screaming necessary.'

'The better path to where?'

2

And it's harder and harder each year; harder for Jamie to achieve this balance, this is what he finds; and his body – and blood pressure – suffer in the struggle.

'Does it need a solution?' she says, with further disinterest as Jamie continues to prowl. His restless pacing, not uncommon, irritates her; patients at least sit still, she makes sure of that. But Jamie holds so much in, he always has; and he currently resembles a bomb in the room, detonation imminent. They used to laugh about it, make a joke of it, or she did at least . . . but not now, not these days, for the laughter between them has stopped; and Cressida can't stand much more of this.

'Might this mystery issue not just go away during the long summer holiday, Jamie?' The school has just broken up for eight weeks, which leaves her a little envious . . . though Jamie claims there's no break for him, that there's always work to do. 'Eight weeks and a bit of sun can change things. Nothing really matters that much in my experience.'

'This does, dear. This matters – oh, yes!' It was an angry 'dear'. 'And it's not going away – it's hardly got started . . . and the Japanese don't like this sort of thing.'

'The Japanese? I thought they must be involved in some manner.' Cressida is well aware that the Japanese are the new moral yardstick at Stormhaven Towers . . . they've replaced God. If the Japanese like it, then it's good. And if the Japanese don't like it, it's bad. Morality is quite simple now.

Jamie goes to his study; Cressida is proving no help at all. He needs time to think, though his thoughts don't help. His thoughts are a loop of panic about how this will all be perceived, old fears dressed in new clothes – and no fresh thought arriving to break the loop. And yes, Cressida is busy – he knows that, as he gazes out of the window at the manicured lawns and newly planted saplings by the school gates. He shouldn't judge her, she has her own concerns, running a successful medical practice in Church Street . . . He just wishes – he really just wishes . . .

Almost immediately, his mobile strikes up a tune, a short excerpt of Bach. Jamie brings the text onto the small screen . . . and goes pale as he reads. Where had this come from? She'd seemed fine

3

when he last saw her! And what exactly is he to do? Well, he'll have to go – he'll have to go and meet with her. It may be nothing, one can't tell – but at least it's a different worry . . . and one requiring action, which is a relief in itself. He needs to do something.

With the decision made, he returns to the front room where Cressida is still on her laptop – healing hands punching figures onto the screen. Whatever your diagnostic skills as a GP, you have to be good with IT.

'I need to go out,' he says firmly.

'OK. Urgent?'

'Very urgent.' Words spoken with self-importance, as if this is not a matter he can discuss with the likes of her. 'I'll be back soon.'

She doesn't reply, but continues with her statistical analysis of patient footfall in the surgery. It isn't just schools who review their practice; Cressida just prefers to do it alone – and via statistics, a truer sound than any human voice. Jamie gathers his things and wonders about a kiss before he leaves – perhaps on the top of her head, affection without intimacy. But he decides against it, she might think it odd . . . or just not notice. It is as if she doesn't notice him sometimes.

'A dead relationship but a functioning marriage,' was how he'd described it to a friend, after one bottle of wine too many. But maybe this is normal for a marriage – stability of life trumping alienation of the soul; and really, he'd dug this hole for himself by choosing to marry her, so who else was there to blame? It had seemed the easiest thing to do at the time. 'No one else to blame, Jamie!' he'd say to himself in further self-punishment.

He pauses for a moment at the door and looks back into the room, so desirably furnished; and such warmth in the sun through the large patio window. He feels almost unbearably sad, a moment of excess which he must flee.

'Remember when we talked, Cressida?' he says, eyes watering. He holds his pose for a moment, before turning to leave. She doesn't look up and he shuts the door quietly behind him. And pausing for a moment as she sits there – sunlight streaming across the cream and rose carpet, across the expensive parquet flooring – she could. Cressida could remember those days, the days when they'd talked, happier days, *talking* days ... though it was a long time ago now. Their conversation had withered as their bank balance had grown.

And a little over three hours later, the body of Jamie King, head-master of Stormhaven Towers, was found splayed on the rocks, at the foot of Stormhaven Head – at skewered rest by the white cliffs he loved to walk with rucksack and stout shoes in the holidays.

He was hardly the first unhappy soul to end it all here. But suicide – it was a shock for those left behind, the cold ripples were endless.

'Remember when we talked, Cressida?'

ACT ONE

The annual school review

was a new tradition – if such a thing can be – introduced by the new headmaster, Jamie King.

Opinions were mixed about the new man as the honeymoon afforded to all leaders drew to a close and his style became apparent. Some enthused about this straight-talking dynamo, seeing him as a new broom – someone with drive, just what the school needed in these competitive times, when private schools were like rats in a bag. Others were less keen on this insensitive hustler. They found him rather pushy, rather negative compared with his genteel predecessor, Maurice Stone, whom everyone liked – even if the school was flatlining under his rather vague leadership. He would walk some way around a nettle rather than grasp it.

Maurice had been a teacher at heart, and had smelled of blackboards and chalk; whereas the new breed of school heads – and this included Jamie – were primarily businessmen. Oh, they kept a few academic tomes on their office shelves ... but these were for show, for parents mainly. The *Financial Times* was more useful reading.

'I wish you the best of luck,' said Maurice kindly over a slightly awkward tea and biscuits, an unofficial handover from the old head to the new.

'Thank you,' said Jamie.

'There was strong competition for the post,' said Maurice, with a sad smile. Jamie nodded humbly. 'Just never forget ... well, just never forget that Stormhaven Towers is a *school*, old boy.'

Jamie smiled at this well-meaning but deluded educational dinosaur.

'If we're to survive, Maurice, I must never forget it's a business – old boy!'

Maurice may have winced, but things had changed from the old days. Could he not see that? This was now a very competitive

9

marketplace, full of high rollers like Eton, Harrow, Winchester – these schools were the envy of the world. The Russians and Chinese begged for places. Well, Jamie intended to cut a dash, make the big boys take notice, stir the water here on the Sussex Downs . . . ruffle some feathers if necessary. And the School Review Team was just the start.

Their 'Grand Review of the Year' was undertaken at the end of the summer term. The students had gone home – and teachers across the land breathed a huge sigh of relief, contemplating long weeks of summer freedom, with no marking, no assemblies . . . and no performance reviews. Jamie was very hot on performance review – the main purpose of which was to make staff feel inadequate, make them try harder in the coming year . . . to push themselves and to push the students on whom their jobs depended.

'Where are we now? Where have we come from? Where are we going?' Jamie would say, as the School Review Weekend approached. Maurice Stone had never asked questions like that; they seemed almost impolite. But Jamie was high energy, and sometimes looked fit to burst, with his slightly pickled red skin. Did he drink too much?

'The End of Year Review is a way of looking after the business,' he'd say. 'And every business needs looking after.'

'Don't you mean "school", Headmaster,' said one of the old guard.

'If I'd meant "school", I'd have said "school", Christopher. Welcome to the twenty-first century!'

The shape of things to come had become clear on a Staff Development Day in January. Jamie had felt it was time to lay his cards on the table.

'Things are changing, my friends,' he said to the teachers, gardeners, administrators and cleaners of Stormhaven Towers, gathered in the rather run-down school theatre. He wanted everyone to hear this and he took centre stage, quite literally, to tell them. 'The globalized educational marketplace is a different world from the one in which Stormhaven Towers was founded – and we need to join it . . . or *die*!' There was some awkward shifting in the ranks, but Jamie had carried on. These people needed to get real. 'The arrival of wealthy and demanding foreign parents – along with the wealthy

10

and demanding English ones! – means that many schools out there are now equipped beyond our wildest dreams. Take Westminster school—'

'But we're not Westminster, Headmaster,' said Gerald, who'd had enough and would soon be leaving.

'No – but we could be, Gerald – that's just the point. We could be!'

'We'll never be Westminster school,' said Geoff Ogilvie, Director of Boys. 'For a start, we're not in Westminster – we're in Stormhaven! There's a difference.'

There was some laughter which disappointed Jamie . . . he'd be patient.

'But have you seen their science labs, Geoff?' he asked, with almost messianic vigour. Geoff taught science, this would engage him. 'It's like NASA in there, and their theatre, well – it beats the West End.'

'We've done some good shows in this theatre,' came another voice.

'But we could do better ones! And their music centre – their music centre has a recital hall, a recording studio and practice and rehearsal rooms! And what have we got?'

'A happy school?' Some of the staff were beginning to feel a bit battered.

'A school that's going nowhere! Westminster's art block is like a Saatchi gallery.'

'What's a Saatchi gallery like?'

Well, if he was honest, Jamie didn't know. It was just something another head had said to him: 'Westminster's art block is like a Saatchi gallery, Jamie. The rest of us are still in the Dark Ages!'

Jamie wasn't an art man himself. He'd read business studies at university. But that question this morning said it all: 'What's a Saatchi gallery like?' Here at Stormhaven, the staff were out of touch, they didn't know about a Saatchi gallery or sense the brave new world of education out there. Educationally, they were like the Flat Earth Society, out of sync with the new ways, clueless about recent developments – and in particular, the possible money from abroad. They still dreamed of the old tumbledown institutions

11

where they themselves were educated – parochial little boarding school worlds with eccentric but largely unemployable schoolmasters covered in chalk dust imparting their random and limited genius to the thick and brilliant alike.

No, things were going to change at Stormhaven Towers, Jamie would make sure of that. It was his way – or the highway.

And so they gathered,

the chosen ones, for a residential weekend at the end of the summer term. Everyone was tired ... of course they were tired. Shattered. The final week of the school year was an exhausting – and somewhat hysterical – succession of sports days, leaving services and prize-givings. But the headmaster had not allowed anyone to be tired until now. One week before the end of term, he'd gathered them all in the common room and explained the situation: 'You're not tired!' he'd said to the weary faces before him. 'There's nothing more tedious than tired staff! The children are tired, hollow-eyed with exhaustion – but you're not tired! Why would you be tired? This is your job! So no tired talk in the common room, please!'

There had been plenty of that of late. He knew the worship of weariness when he saw it – and he was having none of it. 'You're not here to moan or to slack, counting off the days. You're here to give the students a bloody good send-off – 'scuse my French!' The final comment about his French did not go down well with either the language department or the chaplain ... but he'd made his point. They weren't tired, and if they felt tired, they still weren't tired. In fact, anyone who was tired was a wimp.

But term was now over, with the review team only a weekend away from their own holidays. And to be honest, it was quite fun in a way – 'like going away to camp,' someone said. They each slept in recently vacated students' rooms, 'to earth the discussion'. Jamie loved his little student room. It reminded him of university and a girl called Lola ... good memories but different days and not his concern now. 'Let's leave the comfort zone of our homes,' he'd say, 'and understand what it's like to be a student here!'

It was also designed to humble the participants, just in case anyone thought they were superior. They each had to make their own beds – including the head – with the fresh sheets provided, courtesy of the large cupboard on Matron's Landing. 'No special measures for me!' he'd say. He was glad to have a room of his own for a couple of nights . . . making his own bed was a small price to pay.

*

The list of those invited to attend had appeared on the common room noticeboard two weeks previously. (And it wasn't an invitation you refused if you wished for a pay rise . . . and everyone did.) Those chosen were quietly pleased; those not chosen, quietly distressed . . . though the distress did not stay quiet for long, it tended to speak its pain somewhere, in dark mutterings away from Jamie's ears late at night in the common room bar.

And this is what the list revealed:

Those invited to be part of the School Review Team are as follows:
The Head – Jamie King
Head's PA – Jennifer Stiles
Chaplain – Father Ferdinand Heep
Director of Wellbeing – Bart Betters
Director of Girls – Penny Rylands
Director of Boys – Geoff Ogilvie
Bursar – Terence Standing
Head boy – Crispin Caudwell
Head girl – Holly Hope-Walker

We will undertake our review of the year on the weekend of 1–3 July. All submissions by those not on the team gratefully received. Honest opinions welcome! Submit to the Head's PA, Jennifer Stiles, by the final Wednesday of term.

'I've been submitting to Jennifer for the last seven years,' said one depressed teacher who found her to be an impossibly high wall between himself and the head. Her nickname in the common room was 'Access Denied' – reduced to an ironic 'Access'.

It had been
an awkward morning.

The review weekend was under way but struggling. There had been some *get-to-know-you* games, which no one had enjoyed. 'Quite cringe-making' was the bursar's assessment, for he wished to know no one here. Why would you want to know anyone at work? And then came the ubiquitous 'buzz' groups with the hope of some blue sky thinking. But the sky remained grey for the future of Stormhaven Towers.

And now it was lunch time on the Saturday and headmaster Jamie King found himself sitting with Geoff Ogilvie, Director of Boys, teacher of chemistry – and a long-standing member of the school leadership team. At fifty-one, he was in his teaching prime; this was what he felt. So why was he uneasy? He'd gone to Exeter University and while he'd been happy enough there, the best of times in many ways, yet thirty years on he hadn't quite recovered from his failure to get into Oxford ... where several of his more stupid contemporaries went, people from the right schools, and called 'Sebastian' or 'Torquil'. Geoff hated them, in a way.

And now Jamie leaned forward with some difficult news for him: Geoff was for the chop – or a sideways move at least, which was the same. When you're fifty-one, a sideways move is the end of the promotion ladder. From here on, you're just seeing out your time.

'Geoff, I'm thinking about another role for you,' he said. These were not words you ever wanted to hear from Jamie. 'I'm thinking of giving you a break from the firing line for a while. You've been taking the bullets for too long. Let someone else feel the sting!'

'I don't mind the bullets, Headmaster.'

'Someone younger, perhaps.'

'I like being in the firing line.'

He wanted to make this quite clear.

'Fresh ideas, Geoff.'

'I'm only fifty-one.'

'Exactly. You can't buy that sort of experience – and I want us to use you in a more wide-ranging portfolio.'

'A more wide-ranging portfolio?' thought Geoff. In other words, a nothing job with a meaningless title.

Geoff had sensed danger in the air for some time, like manure caught on the wind; yet when it came, it came from nowhere and without warning . . . and he was stunned to receive the news. Jamie just kept on talking – it was all sorted in his mind apparently. Geoff would be given a swanky new title, the head was good at those; but it didn't mask the truth that this would be a downwards move – his trajectory from here on, surely?

'I'm fifty-one and it's all downhill from here, is it?' he asked.

'Get a grip, Geoff!' said Jamie, feeling a brief sense of payback for Geoff's comments about Stormhaven Towers not being Westminster on the Development Day in January.

But in the end, this wasn't personal. The head merely wanted a younger man, more energy and equally important – certainly for the bursar – cheaper. Geoff was at the top of his scale and therefore an expensive, as well as a failing figure in Jamie's eyes. They sat looking out across the well-kept college lawns. Geoff saw the empty years ahead of him and had to express his fears; he'd appeal to the head's good nature.

'It's not easy finding a headship in your fifties, Jamie.'

He'd felt for some time that he should be looking to advance himself, to leave Stormhaven Towers. But he never had, because he was happy doing what he was doing. He'd felt respected and valued. Maurice Stone had listened to him, set great store by his opinions. They'd drunk whisky together, a member of the unofficial inner circle, which every leader gathers. But that meant nothing now . . . was perhaps even part of his downfall. Was he seen as too close to the old guard?

'No, Geoff – but I can't help that.'

'Or a deputy headship.'

'You won't get it, no.' Jamie shook his head sadly. 'Not a chance in hell. No one wants a head or a deputy in their fifties, not these days.' Jamie was forty-one – thirty-nine when he was appointed. 'And you're not married, of course, Geoff – or not any more.' He didn't like to mention it. 'And single teachers these days . . .'

There was no need to continue. Geoff remained silent.

'The thing is, Geoff, you sat around for too long drinking Scotch with the old time-server, Maurice – that's the fact of the matter.'

'I've hardly sat around, Jamie!' The nerve of the man! 'I've worked hard for this school, every hour God sends. I thought we were a team, you and I.'

'And we are a team, Geoff, but every team needs new signings. And this is what football clubs call "the transfer window".'

'I'm being replaced?'

'The school can't be a care home for the faint-hearted.'

Geoff was stunned.

'The *faint-hearted*? Is that what I am?'

'You never chose to progress, Geoff.' He turned towards him now, face to face, man to man. 'Look, no hard feelings – and I don't want to be the one saying this, but someone has to! You didn't take that risk. That was a choice you made.'

It needed to be said. Jamie didn't feel good saying it, but he had to speak his mind.

'I was just doing a job I liked . . . and did well, as you always said.'

'But you never progressed, Geoff. And if you don't make the change, then the change makes you.'

'Ah, the deity of change! Not a shrine I worship at, Headmaster.'

'And Holly thought we needed someone younger.'

It wasn't the most sensitive of remarks.

'Holly? What the hell does *Holly* know about it?'

He very nearly said something stronger. Holly was the retiring head girl and part of the School Review Team . . . and they'd hardly ever met. What right did she have to comment on his leadership qualities?!

'She's allowed a view, Geoff. Everyone's allowed a view.'

'I mean, at least ask Crispin – he's a boy, after all. And I'm Director of *Boys*.'

'Crispin is stupid, Geoff – affable, sporty and stupid. He'll probably end up in the City.'

Geoff was in turmoil, unsure what exactly had happened in the last five minutes.

'It's as though I suddenly don't know you, Jamie.'

'You've just got to wake up and smell the coffee, Geoff.'

Geoff hated that phrase. What coffee should he be smelling? And who said he was asleep?

The head did not rate

Bart Betters either. He was the useless Director of Wellbeing – but how to remove him? It wouldn't be easy.

'What in God's name is a Director of Wellbeing?' had been his first reaction on taking the job. What was the school doing wasting its money on a post like that? Since then, his opinion of Bart had slipped further down the slope of regard. Bart believed everything could be solved by a walk in the forest or building a tree hut – a re-engagement with some version of ancient England that had only ever existed in his imagination. Had he forgotten how murderous everyone was in the fourteenth century? It wasn't all woodcraft, flower circles and mindful breathing in the merry month of May. But Jamie had to be careful. The Chair of Governors, Sir Digby Cork, had been key in Bart's appointment, believing it put them ahead of local rivals.

'A Director of Wellbeing, Jamie!' Digby had said at one governors' meeting, when they both held a large gin in their hands. 'It has a certain cachet, don't you think?'

'If by that you mean a wild waste of money, then I agree entirely, Sir Digby.'

He had said it with a hearty grin, a loud laugh – and a body swamped with frustration at this absurd waste of a salary. A *Director of Wellbeing*? Why didn't his staff just grow a chin? And did the students really benefit from a nanny figure running breathing courses? *Breathing courses*, for God's sake! Weren't they breathing already?

And now, with the term over, here was Father Ferdinand, the school chaplain, complaining about Bart. Jamie looked at him as he spoke: balding, meticulous and trapped inside his dog collar.

'I'm concerned about our Director of Wellbeing,' said Father Ferdinand Heep, in a voice of mannered concern.

'You mean you're furious?' said Jamie. If the Church said it was concerned, it usually meant it was furious – but didn't like to say. Jamie would pacify him: 'Look, Father – it's just a job for a teacher who can't teach, we all know that.'

'You show insight, Headmaster, but will that lead to action?'

'I think Maurice employed him as a favour to a friend – and in some misguided bid to be modern, knowing full well he wouldn't have to live with the consequences. Devious old soldier.'

They were standing by the coffee machine between afternoon sessions, and the chaplain was pressing the head about his own position in the school. He wanted it clearly established that the chaplain was more senior than 'the Wellbeing fellow'. Ferdinand felt it was high time for action with regard to the whole wellbeing thing. The head needed to declare his hand on this one, with no more dithering. Stormhaven Towers was a Christian foundation, after all – not some Buddhist outpost on the south coast, worshipping the questionable god of mindfulness. Oh, and why couldn't *he* be a Director of something as well? Everyone else was a Director of something! This was another matter Father Heep wished to raise. Did 'chaplain' adequately reflect his status in the school? He thought not . . . and felt now was the time to make a stand. His confirmation classes – surely the ultimate barometer of the health of the school? – were getting smaller and he felt Bart Betters was to blame.

'This is a Christian foundation, Headmaster.'

'I know, Ferdinand, I know . . . but the truth is, there are other interests in the matter.'

'Interests other than God's?'

Give it to him straight, thought Ferdinand – but the head eased past the lunge and offered another in return.

'Well – not everyone's as keen on the chapel as you are, Father. Changing times and all that.'

'*Changing times?*'

'It may have started out as a school for the children of impoverished clergy – but it sure as hell isn't that now!'

Unfortunate phrasing, but he'd made his point.

'Perhaps it's the thirty thousand pounds a year fees that put them off,' said Ferdinand drily.

'We have to pay for your large house somehow, Chaplain.'

Touché.

'Your tone was a little different in the interview, Headmaster,' said the chaplain, slyly.

And it was true, he hadn't said these things in the lengthy interview process. Spread over four days, it had been something of an endurance event. He'd met pupils, staff and governors in various settings; taken lessons, given a PowerPoint presentation on his vision for the school. They'd wanted to meet Cressida who, to be honest, had been pretty magnificent. And he had endured a one-to-one interview with the chaplain, Ferdinand, when he'd spoken all kinds of nonsense to get the priest on board.

But nonsense and editing are a key part of any interview. You say whatever they want to hear – and edit out what they don't. You do everything you need to do to get your hands on the wheel of power. And only when your hands are there do you reach down into the weapons box and wield the axe. Ferdinand Heep had had his moment of power over Jamie. He wouldn't get another.

But removing the chaff hadn't proved such a simple task for Jamie. During his first eighteen months in post, the axe remained in storage, unbloodied and unused; both Ferdinand and Bart remained in senior management positions, imagining themselves important – each clamouring for authority over the other.

And then, as the afternoon session approached, Jamie perhaps went too far and declared too much of his hand to the chaplain. For when Ferdinand continued to press him about Bart – more mannered concern – his frustration spilled out. He'd put this stupid priest in his place.

'If it was up to me, Ferdinand,' he said, leaning closer to him, smelling the common room coffee on his incense breath, 'I'd get rid of you both.'

At that moment, head girl Holly Hope-Walker walked past them, looking demure, her blonde hair carelessly falling over her shoulders. She wore a Stormhaven Towers tracksuit, blue and gold – and looked stunning.

'Hello, Father Heep!' she said, in a manner too suggestive for her years.

'Hello, Holly.'

Heep seemed nervous. Why was he nervous?

'Taking the headmaster's confession, are you?' she asked. 'That would be interesting!'

Jamie laughed heartily and said: 'Eternity's too short!'

'Though not as interesting as *your* confession, Father!' she added. 'We'd all love to hear a priest's confession. Where would you begin?'

'We are as everyone else, Holly,' said Heep with careful humility. 'Sinners all.'

'Well, *I* know that, Father – I was just wondering if everyone else did!'

She laughed teasingly and moved on.

'Confident girl,' said Jamie. 'I wish I'd had a little more of that at her age.'

'It's not always a virtue, Headmaster,' said the chaplain, primly. He had his own views on Holly.

'And of course dangerously attractive, eh?' She was eighteen and leaving the school – so Jamie could admit these things now. 'But then I don't suppose priests can allow themselves such thoughts.'

Ferdinand made no reply.

'You're not gay, are you, Ferdy?' asked the head, in something of a whisper . . . and the chaplain's face filled with shock . . . or fear? 'Well, don't look so surprised! I mean, I wouldn't mind. And a lot of you are, aren't you?' It seemed every other clergyman was gay in this part of the world. 'Or is there a secret woman somewhere, someone you keep hidden away from public view?'

On these review weekends, the head went casual. Term time found him in a suit, tie and shiny shoes. But he could dress down and did so now: sailing jumper and beige chinos, soft sole suede shoes; and with casual dress came more casual conversation, the chaplain had noticed. This was not a chat he would have had with the head a week ago, when the 570 pupils were still around, scurrying through the dark corridors of Stormhaven Towers – while earning the school such vast sums every year. Where do people find thirty thousand pounds to spend on a year's education?

he often wondered. He'd never earned that sum in a year – let alone have it to spend on a child.

'Married to the Church,' said Ferdinand, attempting to close the conversation down.

'Yes, I've always wondered what that means,' said Jamie, 'what with all those court cases – you know the ones I mean ...'

Penny Rylands was Director of Girls

and had been for five successful years, this was the feeling. She was also head of the English department, or 'Head of Poetry' as Geoff called it. So she'd come a long way but she wanted more. In the long term, she wanted the headship; but in the short term, Geoff's job would do.

'If Geoff's going, then it makes sense,' she said to Jamie as they walked in the front quadrangle, known as 'The Uppers'.

'Where's Geoff going?'

'I mean, being sidelined.'

Jamie took this in.

'You're very well informed, Penny. You didn't get that from the dull poems of T. S. Eliot. Does anyone have a clue what he's on about?'

More importantly, how did Penny know about Geoff's impending demotion? He hadn't told anyone. He looked at her again. She was an excellent teacher, of course, and a peroxide blonde who could sometimes look a little like Myra Hindley ... which was unfortunate. He didn't mention this to her; it wouldn't have played out well. He did sometimes call her 'Myra', but only with Jennifer or Cressida.

'No secrets in this place, Jamie,' said Penny. 'I know everything.'

'So it seems,' he said and felt discomfort as if his life was under scrutiny. He didn't like the idea of there being no secrets, of Penny possessing a window into his life.

They strolled in the late afternoon sun, before the final session of the day.

'You won't be here forever, Jamie,' said Penny.

'I beg your pardon? I plan to live for a while, you know!'

'I'm talking about the headhunters.'

'What headhunters?'

'Bigger schools, better schools, more prestigious schools – this isn't Westminster, as you made very plain in January.'

'You don't say,' said Jamie, laughing. And one glance across at the crumbling art block reminded him of the fact.

'I know they've been knocking on your door already – you know, the heavyweights.'

'I'm sure I don't know what you mean, Penny,' he said with an enigmatic look. He liked the idea of the heavyweights knocking on his door. Perhaps that would make Cressida think differently about him, for a start.

'I think you do, Jamie. I think you know very well. And when the time comes, the right time for you – I mean, I'm in no hurry.'

'Hurry for what?'

'But whether it's Marlborough, Winchester, Harrow who take you away – they're all possible – I want to succeed you here.'

'You want to be head of Stormhaven Towers?'

'Yes.'

Jamie didn't know how to react, though he knew he was instinctively against the idea.

'Does that offend you?' she asked.

'Not at all.' It did offend him. He could feel the hackles on the back of his neck rising. 'I like you and your ambition, Penny, you know that.'

And he did like Penny and her ambition; no harm in chasing the crown, something to be admired. She'd make a good head somewhere – but perhaps not at Stormhaven Towers. Promotion from within could be tricky in schools, he'd seen it fracture common rooms. And whisper it quietly, but not everyone on the governing body wanted a woman. How would that play abroad, for instance? Would the Russians want a woman? And Dubai? And then again, did *he* want a woman? If she was a success, that would cloud his own legacy in the school, with 'female power' grabbing the headlines, saving the day and so on.

'So, support me,' said Penny, decisively. 'Make me your deputy, with the Director of Girls and Boys posts rolled into one. Make me next in line.'

25

'I can't anoint you, Penny!'

'You can in a way, Jamie. It's in your power.'

They arrived at the chapel door and Jamie felt a sudden desire to go inside.

'Fancy some holy quiet?' he said. 'Or at least quiet – we can take or leave the *holy*!' That was another line he hadn't used at interview.

'Why not?' said Penny.

Jamie pushed at the large wooden door which swung slowly back. They stepped inside the high-ceilinged Gothic interior ... acres of still space above them.

'It has its own power,' said Jamie.

Carved stalls surrounded them as they stood still for a moment – seats for the great and good, while in the middle, endless rows of wooden chairs for the pupils. Old war flags hanging from the walls, the smell of hymn books and incense ... and a long way away, up at the altar rail, a familiar figure lying prostrate on the floor.

'Now there's a surprise,' said Jamie, genuinely shocked.

'Is that *Terence*?' said Penny.

Terence Standing was the bursar and she'd never seen him like this. He was always so organized in every way, financially and emotionally ... life an exact equation. But this figure, though some distance away, was clearly sobbing.

'I believe it is,' said Jamie. 'Not normally one for the high church stuff. He must be in real trouble with God!'

Terence was a well-known fundamentalist of the evangelical persuasion. He was not given to incense or talk of the Virgin Mary, whom Ferdinand mentioned quite as much as Jesus ... if not more. 'You just need God's word!' Terence would say to anyone who asked, which wasn't many. And not for him the lofty cathedral architecture and grand altar. He'd go to church on Sunday in what was little more than a tin hut in a field, near the quaint village of Barcombe.

'Well, just so long as he's not embezzling the school's money,' said Penny.

But the sound of weeping in the empty chapel, the guttural sobbing, was unsettling.

'When men cry, they really cry, eh?' said Jamie awkwardly.

'Yes,' said Penny, who, though unmarried, knew all about men's tears.

There was another pause. Jamie looked at his shoes.

'So?' said Penny finally. She'd had enough of the drama at the altar. She needed to know about her future here; and Jamie knew this was decision time, knew that he'd have to tell her.

'Penny, I'll support you as much as I can, of course I will.'

'I sense a "but".'

'And you'll make a fine head – a very fine head, I've always thought that.'

Not wishing to disturb Terence's obvious anguish, they'd stayed near the door, sitting alongside each other, gazing heavenwards at a stained-glass window of some saint or other.

'*But?*' said Penny.

'But, well, should it be here, at Stormhaven Towers?'

'Yes.'

'That's my only question. Does it have to be Stormhaven Towers?'

'It does.'

'Is that what will be best for you?'

'It is, yes. I want it to be here.' She was quite sure and Jamie recognized that determined look – just not on *her* face, which was strange.

'What's so special about this place, Penny? There are plenty of other schools – schools less lumbered with mausoleums like the one we sit in now. Don't you hate the smell of hymn books?'

'I've known worse.'

She'd known much worse; she'd known the breath of an alcoholic before the violence began . . . the violence of a man who'd lost his way and knew only how to destroy those closest to him. She couldn't help him now. He still hurt others from the grave, the dead do this – but she couldn't help him. All she could do was try to put things right, and this Jenny was determined to do. There was a pause, like a break between rounds. They both looked straight ahead.

'I don't know if I believe in God,' said Jamie. 'I can't say for sure – but the one place I never find him is here.'

He gesticulated around him, wanting to make his point ... but Penny felt only anger rising.

'I want to be head of Stormhaven Towers,' she said, voice raised. 'That's all I want to say — and you're either for me or against me.' She then rose to her feet and brushed her skirt, as if covered in crumbs. She looked down at the headmaster, who remained seated.

'Then I'm against you,' he said, his voice raised in return. If she wanted a battle ...

'*Against* me?'

'I'm against you!' He felt discomfort; he liked Penny, had no wish to fall out with her. But she must see her desire was an unworkable plan. 'What can I say, Penny? I can't lie — we're in a church, for God's sake!'

'I sense my detective days are done,'

said the monk – though he wasn't a monk, not now. These were different days, even if he had kept the habit.

The woman next to him on the stony beach smiled but said nothing. She was a striking thirty-something – dark haired, olive-skinned, thirty years younger than her companion ... and a police inspector, for her sins.

'Well – *are* they done?' he persisted. 'My detective days?'

'I can't promise you anything,' she said.

'I'm not begging,' he replied, pulling back now, feeling patronized.

'Sounds like begging to me,' she said, looking out on the green sea – but without enjoyment. People did go on about the sea ... about how healing it was to stare out into the watery expanse. But to Tamsin, it was very similar to land – just a bit emptier, which wasn't a good thing. Empty wasn't good for Tamsin.

And he *was* begging – passive begging, Peter could see this. He was formerly Abbot Peter of the Monastery of St James-the-Less in Middle Egypt, just along from Mount Sinai. But life had brought him by strange chance to retirement in Stormhaven, on England's south coast. This hadn't been his idea and whether it was a good one was still open to question. It was a town famous for its white cliffs – the Seven Sisters stretched majestically towards Eastbourne. It was also quite well known for its profound dislike of tourists.

'We're a town by the sea, not a seaside town,' as one local put it, soon after his arrival from the desert. There was only one hotel, hidden away, with a few discreet and choosy B&Bs ... because Stormhaven liked to keep itself to itself. Let Prague – or Blackpool – clear up the sick after the hen parties, the stag dos and 'I'm divorced!' weekends ...

'I was pretty good,' said Peter. 'I mean, I was a good detective.'
He was now in his mid-sixties but a keen runner along the South
Downs Way and lean in both body and thought.

'I've had worse partners,' said Tamsin nibbling a tasteless cheese
roll, provided by the abbot. This would hardly have been her choice
of picnic fare. Had the monk not heard of Waitrose? This cheese
roll would not have got through *their* door . . .

They sat together on the shingle beach of Tide Mills, just along
from Stormhaven – and for Tamsin, it took the biscuit for desolate
settings.

'Wonderful, isn't it?' Peter had said and she hadn't replied.

Tide Mills was famous in the area, unaccountably so in Tamsin's
eyes. It was formerly a mill village, using tidal power – but
abandoned in 1939 when the workers' cottages were declared
uninhabitable. Only the haunted ruins now remained, offering
shelter from the wind but not the rain. And perhaps a metaphor
for Peter's life? The thought had crossed his mind as they
carried their picnic to the shingle beach. A haunted ruin of some
historical interest – but destined only for slow, remorseless
decay.

And if the truth be known, and occasionally it is, Peter had
been a very good partner to Tamsin in the police business. He'd
proved himself more than useful in recent investigations, he was
quite sure of that. And how had he got the chance? Through
the 'Special Witness' scheme. It was an idea currently being
trialled by the Sussex police force, 'to promote a more earthed
and insightful investigation', as Tamsin had once told him. She
described the matter in a strangely neutral fashion, as if it was
nothing to do with her – presumably in case it failed. 'As part of
an experiment, a member of the public who is recognized as a
trusted citizen of the affected community can now be brought in
to assist the police.'

'A trusted citizen?'

'Their words, not mine.'

'Still, I'll take the scraps of approval.'

In some ways, Peter was the father she'd never had and the
father she still wished to punish.

'The special witness is involved in all aspects of the case,' she continued, 'kept fully informed of developments and works closely with the leading officer in the enquiry.'

And so it had been. He had worked closely with the leading officer – DI Tamsin Shah – and the abbot had enjoyed the adventures, if not the terror they brought with them. But that was then ... and the cases now appeared to have dried up like seaweed too long in the sun. They hadn't worked together for over a year and as Peter had said to a neighbour recently: 'We don't always know when we've been sacked. The awareness creeps up on us slowly and uncertainly.' And so it had been with his detective career.

'The fact is, Peter,' said Tamsin, grasping the nettle, 'it's not everyone who wants a monk on the crime scene.' Peter nodded. 'Comments get made.'

Chief Inspector Wonder, her boss, had certainly made them when he first heard of their partnership. He'd asked someone to remind him which century they were in.

'And how is our dear king, Henry III – bearing up, I hope?'

They'd all laughed at that back at the nick.

'But what about you, Tamsin?' asked Peter, seeking the more crucial truth. 'How do you feel about a monk on the crime scene?'

'How do I feel?'

She could never answer that question. Feeling was not a close friend.

'Do you want a monk on the crime scene?'

'Any old monk – or a monk of my choice? And there's a phrase I never imagined myself using.'

'Stop avoiding the question.'

He accepted the predicament she referred to, however; it had the bleak ring of truth. He was being judged for his clothes – for while he'd given up many things since leaving the desert, his monk's habit wasn't one of them. It kept life simple, no tedious trying on of outfits in godforsaken clothes shops.

'Don't judge a book by its cover,' he said, trying to regroup.

'Is there another way?'

'I was useful, Tamsin, you know I was useful.' And now he looked out towards Newhaven and the incoming ferry, gliding silently through the sea. It was this very ship, the *Seven Sisters*, which had brought him to these shores ... the last leg in his journey from the desert. So a last link with the big sand ... and a first link with Stormhaven. Was he grateful or sad as he watched it enter the embrace of the harbour walls?

He'd previously helped Tamsin on three cases: the first was a nasty crucifixion – well, there was never a pleasant one – at St Michael's. The vicar had been nailed up in the vestry. The second was a vicious murder at Henry House, a local therapy centre and the third, a killing onstage at Stormhaven's Bell Theatre – with both Tamsin and himself in the audience. The theatre business he'd solved single-handedly, there was no question about that. Tamsin had been in psychological meltdown. And all three cases had involved him in a high degree of personal risk. He didn't want a medal, that wasn't the desert way, but some appreciation would be nice ... so really he *did* want a medal. DI Shah, however, did not major in appreciation. She offered her staff the motivational sandwich of praise–blame–praise, without the praise.

And so things had drifted between them, for it was work that brought them together. And that might have been that, between Tamsin and himself. Peter placed solitude above relationship. But a further surprise on leaving the desert was the discovery of a previously unknown relation. The police inspector he now sat with in a brisk south-westerly wind was his niece; and this was why they were sharing a cheese roll. With relatives so thin on the ground, Peter attempted to maintain at least annual contact – even if his detective days were gone.

And yes, that thought did sadden him ...

'We each have one wish

for the school,' said Jamie King, the headmaster. 'So what is it? What's our one wish, our vision, for Stormhaven Towers? A good question, eh?'

They'd all enjoyed a drink or two from the common room bar. This included the head boy and head girl, Crispin and Holly, for term was over, they were adults now and with the review weekend out of the way, they'd be off into the big wide world. Crispin had enjoyed a beer and Holly, a gin and tonic. For Jamie King, it was strange to see this young woman standing there, in the common room, with a drink in her hand. It was a coming of age – though she remained in her Stormhaven Towers tracksuit.

'You've come a long way,' said Jamie, moving towards her and placing a fatherly hand on her shoulder. This made Holly flinch slightly and he pulled back.

'It's Stormhaven Towers that has enabled that,' said Holly, smiling again. 'I'll always remember the place fondly. I've learned so much.'

And she had learned much, though not perhaps from the traditional curriculum; she'd learned how to survive – and how to earn.

'Boarding school teaches the art of survival,' said Jamie, briskly. 'You learn to use the rules to your advantage. You discover where others are weak and you use their weakness to make yourself strong.'

'Er, yes,' said Holly, blushing a little.

'I'm glad you'll remember us fondly,' Jamie had said. 'And the place will always remember you fondly, Holly!' He would certainly remember her fondly and the apple blossom scent of her hair.

'So our one wish for the school?' he asked, once they were all seated. 'Serious or outlandish, they all count!'

'Be careful what you wish for, Headmaster,' said Geoff.

33

'And keep it snappy, all right? We don't want the Ten Commandments or anything!' said Jamie, making sure he didn't catch the chaplain's eye. 'And if I'm to get the ball rolling – which is what I'm paid to do – I'd just echo the strapline on our school publicity: *Excellence by the sea*. That's my wish for Stormhaven Towers: Excellence by the sea! And it's my role to drive excellence ... and to give the last rites to anything less than that!' Short and sweet, he decided to leave it there. He'd dropped the bomb he wished to drop. 'Holly, how about you?'

They were sitting in a circle of chairs in the common room, where generations of teachers had gathered to sulk, gossip or seek the safety of a newspaper between lessons. The savagery of teenagers – and the scrutiny of their pushy parents – was not borne easily by all. Students, of course, were never allowed in here, this was not their space – it was almost mythical ground. So Holly had never entered the common room before; but if she felt ill at ease, it didn't show.

'A place of truth,' she said simply in answer to the question. Ferdinand choked a little. 'My wish for Stormhaven Towers is that it's always a place of truth.'

There was a short pause for silent admiration and grunts of 'hear, hear' and 'quite, quite'. Though all were thinking the same thing: Who among the adults gathered here would have proposed such a wish for the school? A place of truth? The innocence – and ignorance – of youth! Geoff Ogilvie – soon to be demoted from his position as Director of Boys – went further: he hated Holly in that moment. And what in particular did he hate about the head girl? So many things. He hated her brilliance, her confidence, her youthfulness, her glamour, her assurance. It made him feel old, disappointed ... and disappointing. And he hated the head as well; he hated him for being all over her, just like the weasel chaplain Ferdinand. Geoff had always wondered about those two, the chaplain and the head girl. But then he was now wondering about a lot of things as he surveyed the ruins of his life.

Bart Betters, Director of Wellbeing, was impressed by Holly's words. He liked idealism, he liked things staying positive; it made him feel better. And he'd been about to say, 'Out of the mouth of

34

babes!' But he held himself back for Holly did not look like a babe, or not that sort anyway – and then peroxide Penny Rylands, Director of Girls, took control: 'I think we all wish for that, Holly ... "A place of truth" – absolutely.'

'I'm not sure you do, Myra,' said Jamie to himself.

'As for me,' continued Penny, 'my vision for Stormhaven Towers is simply "Making Lives Better" – pupils, parents, staff; past, present and future. The Towers should be "making lives better".'

There were some nods in the circle because disagreement was difficult with something quite so obvious and bland. The alternative was 'making lives worse' which, while a truer assessment of the school in some eyes, was not an inspiring vision.

'Christ-centred education,' declared Ferdinand, almost talking over Penny, so keen was he to be heard. He wished his voice to be the decisive one in this meandering meeting. Where is God in all this? he wondered. 'That's my vision for the school: Christ-centred education!'

'Very good,' said Jamie, to fill the awkward pause.

'But what does that actually *mean*?' asked Geoff, frustrated.

'I would have thought it was fairly obvious,' said Ferdinand.

'Not really. I mean, I hear it said – but what does it actually mean? Do we really have any idea what curriculum Jesus would want for a twenty-first-century school in the West? Does he have a particular view on the International Baccalaureate or strong feelings about how many hockey teams we should put out? Or whether we should make the fees thirty-five thousand rather than thirty thousand?' He paused. 'Or whether change is always best?'

Jamie intervened: 'I think this is a time for sharing our visions, Geoff, not debating them. You're sounding a little miserable, to be honest!'

'It's being miserable that keeps me going, Headmaster.'

'Mindful of now,' said Bart Betters, with the quiet determination of ancient England behind him. He had no wish for more misery from Geoff, who was a rather negative soul at the best of times.

'I'm sorry?' said Jamie.

'My vision for Stormhaven Towers: "Mindful of now" – because what else is there?' asked Bart. 'Mindful of the nowness of the woodlands, the nowness of ourselves, the nowness of others – the nowness of this moment.' He paused for effect – and then glanced at Ferdinand who looked away.

'The nowness of Italy,' said Penny playfully and there were some smiles. Bart was always going on about Italy – it was a running joke in the common room when they had a moment to laugh, during the term-time madness.

Bart replied: 'I'm being serious, Myra – I mean, Penny.'

Ooh, that was awkward . . . very awkward. So awkward it almost made Jamie laugh. Bart blushed as did Penny . . . only she blushed with rage. Her fury was like an acid inside.

'Geoff, we haven't heard from you,' said the headmaster, wishing to move on. He hadn't heard the word 'nowness' before . . . was Bart quite mad? 'What's your wish for Stormhaven Towers?'

'Loyalty and honour,' replied Geoff, slightly tight in the throat. He was too angry for calm. 'What's a school worth without loyalty and honour? It's not worth a scrap.'

'Quite,' said Jamie.

'A good head,' said Jennifer, looking up from her note-taking. She was the head's PA and he liked to hear her views. He was always asking what she thought when they were alone in his office.

'But I'm not a teacher,' she'd say.

'Nor are half of them,' Jamie would reply naughtily . . . and they'd laugh.

And here she was now, offering her thoughts again, a handsome woman in her late forties, executive wardrobe, never a fibre out of place . . . glasses on a delicate chain round her neck. Mind you, not everyone thought she should be a member of the review team. It seemed a bit odd, but it was Jamie's call . . .

'That's my wish for Stormhaven Towers,' continued Jennifer. 'That the school always has a good head.' Some called her cold – others, merely efficient. You didn't like Jennifer; it would be hard to like her. But everyone knew you kept on the right side of her; she could damage your career, with a voice so close to the throne.

'She has the ear of the king,' observed Terence to a friend at church. 'Which gives her a power way beyond her pay grade.'

And the truth was, she'd damaged many down the years with her interventions – and some quite badly. 'Access denied' was not her nickname for nothing; and she'd become increasingly proprietorial of Jamie these past few months, as if he was hers to control. But she was happy to speak now and say more than she'd ever said in public: 'What I see from my position as PA to Jamie is this: everything emanates from the head. He's the start of everything. It's not that the rest of you aren't important' – nervous laughter from the circle – 'it's just that if a school has a good head, then everything else flows from that.'

And with that said, she returned to her note-taking.

'Right! Well, the cheque's in the post, Jennifer,' said Jamie, slightly embarrassed but also pleased. 'And let's hope I'm one of the good heads you're referring to.'

Jennifer smiled, without looking up.

'Crispin? Do you have anything for us?'

Jamie hoped for nothing too stupid from the head boy – but he wasn't holding his breath. Crispin was clearly uncomfortable in the spotlight; he wasn't a bright boy and was obviously struggling in this exalted company. And because he didn't know what to say, Crispin just picked up on Jennifer's wish for a good head.

'Jennifer wants a good head, which kind of makes sense,' he said. His skin retained the legacy of acne beneath mousy brown hair.

'That's your wish too, Crispin?'

He blushed a little at the attention.

'In a way it is. I just suppose it depends on what you mean by "good". Is a good head a good husband, for instance? Or is that different?'

He offered a half-smile to defuse any sense of offence.

Suddenly everyone was listening.

'What do you know of Stormhaven Towers?'

she asked.

'Why?'

'Could you just answer the question.'

'If you tell me why you ask it.'

'Why do you need to know why I ask it?'

'Because you know exactly why – but you're hiding the reason from me. I'm simply levelling the playing field.'

Abbot Peter's broken doorbell had rung falteringly. Standing on the doorstep was Tamsin, or DI Shah, in uniform.

'We have a situation there.'

'Has a parent choked on the fees?'

'The headmaster is dead.'

'That's a problem.'

'Apparent suicide.'

Peter sighed.

'Well, it's allowed. I mean, not encouraged – but allowed. If you have to go, you have to go.'

'He died five hundred yards from where we stand,' said Tamsin, looking to make some impact. Peter managed a sage nod of the head.

'He should have dropped by, on the way,' said Peter. 'I mean, I wouldn't be offering a bed for the night. But we could have talked, shared our despair over a cup of tea.'

'That's really pushing the boat out, Abbot.'

'It could have included a biscuit. I'm not saying it would have saved him—'

'He jumped from Stormhaven Head.'

'Well, he would have, wouldn't he?'

It was a popular seafront walk. You strolled past the Martello tower and the tea hut, along by the beach huts and then up the sharp incline of the white cliffs, the beginning of the Seven Sisters, rising majestically out of the sea. When you reached the top – and no one managed it without some sense of exhaustion – you'd arrived at Stormhaven Head. Around you were the finest of views – views across the Downs, across the town or out to the sea ... and with a long drop to the rocks below. An actor from a TV soap was the last sad soul to make the leap; it made some of the papers, a few column inches ... financial troubles had done for him, apparently, though no one really jumped for money.

'But we're not sure,' added Tamsin.

'Not sure about what?'

'There may be more to it than suicide. Forensics think so.'

'And I'm very happy for forensics,' said Peter, still filling the door space, and still barring the way inside. 'Give them my love, or whatever's appropriate in the circumstances – but what has this to do with me?'

He could guess ... but would not make it easy.

'Can I come in?' she said. 'It's a traditional courtesy to relatives.'

'They're not usually dressed in police uniform ... or is this a fancy dress party I know nothing about?'

'I just knew you'd come as a monk.'

Peter smiled, relented and stood back to allow her into the small front room. Peter's two-up, two-down – with a study extension at the back – was in a small row of houses fifty yards from the shingle and the cold green sea. His doorstep was a windy place to stand and Tamsin was glad to be inside ... not an outdoors girl, never had been.

'Tea? Coffee?' asked Peter, moving towards the kitchen. He preferred coffee alone, a private pleasure. But his guests could still enjoy one; he'd sip a glass of squash in solidarity. His neighbour – who had a car, bless her – went to the Lidl in Newhaven and kept him well supplied with most things. People said Lidl lacked variety; they had clearly never lived in a monastery.

'Coffee,' said Tamsin.

'Right.'

'Decaff.'

39

'Sorry?'

'Decaff.'

'Ah.'

There was clearly a problem.

'Normal will do.'

'Good. I'm not sure Lidl do decaff.'

'Everyone does decaff.'

'I'll have to take your word on that one.'

'This isn't the desert, you know.'

Though for Tamsin, that described Stormhaven perfectly . . . a cultural desert at least. She'd never buy a house in the town time forgot.

'But what's the point of decaff?' asked Peter. 'I mean you either want coffee or you don't.'

No answer came as he found a mug and put a rounded spoon of caffeine granules in it. The abbot preferred two spoons himself. The tea had tended to be weak in the desert but the coffee, thick and black. No sleeping on the psalms at his monastery! And presumably, in time, his niece would get around to saying what had brought her here . . .

'I was wondering if you were up for a small investigation,' she asked on cue. Tamsin spoke over the boiling kettle, a noisy affair.

'I'm sorry?'

Slightly louder. 'I said, I was wondering if you were up for a small investigation?'

Peter returned to the front room and placed her drink and digestives on the small crate which passed for a coffee table.

'Why the change of heart?' he asked.

Only a few days ago, at their Tide Mills picnic, Tamsin had turned him down, pushed him away. Humorous police comments about monks at the Lewes HQ seemed to have put her off the idea of another partnership. She'd been cold to his pleading. So which tectonic plates had shifted – and why?

'A yes or no would suffice,' she said. 'Not that you're begging, I understand that.'

'I'm not begging, no.'

There was a silence between them. Tamsin sat in the one comfortable chair, Peter on a large wooden crate formerly used in the packing of herring. He'd found it on the shore and given it a wash, a polish and a home. The smell of fish was less striking now and it had proved a solid piece of furniture. But mainly, it was free – for Peter needed to be thrifty. He hadn't returned from the desert with money, because you don't make money there ... you pray. And he'd found it hard to earn any in Stormhaven, other than presiding at the odd funeral, when a vicar was unavailable. He was a rarity in that regard: someone never sad to take a call from the undertaker.

'The school, it's eerie,' said Tamsin, letting down her guard a little. 'There's this huge chapel which emerges from the rocks – have you seen it? It's like some Gothic misogynist monster.'

Abbot Peter smiled. He'd noted the chapel from a distance on his coastal runs. Quite a landmark.

'You want me to hold your hand amid the ghosts and ghouls?'

'Religion is your world, not mine.'

'It's not really my world, Tamsin – the landscape of life is too large for religion to comprehend. But it's not a world that scares me, if that's what you mean. That particular emperor has no clothes from where I stand.'

Peter was thinking about money. He was aware he'd need cash to repaint his green front door, which suffered terribly in the salty wind. He was aware also that he'd enjoy getting under the skin of Stormhaven Towers. They had never invited him to preach since his arrival from the desert. He'd met the chaplain once – Ferdinand someone – an intense figure, given to the manicured speech of the control freak. He'd once said to Peter: 'We must get you over, have you in our pulpit, and sooner rather than later, Abbot.' But he hadn't ... he hadn't got Peter over ... hadn't offered him the pulpit and it was much later now.

'So?' said Tamsin.

'You want an answer?'

'Most questions do.'

'Normal rates of pay?'

41

'Yes,' said Tamsin, smirking at the outbreak of greed. Special witnesses were given a decent allowance. 'As long as you don't fail me.'

'When did I ever fail you?'

'I'm just saying.'

Abbot Peter was reminded that in previous cases, Tamsin had given him more grief than the actual murderers. The murderers usually turned out to be rather pleasant people – something which could not be said of his niece.

'I'm in.'

'You'll do it?'

'Why not? I need some paint.'

'Good! Yes, very good!' she said. There was a moment of connection between the two, shared excitement at what lay ahead. Tamsin was up from her seat, and Peter rose too, though they didn't quite hug; they had never quite hugged. And then she was gathering her things, muttering about how she must be on her way, and that she'd be in touch later that day when she'd spoken with the chief inspector.

'Just don't fail me,' she said as she left, her coffee barely touched – which even at Lidl prices was a waste.

There had been unpleasantness

before they broke for some free time on Sunday afternoon. Bart had wanted to raise the matter of the negativity of the Senior Management Team. He wanted to say how some people – mainly himself, to be fair – found it oppressive.

'I don't know what you're talking about,' said Jamie.

'It's just that some people feel that senior management—'

'Do you mean me?'

Bart did mean him.

'I mean, the message is that we're failing all the time – and it's just not helpful.'

Jamie wasn't taking this, and certainly not from Bart.

'Well, you are, Bart. It's a fact. You're failing all the time.' Bart was affronted. 'There's nothing personal in any of this. But since you ask, what sort of a job do you think you're doing?'

'Well . . .'

'I mean, I don't know your objectives, Bart. What are they? Deeper breathing? More tree dances? And I certainly don't see any outcomes.'

'I meant the school generally, Headmaster.'

'What are you talking about?'

'You say we should be like Westminster, or we should be like someone else . . . when, well, we can really only be ourselves.'

'Is this making sense to anyone?' asked Jamie, theatrically. 'Because I'm struggling.'

'I suppose what I hear Bart saying,' said Penny, stepping into the ring, 'is that it would be good to hear of the things we do well, sometimes.' Jamie looked surprised. 'I mean, we all want to do things better, of course we do, Headmaster.'

'Well, that's a relief.'

'And if it's Russian or Chinese money helping us to do that – then, so be it. But, well – our Learning Support Team, for instance –

they're doing brilliantly, Jamie. Parents pick Stormhaven Towers for our learning support provision.'

'And do you know what, Penny?' said Jamie, attacking her with a stare. 'I'm not that thrilled.' Penny was taken aback. 'I mean, great work and all that, sure. But I'll let you into a secret: the Russians and the Chinese won't be coming here for our learning support provision. They really won't. So I don't want the school to be famous for its special needs provision. I want it to be famous for its academic achievement, for its A level grades, its Oxbridge entrance record, its drama and music facilities, for its sporting achievements – national school football champions, why not? Other schools can do the special needs ones. That's not our market.'

The group sat in stunned silence.

'Now let's take a couple of hours' break,' said Jamie, calming. 'Go out and get some fresh air in your lungs – and I'll see you back here at five.'

'Could I have a word?' said Ferdinand.

'If it's quick,' said Jamie. 'Doesn't sound like good news.'

'It's not good news, Headmaster.'

And when they were alone, in a corner of the empty common room, the chaplain explained the situation, presuming it needn't go any further . . .

It wasn't going well for Tamsin.

She'd imagined this request would be a shoo-in with the chief inspector. She wanted to have Abbot Peter on her team – a formality, surely? Such was her reputation at the police HQ in Lewes – grudgingly bestowed by both lecherous and jealous males – she tended to be left alone, allowed her own way. Only this morning, Chief Inspector Wonder was blocking her path.

'Tamsin, I don't want to be difficult.'

'Then don't be.'

They were in his office, a rather soulless affair. On the wall, a large certificate detailing success for the nick at the 2011 Sussex Gun Show, taking second place in the pistol shooting category. And that was it.

'But, I ask you – the abbot chappie again?'

'Where's the issue?' said Tamsin.

She remained standing, with Wonder wedged behind his large desk, his stomach filling the space.

'Where to begin, Tamsin?'

'I don't know. Where are you beginning? I'm not sure you know – with respect.'

'A monk!'

'A monk with a one hundred per cent clean-up rate – so obviously that isn't bothering you.'

'No, no, well ...'

'Oh, I get it – he's making the rest of the dross employed here feel inadequate.'

Wonder laughed away this absurd statement.

'We've got good coppers here, Tamsin, and you know it.' He leaned back, relaxing a little, happy to engage in banter with such a pretty lady. 'A good copper is nosy – and there's a lot of nosy so-and-sos around here!'

Tamsin had no time for the banter and bonhomie.

'A good copper fears failure,' she said, bringing Wonder up short. 'And so should you.' He reassessed the situation.

'This is not a war, Tamsin.'

It *was* a war; it was clearly a war and had been for a while now with the stakes getting higher by the day.

'No, it's a farce, Chief Inspector – and I certainly wouldn't pay for a ticket.'

'But a monk, Tamsin – really? A monk!'

'He's an ex-monk.'

'Can you be an ex-monk?'

'It appears so.'

She hadn't a clue ... and wasn't interested.

'Well, whatever the niceties of his present position, Tamsin, he dresses like a monk. And I mean, you must see – modern police force and all that.'

He'd already decided to say no to her request. He'd decided to say no before Tamsin even entered his office this afternoon. It was time – and how to put this politely? – that Tamsin was shafted, put in her place, reined in a little. It was all slightly awkward obviously. There were issues here, Wonder was well aware of that ... issues around his behaviour. He'd messed up at Mick Norman's leaving do a couple of years back – of course he had. It had been inappropriate behaviour, that was a possible view – from the women's brigade at least. But really, it was something and nothing ... and he was drunk, for God's sake! It hadn't meant anything – he was a married man and had been for thirty-two years.

But she was an attractive woman, so who wouldn't have hopes? And with a few too many glasses of wine inside him, he'd simply misread the signs, which anyone can do ... especially at a leaving do, when boundaries are put aside for the night, and rightfully so. But ever since then, in some manner or other, she'd held it over him ... and had been allowed a very long lead in return.

No longer, though! This is what he felt, sitting behind his big desk with its leather inlay. Today, Wonder was beginning his fight back. He was going to pull the lead in a little ... he'd remind her that this bitch had an owner.

'The answer's "No", Tamsin.'

'What do you mean, the answer's "No"?'

How could Wonder say 'No' to her?

'Have you noticed that we don't use alchemists at the crime scene any longer – we use forensics! Science rather than charlatans! I'm not having some bloody monk, some mentally sick throwback, trampling over my crime scenes here in East Sussex. End of story!'

'I wonder if I could say something?' said Abbot Peter, who had appeared in the room, unnoticed.

'Who the hell allowed him in?' said Wonder, spinning round in his expensive office chair.

'So what makes you think

it wasn't a suicide?' Peter asked the question both out of interest and to take his mind off Tamsin's reckless driving. It was like being back in Cairo, only without the random camels. 'I mean, it's a popular suicide spot, Stormhaven Head – and really quite a public place for a murder.'

'Well, the first thing is, there's no phone by the body.'

'It might have been washed away.'

'The water never reached him . . . he was found before high tide. And he always carried his phone apparently, never without it. He joked that he didn't want to be out when Eton called.'

'He speaks for us all there.'

Tamsin smiled. She couldn't imagine a more uncomfortable setting for the abbot than the hierarchical and entitled world of private education in England.

'So where is his phone?' she asked, rhetorically.

'Reckoned too dangerous by the murderer?'

'It's a strong possibility.'

The first mention of a murderer and the abbot couldn't help but feel a twinge of excitement. Suddenly there was a target, a figure on the horizon to pursue – instead of vague talk of an investigation. But he'd still have to question the assumption.

'Perhaps he just wanted a break from human contact during his final walk. It's windy up on Stormhaven Head – a phone conversation is a difficult thing up there. And Eton might not have been his major concern if he was about to kill himself.'

'His phone cannot be found at home either.'

'OK. Well, that's interesting.'

That was *very* interesting.

'And there's something else,' said Tamsin. 'There are fibres on his back where one might imagine a pushing hand being placed. A rubber glove – or something similar. Just there – nowhere else.'

'Clever forensics.'

'I had told them what to look for.'

'I'm sure they'd never have thought of that themselves . . .'

Tamsin took one hand off the wheel, and shifted her body, to press Peter's back causing the car to swerve on a tight bend.

'Careful!' said Peter, quite terrified. 'What are you doing?'

'I'm just proving a point – that there was a killer. That's where the fibres were on his back.' But Peter's heart was racing. 'You're just a rather precious passenger, Abbot . . . too long in the sand.'

'Or not long enough.'

'But the fact is, we have the touch of rubber.'

'Ah, thank God for the first law of forensic science,' he said.

'Quite.'

'Or Locard's Exchange Principle as it is more technically called, stating that "every contact leaves a trace". One of my monks was a former forensics bod in the Met.'

'Bully for you.'

'I'm not claiming it as an achievement.'

'But more important than dull nostalgia is the fact that we have a murderer.'

'It does appear so.'

'So read me what we have about Stormhaven Towers.'

Tamsin was driving too fast on the small and curvy road to Newhaven. Coming the other way, at regular intervals, were large lorries off the cross-channel ferry. The abbot was aware they were not missing by much; he winced with each passing.

'I'm not fond of reading in the car; it makes me feel sick.'

'Welcome to the real world.'

'And I prefer to look out of the window. I so rarely have a lift in a car.'

'Do you want this job?'

'You were quite close to that petrol tanker,' he said, trying to sound as casual as he could, given the inner scream.

'Just read the printouts,' said Tamsin. 'We need to be right up their noses from the word "go".'

'We also need to be alive.'

Tamsin wasn't happy with Wonder. She'd won the battle – but had been excluded from the fight, a mysterious mano-a-mano between chief inspector and abbot. What had happened back there? She wanted to know ... but would have to wait. She needed to learn more about the school and had told Carter to print out the necessary information.

The abbot dutifully started to read: '*Bleak House*, a novel by Charles Dickens, was first published as a serial between March 1852 and September 1853, and is considered to be one of Dickens' finest novels, containing vast, complex and engaging arrays of characters and sub-plots ...'

Tamsin sighed.

'He's an idiot.'

'Dickens?'

'Carter. I asked him to do a printout on the Bleake Foundation – Stormhaven Towers is one of their schools.'

'He obviously has a literary bent.'

'Something's bent.'

'He heard "bleak" and thought of Dickens.'

'Whereas I hear "bleak" and think of his future. I mean, why do we call them support staff, when in fact they make life more difficult?'

There was a short pause until Peter decided to risk it: 'You can be quite minimalist in your instructions, Tamsin – quite terse. You may not have explained yourself as clearly as you wished – or thought you had. It's possible.'

'It's also possible he's an idiot,' she replied, fuming at the wheel.

'Stay concentrating on the road,' he said. 'Rage does not a better driver make.'

'Pay peanuts, get monkeys,' she said sulkily. Peter looked out on the passing fields and wondered if she was referring to Carter or to him. His desire right now was to calm her down – she drove more slowly when calm, when she seethed less.

'I do know a little about the Bleake Foundation myself, if it helps.'

'You do?'

'I mean, I'm not encyclopaedic ...'

'What do you know?'

When Peter said he wasn't encyclopaedic, it generally meant he comprehended the matter in its entirety. But then, for the abbot, an expert was simply someone aware of how little they knew.

'Well, it was started by Nathaniel Bleake,' he said. 'He was a nineteenth-century philanthropist. I don't know what he made his money in ... probably child labour of some description. He had seven children himself, though I suspect they didn't work in his factories. There are a few Bleakes still living in the county ... and five schools in the Foundation, strung across the rolling greens of Sussex. Stormhaven Towers is perhaps one of the lesser performers.'

'Why do I always get to work with losers?'

'Shall I continue?'

'Yes.'

'The schools were originally meant for the education of children of impoverished clergy – but with fees for the year now standing at thirty thousand pounds, the impoverished are less involved these days. Decent headmaster, of the driven variety – and of course now I think about it, I met him once.'

'You met him?'

'Some charity event I got dragged along to. Jamie King – a man of energy and professional charm, no question of that. Though whether he was a saint or not, I don't know. I remember he smoked a great deal, drank a great deal, and as far as I could see, always had to be doing something ... one of those people who look like they're going to explode any minute ... restless. You wondered where he found peace. '

'And now he has.'

'Of a sort.'

Silence.

'Do you know anyone else at the school, by any chance?' asked Tamsin. For someone who was supposed to like solitude, she'd discovered Peter did get around. If he was a hermit – which he kept on insisting upon – then he was a notably failed one.

'Well, strangely enough, his wife is my doctor, Cressida Cutting – she kept her maiden name.'

'Is that a problem, Abbot?'

'Don't let feminism make you stupid, Tamsin.' She pulled a face. 'I state it as a matter of record. Just as I also state she has an appalling bedside manner, cold as the February sea.'

'You don't seem to like her.'

'On the contrary, she is everything I need in my GP. Appalling bedside manner – but a very sharp eye for the correct diagnosis and I'll settle for that. Bedside manner is overrated, so there's hope for you yet ... which reminds me, I've also met Father Ferdinand Heep, the school chaplain.'

'So what's the dirt on him?'

Peter looked disappointed.

'It's not dirt, Tamsin. Why does information have to be dirt?'

'Because it usually is. The more you discover about someone, the less impressive they become. People present a virtuous facade; but as more and more information is discovered, there's not much left of the facade, believe me.'

Peter couldn't disagree ... though he had met the occasional soul who'd become more wonderful through the knowing, rather than less ... but that was back in the desert, not in Stormhaven.

'I did notice,' said Peter, 'that he was caught up in his own little battle with someone called Bart.'

'That's dirt.'

'A slightly grubby truth, perhaps. He really didn't like Bart, who was the school's Director of Wellbeing.'

'*Director of Wellbeing?*' Tamsin almost veered off the road in amazed disdain. 'Tell me you're making that up.'

'Bart Betters is his name.'

'It's getting worse.'

'He likes woodcraft, mindfulness, ancient England, that sort of thing. And he sings folk songs, long ones – which is probably where I part company with him.'

'So you've heard him sing? You're not Simon Cowell in disguise, are you?'

'There's a farm in the village of Spithurst.'

'And?'

'It's well known for its nightingales.'

Nightingales would calm Tamsin.

'Can we stay with the murder?' she said. 'We'll be at the school soon.'

'I bought a ticket for an event there. I was part of a group that came in search of the nightingale and its marvellous song.' This was not a group Tamsin would ever join. 'We didn't have them in the desert, being so far from Berkeley Square.'

'Berkeley Square?'

'It doesn't matter.' Another failed joke in the history of the universe. 'It was a night event, part of Brighton Festival. We arrived at the farm at nine and sat round a large and rather engaging fire enjoying herbal tea and oatcakes while darkness fell and the stars appeared.'

'Sounds like a complete nightmare.'

'And the thing was, our leader for the night was Bart Betters.'

'Is that his real name?'

'He spoke a little about nightingales; he'd obviously read up on them. They fly to Africa for the winter, apparently, and have an unusual larynx.' Tamsin sighed . . . not far now to the school. 'But he seemed most interested in singing folk songs. I wouldn't have minded one brief one, but these came one after the other, each with eighteen endless verses – possibly more – about young love in ancient England –

> A country boy did espye a maiden,
> And in his heart, she made her claim,
> Beneath the oak, he wondered dearly –

'That's probably enough,' said Tamsin.

'Be grateful for the power of edit – because there was none that night, I can assure you. We left the camp fire at about eleven after more songs and walked on into the forest, a silent troupe listening to the night silence.'

'I prefer to do that from my bed.'

Tamsin had recently moved into an expensive flat near Hove station, which was both Brighton – yet not Brighton. Hove was a community of its own, while just a few minutes away from the 'happening' metropolis. It was sometimes called 'Hove, actually' from the oft-used response by people when asked where they lived. 'I live in Brighton – well, Hove, actually.'

But Peter was still in the forest, in search of the nightingale.

'And then finally, at midnight, after a further walk, we reached the Promised Land: a nightingale singing! It does it to mark its territory, apparently – but we could pretend it sang in sadness or delight. And we were just standing in holy awe at the sounds – so much variety of tune and tone – when Bart gets out his guitar and insists on singing again! "It's like a duet with creation, guys!" he said – though we didn't hear much of the nightingale after that. It was mainly Bart and his long dirges written for a time when no one had anything else to listen to.'

'You don't like folk music, do you?'

But before Peter could respond, Stormhaven Towers was upon them – and their hearts jumped in unison.

'Look lively,' said Tamsin as they drove through the large school gates. They featured two stone seagulls, looking down from their perch like disapproving Caesars, eager to swoop on new arrivals with their cruelly curved beaks. The grey flint buildings appeared calm in the sunshine, untouched by recent upset; and the mowed lawns lay immaculate, much tended. A gardener was clipping their edges even now.

'A gardener died here last year,' said Peter as they drove past the bent figure. 'I remember reading about it. Something of a mystery, as far as I remember.'

'Not our case,' said Tamsin, cutting the conversation dead. Her mind was on the headmaster, nudged into dreadful flight, hurtling down towards the rocks . . . and sent there by someone waiting for them now, in the school; this was her feeling.

'The killer's waiting for us in there,' she said, nodding towards the school.

'Well, it's possible.'

'And at this very moment, they think they can get away with it.'

Peter smiled.

'Then we must disavow them of that notion.'

'We must what?'

'I suppose the chapel is fairly magnificent,' he said, gazing upon the edifice on their right. 'If you like that sort of thing.'

'I don't.'

'No.'

Tamsin parked the car in one of the many vacant spaces. This was the holidays . . . and this was a crime scene. In fact, what the hell was the gardener doing? She'd have a word with someone.

'Why do I feel like a new boy all over again?' said Peter, sensing nervousness from way back reappearing in his body.

'This is when the adventure begins!' said Tamsin. 'Are you ready, Abbot?'

'I'm never ready,' said Peter. 'How can we ever be ready for the unknown?'

'Has anyone seen my phone?'

asked Jennifer Stiles, former PA to Jamie King, head of Stormhaven Towers. The gossip was that he had jumped off the cliff at Stormhaven Head, a tragic suicide ... and one which you'd never have expected.

'But then do we really know anyone?' someone said.

It was all very unsettling ... and the School Review Team were gathered in the common room to meet the police. No one quite knew what they should be thinking or doing and Jennifer's phone was a welcome distraction. A mislaid phone was more manageable than death – especially the death of someone who twenty-four hours earlier had been sitting among them, talking about the school's future ... while planning an end to his own, it appeared, with a leap from Stormhaven Head.

The presence in the room of his wife – well, widow – Cressida Cutting, just made everything worse. She'd been asked to attend but had arrived in the common room quietly. She placed herself in a corner, away from the others. The unspoken message from her was simple and clear: 'Please leave me alone in my grief.' Or maybe just 'Please leave me alone.' She was that kind of person. The message she gave off, ever since she'd arrived at the school, had always been one of distance. And no one had seen her in the common room before, which merely added to the strangeness of seeing her there now.

Then Jennifer arrived and without seeing Cressida, raised the issue of her phone.

'When did you last have it?' asked Bart Betters, Director of Wellbeing, who liked solving other people's problems. (*Director of Rubbish Solutions* was one of the less polite names given to him by his colleagues, who weren't overly convinced of his value. Another was *Director of Fresh Air*.) He was currently doing his stretching exercises on the floor. He quite often did this during coffee breaks.

Like breastfeeding, people had got used to it, though why he couldn't go somewhere more private . . .

Bart said that bodywork was better for wellbeing than reading all the negative news in the papers, which arrived in the common room daily.

'I don't know when I last had it,' said Jennifer in irritated response to Bart's question. 'If I knew that, I'd know where it was.' Did Bart really think she hadn't already considered that? 'It disappeared at some point yesterday. I just thought it would turn up.'

'And it will turn up,' said Bart. 'Let's be positive − think what would Buddha do?'

'He didn't have a phone.'

'No, but I mean . . .'

'Do you want to borrow mine?' asked head girl Holly, holding her sleek gadget in the air. 'It might be an upgrade.'

'No, I just want mine back,' said Jennifer. Why would borrowing Holly's phone help? 'It's got my photos on it,' she added.

Yes, someone in the room had seen the photos . . . which might make things easier.

'You should always back-up photos,' said Bart, now doing press-ups in the cause of his own wellbeing.

'Here,' said Penny, Director of Girls. 'Give me your bag, Jennifer − I'll find it. I always find your things.'

'I've looked there already,' said Jennifer. 'It was the first place I looked.'

'Then I'll look again,' said peroxide Penny and with that she took the bag from the table and began the search. Cressida watched from her corner, fascinated. Widow or wife, she'd never allow anyone to hold her bag, let alone open it and nose around inside. But then . . .

'It's here!' said Penny.

'What?'

'It had fallen down the side pocket . . . which is surprisingly deep.'

'I'm sure I looked there,' said Jennifer, both grateful and annoyed. She took both her phone and bag back from Penny.

'I told you I always find things.'

57

'Speaking of which – who found, er, Jamie?' asked Geoff, Director of Boys. He was embarrassed at the superficial exchange he'd just watched. Jamie was dead, for God's sake and his widow of a few hours was sitting in the corner. This was hardly the time to be fussing about a bloody phone.

'I believe some people saw the body from Splash Point and alerted the authorities.' It was the chaplain, Father Ferdinand Heep, still in his dog collar, who gave this official news. 'They managed to collect the body in a boat before the tide reached him. A blessing, of course.'

A blessing? thought Geoff. Is the man completely mad? This is not the time to be talking about blessing.

'One doesn't want the body floating out to sea on such occasions,' added Ferdinand as if he heard Geoff's thoughts. He'd gone over to Cressida when she arrived, to offer pastoral support. But she'd seen him coming and raised the palms of her hands to indicate that she wished to be left alone – rather like a cross held up to a vampire. Ferdinand had nodded knowingly – there are stages of grief, as he often said – and returned to his seat. He was disappointed, however – disappointed that his approach had been treated in this manner . . . and so publicly. And Cressida was not especially regular at the chapel services, of course . . . but he would overlook that in the current circumstances.

'Are you two all right?' asked Penny. She was enquiring after Holly and Crispin, the head girl and boy from the previous year. They sat next to each other now, brought together by death. The solidarity of youth seemed important in the circumstances, Crispin in his blue school jacket and grey trousers and Holly in her blue and gold school tracksuit. Their clothing suggested a continuation of term rather than the start of their holidays.

'We're fine,' said Holly.

'And your parents are happy with this?'

'With what?'

Who could be happy with a suicide? It was gross.

'Well, with you . . . with us all being asked to stay at the school – until the police let us go, I mean. Not every parent would be keen. I could name one or two.'

58

'I spoke with my dad,' said Crispin. 'I don't think he realized term had finished.'

Holly put a hand on his shoulder. It felt a bit strange. She couldn't have done it twenty-four hours ago ... but she did feel for him.

'No, it isn't his fault,' said Crispin hurriedly, aware of her hand, now withdrawn. 'He's just opened a new car dealership in Düsseldorf, a lot of travelling ... very busy, I think. He says I must stay as long as the police think fit and help in every way possible.'

In other words, he doesn't care at all, thought Geoff. He was aware of how much Crispin missed his mother, a victim of cancer two years ago – or that was the story, no one was quite sure. The lad had done so well to carry on – without perhaps knowing that he was carrying on, this was Geoff's view. When you're young, you just get on with things ... it's only later the dark birds of rage and despair come home to roost. Geoff's childhood had long been lost in the mist of repression and he wasn't sure he wished to find it again ... if you don't want the sludge, don't lift the drain cover.

'And I was meant to be staying with friends this week, anyway,' said Holly, cheerfully. 'So they're, like, cool with this. And then it's the family holiday to Barbados which I do not want to go on, no way – so I don't mind if we stretch this out a little.'

'Well, we'll see,' said Penny, cautiously.

'Mum's new boyfriend is a total pig,' continued Holly. 'Like, a total misogynist. He says I should respect him because he's an adult ... we don't speak. And I think he fancies me more than Mum, which is embarrassing.'

There was a pause in the proceedings. No one had heard about Holly's home life before. They were weighing her words, various images coming to mind. Ferdinand found it particularly distasteful.

'Do you think you could stop doing your stretching, Bart?' said Penny.

'It's just bodywork.'

There was a light sweat on his ginger brow.

'And it's slightly getting on my nerves,' said Penny. 'I'm not sure it's appropriate.' Her eyes led across to where Cressida was sitting, checking her phone.

'Sure, sure,' said Bart getting up off the floor. 'I suppose it's about the fusion of body and mind.'

'No, it's just irritating,' said Penny, who was missing her garden. Forty-eight hours away from her flowers and she could sense the need in herself for their calming presence. It was a little known passion but 'Myra' – yes, she was well aware of the name – grew all sorts of plants, exotic and unusual, with much loving care . . . and Latin names. She insisted on the Latin names for them all, as if linguistic obscurity made them smell sweeter. For Penny, her garden was a restorative place to be . . . something which could not be said of this common room.

And then Ferdinand, the chaplain, spoke. He wished it to sound off-the-cuff. 'By the way, I want everyone to know that I'm here for you – er, should anyone wish to speak with me in a pastoral capacity. Not easy times for any of us, of course, and we'll all handle this in our own way. But should anyone, well –'

'Are you OK, Terence?' said Jennifer, ignoring him. As the head's PA, she worked more closely with Terence, the school bursar, than most in the room. Staff don't really come across the bursar unless they have contract issues, and even then, he's a rather elusive figure, his wishes communicated by others. This was Terence Standing's approach, at least – strawberry blond hair, always the same length and a man who looked like a banker or someone behind a desk. He had a shiny grey suit, white shirt and red tie, almost a school uniform. He was mid-thirties and slim but well-ready for his fifties, nothing would have to change – apart from some balding perhaps, the strawberry blond thinning a little. He'd not exchanged a word with anyone since arriving in the common room, other than to accept a cup of tea from Geoff, with a quiet 'thank you'.

Penny looked round at Terence. She hadn't spoken with him since their strange encounter in the chapel – with him prostrate before the altar, sobbing. Had he seen her? Had he heard her and Jamie argue? She wasn't sure. But normal service had been now resumed in the ordered world of Terence Standing. He was well under control, back to his organized, methodical self, just not wishing for conversation . . . or not here at least.

Terence wanted to talk to Benedict, if the truth were known; but how was that going to happen, with the police about to arrive? One thing he was sure of: Benedict must be kept out of this, out of view – so he couldn't risk a visit. There was no need for the police to speak with Benedict ... or even know of him. Benedict must stay out of sight, if not out of mind. He'd never be out of Terence's mind.

'I'm fine thank you, Jennifer,' said Terence. 'Just fine.'

And that was the moment. It was then, at three minutes to five on that Monday afternoon, that a further killing at Stormhaven Towers became necessary. Capital punishment was about to make a return to the UK ... and quite right too. It derived its meaning from the Latin, *capitalis*, which meant 'concerning the head'. But this would not be a beheading or hanging; there were better ways. It had only been a glance across the room, but the glance was enough, the eyes said it all – a death sentence in its way. It was as though a judge had placed the black cap on their head and announced that the prisoner would be taken from this court – or common room – to a place of execution.

The killer even knew where that place would be ... after all, they'd seen the photos.

'So this is a public school,'

said Tamsin. 'Where the great and good educate their children.'

'I think it's more the rich,' said Peter. 'The great and good is another list entirely.' As if to confirm the thought, he noticed a large black Porsche sitting elegantly in the sun near the finely carved stone of the school entrance.

'I hope you're not coveting your neighbour's ox,' said Tamsin.

'I feel like one trespassing in a car advert,' said Peter. 'Teachers' pay has clearly improved at public schools.'

'But it's also called a private school.'

'Yes.'

'You know my next question.'

'The public/private thing?'

'Yes.'

They were standing by her car, close to the arched main entrance. The school buildings enveloped them, like the jaws of a lion, waiting to tear them to shreds.

'As always, the answer lies in the past,' said Peter. 'I think it was Eton College who first called themselves a "public" school. The title was to indicate that they were open to the paying public.'

'You mean some schools weren't?'

'The religious schools weren't public – they were open only to members of a certain church. So when Eton declared itself a public school, it did so with a vision of openness and equality . . . times change.'

They had fifteen minutes before they were to address the staff . . . and Tamsin was happy to leave them waiting awhile anyway. They'd been told to gather in the common room at five, but it didn't do any harm for everyone to stew a little. So for now, Tamsin opted for a walk around the grounds, taking stock of the place – while Peter explained events earlier in the afternoon, when he'd arrived at Lewes HQ and disturbed her meeting with Chief Inspector Wonder.

'You shouldn't have been there,' she said. 'That's my place, not yours.'

'I felt I had to visit really, after what you said on the beach at Tide Mills. You had them all laughing at me as an anachronism, jokes about thirteenth-century monarchs, Henry III to be precise.'

'You do know he's not well?'

Peter's anger did not permit a smile.

'And you join in with them, I see.'

'It was just a joke.'

'And I didn't like them laughing at me.' Tamsin's eyebrows arched in shock. 'I couldn't get it out of my head. I heard the laughter at night, when I'd wake at two thirty and listen to the sea. I'd start to hear guffawing coppers drowning out the waves – so I thought I'd pay them a visit.'

'You had to walk into the fire,' said Tamsin, amused . . . admiringly . . . accusingly.

'I always have to walk into the fire,' said Peter. 'I wish I didn't. But I find it very hard to walk round fires.'

'So what happened?' She did want to know. Wonder had been at his bolshie worst when she'd left him, declaring the abbot 'a mentally sick throwback'. And she knew what her boss was like – he could be very stubborn when he wanted to be and quite beyond the reach of reason . . . like a two-year-old in a tantrum. She'd honestly thought the battle was lost. So what had Peter said to turn things round?

'Oh, we just discussed uniforms, really – and discovered a shared calling.'

What was he talking about?

'A shared calling?'

'We're both frontier men, this was my main pitch.'

This wasn't getting any clearer.

'Tell me what happened.'

And so Peter recounted how he'd sat down with Wonder in his chief inspector's office. He'd requested that Tamsin leave, as Peter thought it the better way. So she'd gone off to speak with forensics wondering if either of the two men would be alive on her return. The abbot had spoken quietly and with a smile, you see, which wasn't a good sign. When Peter's voice was quiet, he was angry; when he smiled as well, he was very angry, while Wonder – well, Wonder was behaving like a trapped boar that morning, all sweat, shame and fury. It was hard to see a happy outcome.

'I can give you ten minutes,' the policeman had said, wondering if that was slightly too long to be with this monk. He'd have preferred it if the monk had not heard his comments, of course, that was unfortunate. But he was trying to remain in charge of the situation. He ordered his desk a little, shifting papers, glancing at a memo. He was a busy twenty-first-century man, after all. But while it was his office and he displayed three pips on his shoulder (as well as the dandruff), he did feel strangely unnerved by the stranger facing him.

'I'm grateful for your time, Chief Inspector,' said Peter quietly and with a smile, which reassured Wonder. The monk was clearly intimidated and, let's be honest, out of his depth. He could knock this fellow off course quite easily.

'You have a matter you'd like to discuss?' said Wonder, sitting back in his chair, relaxing now with a renewed sense of power. And then the abbot spoke:

'Grateful for your time, Chief Inspector, though disappointed with your intemperate language about me just now.' Wonder blushed a little.

'It was just banter.'

'The thing is, Chief Inspector, whatever you wish to call it – you call it banter – you spoke confidently, as if you knew me.'

'Well . . .'

'As if you'd reached a considered opinion about me on the basis of that experience – when, as far as I'm aware, we've never met in our lives.'

'Look, it's nothing personal . . .'

'. . . but it is ignorant, Chief Inspector, it's ignorant. And that's a serious charge.'

Wonder felt slightly ill. 'Ignorance is a damaging little fellow,' continued the abbot, 'especially when found in the mouth of someone who, like yourself, aspires to leadership.'

Aspires to leadership? He *was* a leader and had the pips and the office to prove it!

'I may have gone a little over the . . .'

'Ignorance kills more people than cancer,' said the abbot, cutting in. 'This is my experience . . . and probably yours. So I never applaud it, whatever mouth it emanates from – even that of a chief inspector.' He paused. Wonder willed for the telephone to ring, the fire alarm to sound, the world to end, anything to break the silence.

'Are we done?' he asked . . . but Peter wasn't.

'And deciding so firmly about someone you've never set eyes on! Really! Perhaps you imagine it's acceptable behaviour because I'm only a monk? So is it equally permissible to dismiss the over-weight as stupid?' Wonder tried to draw his stomach in, without great success. 'Is permission given for that? I mean, I'm against all labelling myself, Chief Inspector . . . apart from in the food cupboard obviously.'

Outside there were voices in the corridor, and a siren in the distance. But inside the room was silence.

'Look, I'm not a religious man, Mr . . .'

' "Peter" is fine.'

Wonder nodded. He preferred him without a name, preferred him as 'the monk fellow'. But if needs must . . .

'I'm not a religious man, er, Peter . . .'

'And with the greatest respect, Chief Inspector, I have no interest in your religion . . . or whatever opinions you hold on the matter. We're not here to discuss those things, and you're not fit to anyway . . .'

'Well . . .'

'But I am concerned that you use labels to judge people . . . and that a monk is a source of comedy – something about the long-dead Henry III, wasn't it? And all this, simply because he wears a different uniform to you.'

'Well, if we're comparing uniforms . . .'

'Are you aware, Chief Inspector, that the police outfit is the one most commonly used by stripagrams?'

'Er . . .'

What sort of a question is that? Is this man a pervert?

'Yes, I heard a programme all about it on the radio,' said Peter, 'very interesting. Do you have a radio? My best-ever Christmas present. You might still be able to catch it . . . it may be a podcast. But what we discovered was this: that up and down the country, the police uniform has a comedy all of its own, at parties of one sort or another . . . both with and without a truncheon.'

Wonder shifted uncomfortably.

'Yet still you wear the uniform and look very smart, Chief Inspector – all the while hoping, I suppose, that not everyone will reckon you an exhibitionist or cheap sexual entertainer, about to remove his trousers and wave his private parts in the face of the audience. Not everyone in a police uniform is a stripper!'

'Quite.'

What was he meant to say to that?

'I certainly don't see you in that way, Chief Inspector. No, I reckon you a good man. Indeed, I'd go further than that and call you a "frontier man" . . . definitely a frontier man.'

'*A frontier man?*' said Wonder, with some relief, glad to be away from the hen party. Wonder loved Wild West movies and the *High Chaparral* – he had the box set – and warmed to this notion. 'Well, that is a description I recognize, er, Peter. It does feel like a frontier sometimes – and a bloody difficult one, 'scuse my French!'

This was better.

'Consider it excused,' said Peter warmly. 'And I agree with you entirely. Here you are at the painful frontier between law and the breakdown of law. And as you say, it's a hard frontier to tend.'

'Has its moments, I can tell you!'

'I can imagine – and what a job you do. That's why you need the uniform, of course, which some might laugh at as a stripper's costume . . . but we know otherwise.'

'Quite.'

'It's something to be proud of, to treasure, it's a mark of honour, the uniform of the frontier man acting almost like – well, a wall I suppose, a wall between two different worlds, between law and no law. A noble uniform indeed!'

Wonder nodded; this fellow wasn't completely mad – eccentric, perhaps, but he understood one or two things about policing ... more than the local press, for a start.

'Yet also a point of connection,' said the abbot, changing tack.

'What?'

'The wall becomes the conversation. Don't you think so, Chief Inspector?'

The wall becomes a conversation? Where is he going now? Strange bugger, this one.

'Do you know the story told by the philosopher Simone Weil? I'm sure you do.'

He'd never heard of him – or her. Simone ... probably a woman, though who could tell with those philosopher fellows?

Peter continued. 'She tells of two prisoners in adjoining cells and how, over a long period of time, they learn to talk to each other by tapping on the wall. The wall is the thing that separates them but also a means of communication between their two different worlds ... like a police uniform.'

Wonder nodded sagely.

'And similar also, I suppose, to the uniform of the monk,' said Peter, 'the dress of another frontier man, who stands on the boundary between the visible and invisible world ...'

There was a knock on the door.

'Time's up, Abbot, I'm afraid,' said Wonder, with pleasure that was hard to hide. 'That'll be my next appointment, a local councillor.'

'I see.'

'Rather a long list of visitors this morning – but then, what's new?' He was playing the world-weary executive, implying that while the abbot had all the hours God sends to sit around discussing uniforms and frontiers and the like, he certainly didn't ... he had a police HQ to run! 'Roll on retirement, eh? And endless days of golf!'

A vision of hell passed through Peter's mind.

But the chief inspector wished Peter gone. He was waiting for him to move, to get up from his seat, to take the hint – but Peter didn't move. So Wonder attempted closure on the matter in hand. 'I mean, I'm not against your involvement in the case per se,

Abbot,' he said, rising in a manner that clearly said the meeting was over. 'We can think about it.'

But still Peter didn't reckon the meeting over, because that wasn't enough – not what he had come for at all. He hadn't got on the bus from Stormhaven to Lewes – a journey of over thirty-five minutes – for some ongoing conversation to be continued at a later date, for the matter to be brushed under the carpet of time, to be resolved at another man's whim sometime between now and eternity's end. No, Peter had come for a decision.

'I'm glad to have your authorization, Chief Inspector,' he said. He now rose from his seat, looking Wonder in the eyes. 'Frontier men need to stick together.'

Had he given the monk permission? Wonder wasn't sure that he had – he'd merely been playing for time, postponing the no. He'd have preferred to put it in a letter than speak it face to face. Only now, the no was apparently a yes ... and he didn't need an argument in front of the councillor, who'd come right on in and now stood watching.

'Oswald, good to see you!' said Wonder, in his most clubbable, man-of-the-people manner. Policeman and councillor shook hands ... and Peter left as quietly as he had arrived.

'Thank you, everyone,'

said Tamsin to the assembled company in the common room. 'My name is DI Shah and I'll be handling the investigation into the death of – the headmaster here.' Hell – she couldn't remember his name! What was his name? But she had their attention – you do in a murder case, at the outset. The truth is, they're excited. Some want the gossip about the death . . . their friends want to know. Others aren't quite here, imagining they're in a film or a TV series, almost an out-of-body experience. Perhaps one or two experience grief – though it's more likely to be shock in disguise. But all are glad to be here in some manner – apart, perhaps, from the widow in the corner, who betrays no emotion at all. And while there are some earnest faces on show, none will stay earnest for long. Soon, each will be contemplating the lies and evasions necessary to keep their messy little lives out of the wandering searchlight. Lift the lid on a murder and you lift the lid on much else besides . . . much that isn't pleasant. Tamsin is aware she's talking to a determined bunch of deceivers.

'And I don't want to keep you long this evening,' she said kindly. 'It's been an exhausting day, I have no doubt. But as you know, since the sad death of the headmaster . . .'

'He has a name,' said Cressida.

'And you are?'

'His wife . . . his widow. And his name was Jamie.' Tamsin remembered now. Jamie King, that was it. 'And *my* name is Cressida, by the way. Just in case it matters.'

Bitch, thought Tamsin.

'The sad death of Jamie King,' she continued, relieved she had the head's name but raging at the intervention. She'd not forget that little hatchet job by Cressida. 'And for the immediate future – and I apologize for any inconvenience caused – we're going to ask everyone here to stay in their current accommodation in the East Wing.'

People took this in. No one had ever done this before, been caught in the aftermath of murder. No one knew what was coming next . . . ordered lives, guided by bells and curriculum, were now adrift on a sea of unknowing.

'Are we to deduce from all this that you believe it may not have been suicide?' asked Geoff. He'd like some sort of anchor lowered into the water, some sort of certainty. 'I'm Geoff, by the way, head of chemistry and Director of Boys.' Tamsin nodded acknowledgement. 'Oh, and one other request – please don't say that you're "ruling nothing in and ruling nothing out" because we deserve more than some dismissive and meaningless cliché.'

Tamsin noted another enemy. Cressida – and Geoff. She was not used to being challenged so early in the proceedings. This was the problem with literate people; they lived in a climate where being pushy was reckoned a virtue deserving of applause.

'I take your point,' said the abbot, who had so far sat unnoticed . . . as much as a monk can stay hidden in a school common room in early July. 'We don't want clichés. But I do like the old police mantra,' he said. 'I don't know if it's still around these days, times change! But how did it go? "Assume nothing, believe no one, check everything." It's the only way to proceed in any investigation, surely? And it's how Geoff the scientist proceeds, I have no doubt of that . . . ruling nothing in, ruling nothing out . . .'

Geoff was reluctantly calmed.

'We're asking everyone to remain on site,' said Tamsin, wanting to get on with things before another interruption. This wasn't a debating society – it was a crime scene. 'Unless exceptional circumstances arise, of course.'

'And what would they be?' asked Bart, flippantly. 'Someone chasing us with an axe?'

'Few murders are committed with an axe, Mr . . .'

'Betters – Bart Betters.'

So this was Bart Betters, the folk song man.

'In fact, Mr Betters, there were no axe murders in England last year, or indeed the year before.' Kill him with calmness, thought Tamsin. 'But for your own safety, all rooms will please be locked after eleven.'

'For our own safety?' said Terence, the red-tied bursar. 'That sounds rather melodramatic! Are we to glean from that comment that the killer is in this room?'

'As the abbot suggested, er ...'

'Terence. Terence Standing.'

'As the abbot suggested, Mr Standing, let's assume nothing for now. We just want to get to the bottom of recent tragic events, as do you. We're all on the same side and would appreciate your support in this.'

'And who's the monk?' asked Bart. It was the elephant in the room, the question others had been aching to ask. 'And I suppose *why* the monk? So two questions!'

'This is Abbot Peter who'll be helping me with this enquiry.' She'd forgotten to introduce him, which was a mistake. 'In Sussex, we've learned that sometimes a member of the public can be a significant aid in an investigation, especially when they have an aptitude for people and local knowledge.' Raised eyebrows surrounded her. 'But let me reassure you that Abbot Peter has no power here other than to be another pair of eyes and ears. Does that answer your question?'

'I suppose,' said Bart, dubiously. 'But it still seems a bit weird.' He snorted a little laughter, derisive.

'And you aren't?' said Ferdinand, surprising himself, though for once, he felt some agreement from those around him. As if Bart wasn't a bit weird! He carried no particular candle for the abbot – but he didn't like to see the Church under attack, especially not from the crypto-Buddhist wellbeing mob.

'We have met before, you know,' said Peter to Bart. 'You may not remember. It was round a fire on a farm in Spithurst.'

'Oh?'

'Yes, we listened to the song of the nightingale ... and to other songs from you.'

'Ah, well – I trust you enjoyed it!' said Bart, warming a little to this fellow.

'The nightingale was wonderful,' said Peter appreciatively.

Tamsin felt a speedy end to this banter would be good for all parties. She knew Peter was merely trying to defuse things.

But Tamsin had a keen eye for drift, and this was dangerously close.

'We'll be interviewing you all tomorrow. The times are up on the noticeboard. In the meantime, we'd like to keep the common room as a place where you can still gather, should you wish. And can anyone suggest a venue for the interviews?'

'There's a waiting room behind reception,' said Penny, Director of Girls.

'That sounds perfect,' said Tamsin. 'The waiting room it is. And just so you know, for the duration of the investigation, Abbot Peter will be sleeping in the East Wing as well. So if you see a monkish figure late at night, it isn't a ghost!'

What? thought Peter. He hadn't been informed of this development.

'Thank you for your patience and cooperation in these difficult times,' she said and duly brought things to a close. No one moved apart from Cressida, who drifted over towards Penny, whispering in her ear, 'Don't mind me – I'm just trying to avoid Ferdinand. I fear another pastoral prowl.' And Penny nodded with an understanding smile. Peter then crossed the floor to speak further with Bart about the nightingales . . . to show there were no hard feelings . . . while Tamsin got into a brief conversation with Crispin and Holly, who were beginning to enjoy the review weekend much more than they thought they would.

'Forty-eight hours of old people!' had been Holly's reaction at the prospect, and her friends had commiserated. 'Can you literally die of boredom?' they'd asked.

Things were looking up, however. They may be in school blazers and tracksuits but they were adults here, not excluded but equal – equals in this strange little show.

'We're actually suspects!' she said to Crispin when Tamsin moved on, 'which is, like, *so* cool!'

'The murderer is the least likely one,' replied Crispin, in a serious fashion.

'What are you talking about?'

'That's what my dad says.'

'Your dad?'

'Yep.'

'Right – and he sells cars . . . so obviously he'll know all about police work.'

'No, he does! We watch murder mysteries together sometimes – well, we used to. He says it's always the least likely one, the one who is very nice and helps the police with their enquiries. It's never the evil one or the nutty one or the oddball or the unpopular one who you want it to be.'

Holly pondered.

'So if we cut out the evil, the nutty, the oddballs and the unpopular at Stormhaven Towers – who does that leave?' she asked, bursting out into loud laughter. Adult heads suddenly turned in disapproval. One shouldn't laugh amid murder, especially when the widow is present. Holly reddened a little and she spoke more quietly: 'And anyway, that's only on telly, Crispin. In real life, the police know the murderer straight away, almost always, within the first forty-eight hours. It's just about proving it. And it's normally a relation.' Crispin looked doubtful. 'No really, it is!'

'You're saying it's his wife?'

'I'm not saying definitely. But by the law of averages, it probably is.'

'Absolutely no way.'

They both looked across to Cressida who had moved to where Penny had sat. She was looking out of the window, as if in a trance.

'Why not?'

'Well, she's a doctor, for a start.'

'So? It's always the doctor!'

'It's not *always* the doctor. It's the butler sometimes.' They laughed. 'Or the Reverend Green with the lead piping in the library!' They looked across at the chaplain, Ferdinand Heep. Holly wasn't laughing now, but serious again.

'Dr Crippen was a famous murderer,' she said. 'He killed his wife.'

'She had lots of affairs,' said Crispin drily. 'Mrs Cutting is nothing like that.'

'How do you know?'

'I just do. And anyway, Crippen was American.'

'Racist.'

'And not even a proper doctor.'

Crispin had done a school project on Crippen and even visited Hilldrop Crescent in Camden, where the murder took place. He couldn't say why he was so interested.

'Harold Shipman,' said Holly. 'He was a doctor – and English.'

Crispin shrugged his shoulders and then had a thought.

'It could be you, Holly.'

Holly thought for a moment. She'd never really talked with Crispin before. They'd had different friends, walked different paths through their schooldays. He wasn't stand-out gorgeous or stand-out anything, really, so he'd got a bit lost in the crowd . . despite being head boy. But he was quite sweet really, that's what she was thinking. She felt playful with him and she hadn't felt that for a long time. School for Holly had been a game – a game she'd survived and thrived in, been clever and smart . . . she'd somehow stumbled upon the key to power. But it had been an oppressive game, each day a battle and this is what she was now feeling as she sat in the evening sunlight of the common room – bad things done along the way. Yet somehow a weight was now removed from her shoulders. How had that happened? Perhaps she'd confess to the abbot – because she needed to confess to someone, that was obvious . . . and he looked nice in his mad clothes.

'And that's cool as well,' she said. 'Like, I could be a murderer. That's epic!' Apart from anything else, it felt like she was a woman at last. 'And I could, you know! I could do it. I could easily have done it.'

She raised her hands as if to attack Crispin, who laughed awkwardly and pulled away. His mind was elsewhere, on the murder moment. He'd been there, you see – the thought had just struck him.

'I was there,' he said to Holly.

'Where?'

And then he hesitated.

'It doesn't matter.' He was suddenly sweating. 'I think I'll go to my room.' He needed to think.

'OK,' she said, and watched him leave.

Holly now sat alone. And then she turned and caught Ferdinand staring at her, as though she was a ghost.

'You might have told me

this was a residential job,' said Peter. They were walking towards the house of the late Jamie King and his widow, Cressida Cutting. 'I would have put up my rates.'

'You don't have any rates. Or none that are negotiable.'

'Even so.'

'I only had the idea as I was talking.'

'And you didn't think to run it past me first?'

'How was I to run it past you in the meeting? You need to go with the flow, Abbot.'

Peter laughed.

'I don't remember you ever going with the flow, Tamsin.' He was right – she never went with the flow. 'You fight the flow every inch of the way, with every ounce of your being. You build a dam or send the flow underground. What you never do is *go with* it.'

'And anyway, you'll love it, Uncle, you know you will – all this boarding stuff.' Peter felt a strong inner reaction. He disliked people assuming what he would feel . . . they were always wrong, and generally attempting only to make themselves feel better . . . as Tamsin was now. 'It'll be like being back in the monastery,' she said, 'with your little cell and a community of oddballs. PC Wilson is bringing your stuff.'

'Wilson?'

'Yes.'

'And how is Wilson getting hold of "my stuff" – breaking and entering?'

'I sent him into Lewes to buy everything you need. They've got good shops there and it won't do you any harm to have some new pyjamas.'

'How would you know that?'

He didn't have any pyjamas.

'I'm guessing.'

75

The abbot considered the unfolding story of his overnight stay and Wilson's shopping expedition. He'd initially felt like the victim of a police stitch-up ... which he was. But he also saw potential in the development.

'I'll need running gear,' he said firmly.

'What?'

'I'll need to run while I'm here – and I'm not going naked.'

'No, that wouldn't be good. Especially not in a school.'

'So?'

'It's the sense of entitlement that disappoints me. It's like the politicians' expenses scandal.'

Peter ignored her.

'I won't be staying over without the running gear, Tamsin. Running keeps me sane.'

'Isn't prayer meant to do that?'

'Prayer and running.'

'You're pushing it, Abbot.'

'No, you're pushing it, Detective Inspector – and I'm responding. I'm the one in the East Wing, going to bed with a murderer down the corridor, possibly next door, while you enjoy the luxury of your little flat in Hove ... which I still haven't seen, by the way.'

'When I've got it all sorted ...'

'Size nine running shoes, Adidas preferably.'

They arrived at the door of the headmaster's house, tasteful mock-Georgian and surrounded by trees. Inside was the widow, Cressida Cutting. They glanced at each other in a moment of camaraderie and rang the bell.

'Let loose the dogs of inquiry!' whispered Peter.

Cressida opened the door,

and without a welcome, silently guided them inside to the front room, where yesterday, Jamie had paced with worry. He'd left with the spoken desire that they should talk together more. And now they wouldn't talk at all.

'Good of you to see us, Cressida.'

'Did I have a choice?' she said with an accusing smile. 'Do sit down.'

Two large sofas offered themselves, at right angles, expensive beige fabric with a subtle Japanese style black and pink print – and a glass coffee table in the middle ground. The room was decorated with quiet luxury, held in the arms of a beautiful walled garden through the large patio window ... though the garden showed some signs of neglect.

'I'm afraid Jamie didn't like having the school gardener in,' she said, anticipating their thoughts. 'He found it intrusive. Everyone needs to get away from where they work – from the staff.'

'Quite,' said Tamsin. She always needed to get away.

'But unfortunately gardens don't tend themselves,' said Cressida. 'I don't know what I'll do with it now – well, I don't suppose I'll be here for much longer ...'

There was a pause.

'It is very sudden and a shock, we do know,' said Tamsin, briefly aware of how difficult this all must be for the woman opposite. Yesterday, she had a husband and a house. Today, she just had the house ... and soon, she would have neither. 'I mean, our visit. But we do need to speak with you this evening.'

'That's fine,' said Cressida, revealing her frustration. In Peter's experience, only the stressed used the word 'fine' to describe themselves or their predicament.

'You were with your husband shortly before he died ... as far as we know, the last to see him before he died.'

'Well, not quite the last – if what you propose is indeed true.'

'I'm sorry?'

'If he was murdered . . . then I wouldn't have been the last to see him.'

'No, of course . . .'

'Though I'm not convinced that he was.'

'We're not proposing anything at the moment, Cressida,' said Peter. 'And we appreciate how difficult this must be for you.'

It was also difficult for Peter, finding a new way to relate to his doctor. In the surgery, it was she who asked all the questions and held all the power.

'It's not difficult,' she said. 'It's just meaningless. The death, the investigation – it's meaningless.'

Tamsin and Peter felt awkward on the sofa. The abbot was also concerned lest his habit stain the beige fabric and the delicate flower print, visible now he was close to it. A trip to the launder-ette was probably due – no, long overdue – and this was not a good place to discover that.

'Look, just ask the questions you wish to ask,' said Cressida, 'and let's get this over with, shall we?'

OK, then, thought Tamsin.

'How was your last meeting with your husband, Cressida?'

'How do you mean?'

'Was it happy?'

It was Jennifer Stiles, the head's PA, who'd tipped off Tamsin that, 'It wasn't exactly the happiest of marriages.' Tamsin had asked for more, but Jennifer refused to explain further. 'I don't think you'll find many who disagree, though,' she'd said.

'I don't know what you mean by *happy*,' said Cressida. 'He was concerned about the review team weekend, an issue had come up and he wanted my opinion about it.'

'What was the issue?'

'He didn't say what the issue was. He was like that.'

'Like what?'

'Jamie couldn't always speak of his concerns – he bottled them up, held them in, unpresented. I see a lot of people like that in the surgery: people who want only a degree of healing. They want relief without the deeper healing of fundamental change in their lives. They want me to mend the outcomes of their poor habits – but not to change their habits. Do you get the picture?' The abbot wondered if he was one of these despised patients – and they *were* despised, he could see. 'It could be frustrating with Jamie because while he wouldn't tell you anything, keeping it all locked up, he'd still be in a mood and demand support ... and get angry if it wasn't there. He didn't want my opinion – he just wanted my sympathy.'

Why does anyone ever get married? wondered Tamsin. And it looks as though Jennifer wasn't wrong; Cressida was hardly in pieces over his loss.

'So he was in a mood and not revealing why,' said Tamsin, reminded of most of the men she knew. 'And then?'

'Oh, he went into his study, I think – I was working. And then he came out a few minutes later, saying he had to go out.'

'Did he say why – or where?'

'No – and I was too busy to care, to be honest. It's possible I wasn't listening too closely.'

Tamsin did not want to like Cressida – she'd been publicly humiliated by her in the common room, which usually meant revenge somewhere down the line. But she found admiration growing for this headmaster's wife ... matter-of-fact and distant, nothing hysterical about her and quite unmoved by the childish self-importance of her husband Jamie King. Not that she was taking sides ...

'And so he left, without saying where he was going.'

'Yes.'

'And you never saw him again?'

'No,' said Cressida. 'And the world is now a very different place, believe me.' She smiled painfully, like sunshine in the rain, as her eyes watered a little. Peter hoped Tamsin would leave it there. But Tamsin never left it there.

'Do you think your husband was the suicidal type, Cressida?'

'Who *is* the suicidal type?' She laughed dismissively. 'Men never let anyone know what's coming, that's why it's such a shock. Women tend to give more clues, more cries for help along the way. But men, only rarely ... they just go out and do the violent deed. And it does tend to be violent. Men don't do drugs and sleeping pills. I see it all the time.'

'In a professional capacity?'

'Of course. They're with you in the surgery one week, friendly enough and then next week ... they've got up one morning, tidied the greenhouse, thrown a rope over a beam in the garage and hanged themselves. Men like the angry, violent exit – leaving a devastated family behind.'

'Do you think Jamie killed himself, Cressida?'

There was a pause.

'What does it matter what I think?'

'I think it matters a great deal,' said Peter.

'It won't bring him back – so how does it count at all?'

'I suppose we're just trying to find out what happened – so we can lay the matter to rest.'

'Do you think I'll be happy when the murderer is found? I won't be – because really, *so bloody what?*' The abbot chose not to reply. It was the first interview; she must be allowed to rule. They could press harder another time. 'He was certainly anxious yesterday,' she added, to break the silence. 'Something had come up that he couldn't solve – but that was hardly new. Things come and go in any community.'

Unfortunately Wonder stays, thought Tasmin.

But Cressida was still speaking: 'I just don't see anyone wishing to kill him. No ...' She broke off, as if remembering. 'I mean, he always said you had to be aware of the "pissed-off and the passed-over" in the school – that was his phrase. They were the teachers whose careers had run into the sand and were going nowhere – yet still in their mid-forties, so facing twenty years of disillusionment ahead, waiting for their pension. But it was their sulking he didn't like – I don't think he imagined they'd kill him.'

She said it deadpan, it wasn't a joke. And then she spoke again.

'I'd take poison. I wouldn't jump.'

Jennifer left her bike

in the gravel car park off the A259, by the blackberry bushes they had picked from as children. One in the mouth, one in the bag and they'd been good days. Well, better days at least ... days of innocence before her father's suffering began.

She walked in the late evening light down the track, which led over the railway line to Tide Mills and the sea. And really, what a day! Who would have thought it – the police saying that they thought Jamie had been murdered? Jamie's death was quite appalling, because she had probably loved him. He'd been a man who knew what he wanted, not frightened to take decisions, a strong man who liked her, depended on her, until ... well, she'd now do all she could, of course – which was why she was here, walking this familiar path in the fading light. They came here as a family, all those years ago. A picnic at Tide Mills was something Dad could manage – and they'd all had to look after Dad.

He liked to tell them the history of the place, it was what dads did ... they hid their feelings in stories. So Jennifer knew how in 1770 a flour mill, driven by tidal power, had opened halfway between Stormhaven and Newhaven – and was called Tide Mills. And how the mill was a success, with a village growing around it to house the workers.

But there was trouble in 1795. Her dad was particularly keen on this particular yarn. It was a little more gruesome than the rest and he liked to frighten his girls. 'Britain was at war with France – that's who we used to fight, the Frenchies. And to guard against invasion, militia groups were stationed along the south coast of England, ready for the fight. But some of the militia at Blatchington – that's the north side of Stormhaven – they weren't happy, were they? Not happy at all. They weren't being given enough food and, in the end, they were so hungry they mutinied!'

'What's that mean?'

'They disobeyed their commanders, charged down into Stormhaven, seized food from shopkeepers at gunpoint – and then proceeded on to Tide Mills where there was flour. Well, two of them were charged with stealing flour from the sloop, *Lucy*, moored there – and another was charged with stealing rum and flour from the mill.'

'But they were hungry!'

'Yes, but that wasn't so clever though, was it? Because along came the troops from Brighton and ...' At this point, he'd try to grab the girls with his hands, and they'd run away screaming. 'They got caught! The five ringleaders were hanged by the neck and the others were transported – sent to Australia where hard labour awaited them.'

But quieter times followed, for the history books at least. The mill closed in 1883, though the village – still known as Tide Mills – continued to be occupied by tenants, now having to make their living elsewhere. Eventually, in 1937, most residents had to leave when their homes were declared unfit for human habitation. It had become a bleak and neglected outpost – and no shops for a good distance in either direction. The remaining tenants were evicted in 1940 as the area was needed for defensive purposes ... the Canadians were lodged there, in case of invasion from a different enemy now, the Germans.

The troubled history of Tide Mills ... yet Jennifer loved this place. These haunted ruins were her childhood and, in a way, her home. Never closed down or cordoned off, they remained a place of play for generations of children; and she knew where to go, the place where they always went. They called it the 'Secret House', hidden from view, with the concrete bench where, as children, they could sit, talk and imagine ... and be free from their parents for a while. Just for a while, they could look after no one but themselves.

There was a chill in the air as Jennifer walked, a night chill – July could still be cold. She now left the track and made for the derelict flint cottages. She stepped through the absent door and into the stone skeleton of the old miller's home, the 'Secret House'. They'd both be back by the eleven o'clock curfew, the two of them, no one need know; it was harmless enough, after all. But what was the meeting about?

And the person following Jennifer – they had been since she arrived – was happy to take her lead. They didn't have memories here, didn't know this place at all really . . . not in the way Jennifer did.

But then Jennifer thought she was meeting someone else entirely.

PC Wilson's shopping

lay on the bed – and he'd done a pretty good job. Peter was not used to so many new items so close together. He tried to avoid shops. Yet here on his bed were toothpaste, dental floss, toothbrush, deodorant, razors, shaving cream, pyjamas – flowery – a red dressing gown, blue slippers ... and a full set of running gear. And it really was very full – including a headband, which suggested Wilson was either a runner himself or married to one. Perhaps they ran with the Stormhaven Striders, the local running club? Peter wasn't sure about the dark running glasses – what would he be doing with those? Dark running glasses were worn by the shifty, by those insecure in their identity, this is what Peter felt – by those hiding from the world.

'But the glasses aside, a very good job, Wilson,' said Peter to himself. The size nine Adidas shoes were a pleasing cobalt blue, the colour of wisdom, while the ample supply of fruit and nut chocolate and a pack of digestive biscuits were the icing on the cake. Chocolate still felt like a treat to Peter. Whole years had gone by in the desert without it, the heat making storage difficult. The monk in charge of requisitions, Brother Titus, did sometimes smuggle the brown gold into the monastery, taking it quickly to the fridge in the scullery. But it never lasted long there, this was his experience. Word got round, as it does in a community, discreet visits were made to confirm the sweet rumours and then came the tasting. In the end, Brother Titus gave up. Unless he could find a private fridge – and where would he find that? – what was the point?

But Peter had no such issues now. His newsagent was well stocked with all manner of delights, his fridge an entirely private place – and with PC Wilson on hand in a crisis, such as now. Here was a most competent police officer, who one day might make a very good butler.

*

It was now ten on his first night in the East Wing at Stormhaven Towers. He had not expected to be there at the start of the day, but then, that was life. 'Where we wake in the morning, we may not take our rest,' as the Bedouin used to say.

He would shortly make a trip to the common room. Wilson's only failure was to remember the kettle Peter had asked for; but while a loss, it was not insurmountable. He could find boiling water in the common room easily enough, and then bring it back to his room for a quiet drink before lights out. 'Lights out!' Hah! It seemed the right phrase now that he was back at school . . . though as the prefect in charge, he did have some extra powers here tonight.

He put his clothes away in the small chest of drawers and laid out his bathroom gear on the glass shelf above the sink. It was a wonder in itself – monasteries didn't have glass shelves. I must get one of these above my sink at home, he was thinking. His sink at home was a crowded place, and a simple shelf above it would ease the crowding. The soap could stay on the sink but the toothbrush and paste could have their own place on the shelf . . . it had not been a wasted day. He then moved towards the door, turned the handle and stepped out into the dark corridor.

Suddenly, a figure emerged from the shadows. Peter froze. It was young Crispin, breathless and terrified.

'You look like you've seen a ghost!' said Peter.

'I *have* seen a ghost!' said Crispin.

They sat in his room.

Abbot Peter had made space on the bed for himself. Crispin sat in the chair by the window.

'I don't believe in ghosts,' said Crispin.

'No,' said Peter, who only did occasionally ... well, he couldn't decide. Tamsin would laugh in his face at the idea, but that didn't mean she was right. The Chinese astronomers saw new stars a long time before the European astronomers did. They were looking at the same medieval sky with roughly comparable instruments ... but they were seeing different things – and why? Because Chinese cosmology allowed for celestial change, for the possibility of new stars in the sky ... while pre-Copernican Europeans didn't. New stars were not possible in their world view ... so they didn't see any. You only hear what you can receive and see what you can accept ... Peter's life was colourful testimony to that.

'But it was no one I knew,' said Crispin, shaking his head.

'You didn't recognize the ghost?'

'No.'

'I could get us a cup of tea,' said the abbot.

'Not for me, thanks. I don't drink tea or coffee.'

He wasn't terrified any more, this was Peter's conclusion and his breathing was now steadier.

'And what were they doing?' he asked.

'Who?'

'This figure you saw.'

'Oh, just walking down the corridor – tilting his head sometimes, like this.'

Crispin twisted his shoulders slightly and angled his head to demonstrate.

'At least he wasn't holding his head under his arm,' said Peter.

Crispin almost smiled. But he was not quite free from the shock and Peter was disturbed. He was aware the East Wing was locked, that no stranger could simply have wandered in. There were two police on patrol somewhere outside – though what they did at night, he wasn't sure. His guess was they'd be paying particular attention to the fridge in the school kitchens. He knew a young constable in Brighton whose night beat was almost entirely shaped by the tea stations along the way. But if the ghost wasn't a visitor, it must be a resident.

'And you didn't know him, you're sure of that?'

'Sure. I mean, I only saw his back – and the side of his face, but ...'

'No one you've seen before. So what was he like? It was a man, you say?'

'It was a man, yes.'

'How old?'

'Old. I don't know, fifty?'

'That's not old, Crispin.' Another joke that failed. 'And what was he wearing?'

'He was pale in the moonlight, his face was white, when he walked past the window, pale face – pale suit.'

Peter would probably have preferred him in tights and a doublet, distant from the murder investigation, separated by the centuries. This ghost sounded contemporary, a more present threat.

'Do you believe in ghosts?' asked Crispin.

'I don't *not* believe in them,' said Peter, clumsily. 'I find the idea of an unhappy soul loitering, adrift from their true time zone, looking for resolution of some sort – well, I find that quite psychologically compelling ... though absurd as well, of course.'

'You don't believe me?'

'I believe you entirely, Crispin. I believe you saw a figure walking down the corridor, tilting his head.' Peter tilted his head in solidarity. 'The question is: who was he ... and what was he doing in the East Wing?' Crispin shrugged. He wasn't so bothered about that. 'So how are you feeling about all this?'

'All what?' Crispin sounded worried.

'Well, it has hardly been a normal day. Your headmaster has been murdered.'

'Are you really sure about that?'

'About it being murder? It's a strong possibility.'

There was a knock on the door and Crispin convulsed in fear. Peter rose to comfort him just as the door opened.

'Well, this is all very cosy,'

said peroxide Penny Rylands, surveying the scene. She was looking at a man and a boy in the man's room, the abbot standing over Crispin. 'Does the Church never learn?'

'I was just . . .'

'I really don't want to know, Abbot. Not my affair – and Crispin's an adult now.' Peter looked at her but she could not look back. Penny was somewhere else, distracted, tense and twitchy. 'And I need to know where Jennifer is.' Peter was thrown for a moment.

'Jennifer?'

'Jennifer Stiles! The head's PA. She's not in her room. Have you seen her, Crispin?'

Crispin shook his head.

'Crispin's had his own troubles,' said Peter. 'He's seen a ghost.'

'And he wouldn't be the first here, there have been sightings before – but I'm sure he'll recover. My concerns are more with flesh and blood.'

'I'm sure there's a good reason why Jennifer is not in her room,' said Peter. 'I have no doubt that in the morning . . .'

'Don't patronize me.'

Penny was snarling tension, like a cornered dog.

'Does she have a mobile?'

'Yes, of course she does. How could the head's PA not have a mobile?'

'How indeed?'

'But I don't have one, since you ask.'

'You don't have a phone?'

'It's gone missing.'

'When was that?'

'I don't know, I had it this afternoon.' And then she paused, puzzled. 'And then it disappeared.'

'I see.'

Was this important?

'Just like Jennifer's – though we found hers in her bag. Well, I found it.'

'I'm sorry?'

He was lost.

'It doesn't matter, we found it.'

'You found what?'

'Jennifer's phone! But it doesn't matter – what matters is that she's not in her room when she should be. And unlike you, I'm worried.'

The angel appeared through the dark

'What's happened to you?' they asked.

'I don't know,' said Jennifer, relieved to her bones to see some-one she knew. Her head was throbbing and she was aware now, or beginning to be aware, that she was lying on the ground, with the night sky above her. There was probably a reason – Tide Mills, now she remembered. She'd come to meet someone or perhaps that was another day.

'Lie still,' said the angel, holding her head with care. 'There's nasty bleeding at the back of your skull – has someone hit you?'

'I don't think so,' said Jennifer, though why she was lying here she wasn't sure.

'I'm going to hold something against the wound to stop the bleeding, so just relax – can you do that?'

'I think so.'

'You're going to be all right, Jennifer. You deserve this.'

'But what are you doing here?' asked the stricken figure, though she didn't remember the answer. Dizziness overcame her beneath the coastal stars and then vomiting. She was throwing up over the Tide Mills cottage, the playground of her youth, though the pathologist – later the following day – would say Jennifer Stiles, the head's PA at Stormhaven Towers, died of asphyxia.

The angel was long gone by then, with wings stained in blood.

'We need to give

the murder investigation a name,' said Tamsin.

She sat with Peter in the waiting room in bright July sunlight, at the beginning of a morning of interviews. They'd agreed to meet early to catch up on events before the questioning began. Tamsin was drinking black coffee and eating a croissant with raspberry jam.

Peter's morning had started a little earlier. He'd already been down to the kitchen, where bread, cereal and boiled eggs were laid out in self-service style by Mrs Docherty on the early shift.

'Never seen a monk close up,' she'd said, busying herself with the cleaning of surfaces. She was mainly employed as a cleaner at Stormhaven Towers, to be fair. Only in emergencies – like the chef demanding unreasonable amounts of overtime – was she sent to the kitchen where boiled eggs were probably the limit of her competence.

'Then be grateful,' said Peter. 'They're better kept at a distance. We haven't met. I'm Abbot Peter. And you?'

'Mrs Docherty.' She was hesitant, unused to revealing her name ... or to anyone being interested. 'So what are you doing here?'

'Helping with the investigation. That's the idea.'

'It's the queen and her dog when the headmaster's murdered!'

'I'm sorry?'

And who were 'the queen and her dog'? wondered Peter.

'I'm just saying.'

'What are you just saying?'

There was clearly a grievance here.

'That it wasn't like this for Gerry. That's all I'm saying ... nothing like this for Gerry.'

'Who's Gerry?'

'I'm not sure they sent anyone when he went.' She was pouring oats into a large plastic serving bowl.

'I don't know Gerry.'

'Well, you wouldn't, would you – because he's dead.'

'He worked here?'

'He was the gardener, Gerry was. Died last year, poisoned, clear as day. They never found who done it, though. But then no one was much interested, were they? He wasn't a nob, was he?'

'A nob?'

'A posh sort. Are you not from this country?'

'I've been away awhile.'

'Should have stayed away. It's going to the dogs.'

'But I'm very sorry about Gerry.'

'Terrible at the end, I saw him. He was here, in the kitchen. Dizziness at first, then vomiting. Though they say he died of asphyxia . . . in the cricket pavilion.'

'The cricket pavilion?'

'That's as far as he got.'

Peter had forgotten about breakfast.

'Dizziness, vomiting, asphyxia . . . that sounds a little like aconite poisoning,' he said.

'That's what it was, monk. Aconite!' He wasn't completely stupid. 'I read about it. They said he was just unlucky with one of those plants. You'd not think gardening dangerous, eh? Not like skydiving and the like. But you never know, do you? There must be a dangerous plant here somewhere.' She cleaned a little more, rubbing hard. 'You don't know when you'll go, monk, that's for sure. I tell that to Mr Docherty. "You don't know when you'll go," I say.'

'We know neither the day nor the hour, Mrs Docherty.'

Peter had taken his coffee, toast and marmalade back to his room to reflect on a troubled night, with both Crispin and Penny so disturbed. He'd watched the sun rise, taken a short walk across the dewy grass, pondered the death of Gerry – and then waited for Tamsin to arrive with her coffee and croissant.

'Does it have to have a name?' he asked, believing there must be a better use of their time.

'All murder investigations have a name, Abbot . . . just like all tornadoes have a name.'

'I've always struggled with mindless destruction being called "Lucy" or "Susannah".'

'When "Chief Inspector Wonder" would do.'

They laughed.

'How about Cliff?' he offered. '*Operation Cliff?*'

'We had a previous investigation called *Cliff* . . . it sort of goes with the territory here.'

'*Son of Cliff* . . . or how about *Cliff – the Sequel?*'

'Now you're being stupid.'

'And you're not? The idea that we have to give the investigation a name . . .'

'And you're being stupid in a habit, which somehow makes it worse . . . I expect gravitas from those clothes.' Peter shrugged. There was something in him which enjoyed being a disappointment. Disappointing his adopted mother had been one of his few pleasures as a teenager. 'And anyway,' continued Tamsin, 'the name of the investigation is supposed to give nothing away about itself.'

'*Tamsin.*'

'Very amusing.'

'You're not laughing.'

'Do you struggle with the fact that I don't talk to you about personal matters?'

'Not in the slightest.'

Perhaps a little.

'And anyway, you do tell me things,' said Peter.

'Not anything important.'

'And what makes one thing more important than another? It's in the tittle-tattle that people give themselves away.'

Tamsin looked at him and remembered why she wanted him here for the interviews. 'The abbot's like a deponent verb,' as someone once said to her. 'He appears passive – but is in fact active.'

'*Rosemary,*' said Peter.

'I'm sorry?'

What was he talking about?

'*Operation Rosemary,*' said Peter. 'My final offer for the name of the investigation.'

He wanted to get on with things.

'Why Rosemary?'

'Does it matter?'

'Of course.'

'It's just a name.'

'No, it isn't.'

Peter raised his eyebrows with regret; he'd skewered himself, he realized that.

'She was someone I once knew.'

'When?'

Oh, to hell with it! thought Peter. He'd tell her ... he'd give himself away.

'She was a nurse in the unit.'

'What unit?'

'And my first — well, I suppose, my only — love. Is that the word? Or maybe obsession.'

'Rosemary was?'

'She rejected me, of course. And whatever she's done since — I have no idea where she is — that will definitely have been her wisest decision in life.'

Tamsin was surprised by this revelation and for a moment, her mind was freed from a tumbling headmaster.

'And so that was that, Uncle — no way back with Rosemary?'

'How do you mean?'

'After she rejected you ... no way back.'

'No.'

'You didn't plead with her?'

'*Plead* with her? Why would I do that?'

Tamsin laughed dismissively.

'It's what people do when they're in love.'

She'd seen it in others — though not known it herself. Love for Tamsin could only ever be a negotiated and acceptably tolerable arrangement between two people.

'I read the letter ...'

'She wrote to you? She dumped you by letter? She didn't say it face to face?'

'There was nothing to say.'

'Really?'

'So I read the letter, accepted my fate, visited the garden of sadness for a while – and then had a relationship on the rebound, I suppose.'

'Oh.'

'There's no need to feign empathy. You don't do it well.'

How much dare she ask? But if not now, when? 'Seize the moment!' as the fat police receptionist would say . . . though which moment – apart from the biscuits – she'd seized in her life was not immediately obvious.

'A relationship on the rebound – who with?'

'The desert,' said Peter.

There was a knock on the door.

'Come!' said Tamsin and in walked Terence Standing, the school bursar who liked to think he had everything figured out.

'I'm sure I can't help,'

he said, before he'd even sat down.

The waiting room, behind reception, was now the interview room and Terence was first on the list.

'Well, don't be too sure, Mr Standing,' said Tamsin, indicating he should sit. She was smartly dressed, white blouse and black skirt, drawing on her extensive wardrobe in Hove.

'It's just that I have nothing to say.'

He sat down in a manner to suggest he wouldn't be here long, that sitting was a slight waste of time.

'Perhaps you have more to say than you know.'

People always had more to say than they knew, though Terence seemed to take it as an accusation.

'I really don't,' he said. 'This will be a waste of time for us all.'

His white shirt was as fresh that day as the day before. Perhaps it was a new white shirt, though the red tie must be the same. He was clean-shaven and trim in beige chinos, red socks and black shoes, which for Tamsin was a disaster. Black shoes and beige chinos? A fashion car crash ... but she had other things on her mind.

'You're sounding rather determined, bursar!' said Tamsin. 'Determined to say nothing – when all we want is a chat.'

'Yes, but it isn't a chat, is it?' he said, rather precisely, as though looking at some faulty figures.

'Then what is it?'

And now he looked like a lost boy in Asda. 'It's about incriminating people, tripping them up,' he said.

'I think you'd best calm yourself, Mr Standing,' said Tamsin. She hadn't expected this display of fear and insecurity. 'No one is out to get you ... or trip you up.'

'In fact, we want you "standing" at all times!' said Peter cheerily. 'May we call you Terence?'

'I suppose.' Only the head called him Terence in the school, he'd been quite insistent about that. 'I'm quite innocent, though.' And with that, he crossed his arms.

'But unhappy,' said the abbot, changing gear. Terence gave a dismissive why-do-you-say-that? look but didn't answer and so Peter continued. 'Innocent, as you say – but clearly troubled by something.'

'I don't know what you mean,' Terence replied. He tried to stare Peter out, a half-smile across his face. It was a challenge.

'It's not a crime to be troubled, Terence.'

'Who said I'm troubled? I am the bursar here, a key post.' He said it as if he was Lord High Admiral. 'And as far as I'm aware, I do a very exact and satisfactory job.'

'*Exact and satisfactory?*' said Tamsin.

'The head always said so. No one gets an unnecessary expense past me.'

'I'm sure they don't.'

'And we're in a healthy state financially . . . and when the Japanese finally give the nod . . .'

'The Japanese?'

'A possible link-up. It's not in the public domain – and neither should it be for now.'

He didn't wish to say more and wasn't pressed, so silence fell.

'And if I keep myself to myself,' said Terence, to fill the space, 'that is my own choice and quite unrelated to happiness, I can assure you.'

Terence's speech was as precise as his accounts. Peter nodded.

'And I'm like you, Terence, in that regard. I keep myself to myself as well. A crowd does not equal happiness in my world!'

Terence looked slightly relieved to find an ally in this matter.

'But I suppose the happy do not lie prostrate in the chapel, sobbing,' added Peter. 'Unless they're crying for joy, I suppose.'

Penny, thought Terence. Who else could have told them? No, Penny was clearly the grass. Well, two can play at that game. He looked down, though, like one deflated; he did not wish to respond. Perspiration appeared beneath the armpits on his fresh white shirt — not a look that endeared anyone to Tamsin, which ruled out most of Lewes CID from her circle of love. But the sweat was interesting. The body never lies and the morning was chill, as summer mornings can be. Tamsin had noticed the abbot was wearing both a T-shirt and rugby shirt beneath his habit.

'It is no crime,' said Terence primly. 'Have you never cried about a sad matter?'

Have you never cried about a sad matter? It was strange how he spoke, childlike and defenceless in a way, but with the veneer of cleverness and control. Peter did not want to push him further for now; he thought he might break and not recover. So instead, they talked a little about Jamie, easier ground for the bursar.

'Was Jamie the sort of man who could fall off a cliff by accident?' asked Tamsin.

Terence thought for a moment . . . he thought quickly.

'Highly unlikely,' he said.

'Why do you say that?'

'Jamie both walked and ran those cliffs — he knew them well.'

'A runner, was he?' asked Peter. Perhaps he'd passed him up there, said good morning to the man. Most runners were friendly and offered a greeting — apart from the ones in dark glasses.

'I think so. He had a running machine at home . . . in the scullery. Cressida showed it to me. He did drive himself hard.'

'But you got on well?'

'When we managed to speak.' Tamsin looked quizzical. 'Jennifer did not always make access easy.'

'Ah yes — I hear she was a little protective.'

It had been a remark Ferdinand once made to the abbot . . . and he passed the inference on.

'A little, I suppose,' he said, as one unconcerned. 'But I learned to bypass her,' he added, pleased with himself. It wasn't as if he was like the others. He was the bursar.

'And how did you do that?' said Tamsin admiringly.

'Quite simple really. I learned which phone number to use.' He spoke with a knowing smile. 'I will say no more.'

'And the sad matter?' said Tamsin, wishing to throw him again. 'The sad matter that took you to the altar?'

'What of it?'

She had thrown him. He was ruffled.

'What made you so sad? It must have been something serious.' Elvis Presley's 'Crying in the Chapel' suddenly appeared in her consciousness – but this wasn't the time to hum the tune.

'It's not something I wish to talk about.'

'But something you'll have to talk about in a murder investigation – Terence.' She sensed he disliked them using that name and so she'd use it as much as she could. 'It's a rather brutal affair in that regard, the things closest to us yet hidden – they have to be shown.'

Terence paused.

'It was my mother,' he said.

'What about her?'

'She's been unwell.'

'Really? Well, to cry in that fashion – and in that place – you must care about her greatly.'

'Of course I care about her – she's my mother! Doesn't everyone care about their mother?'

'No.'

Tamsin didn't, not in any comparable way, at least. I mean, one was polite to her but anything more was a struggle. Terence, meanwhile, was rigid with offence, believing this was none of their business and quite unfair.

'And so where did you get to on your two hours off?' asked Peter, changing the angle again. 'Jamie gave you all a break, didn't he, on Sunday afternoon?' It was while they were all out that Jamie fell, so the logistics of the afternoon, the movements of the assembled company, were of interest. 'He wanted you all to get out, clear your heads and breathe some fresh air.'

'"He probably wants a smoke," was Penny's take on the matter,' said Terence a little bitchily. 'But then we all know what she wanted!'

'*What* did she want?'

'Myra is not unambitious, you know.'

'"Myra"?'

'It's a name people have for her – her hair colour, and the eyes.'

Tamsin nodded.

'So what did you do with the afternoon, Terence? Did you get out and about?'

'I drove to the Long Man of Wilmington,' he said, folding his arms triumphantly, like a card player when they've just declared a good hand.

All three shared some knowledge about the Long Man, though Tamsin less than the other two. She knew he was long and a man – but not a great deal more. Terence and Peter could go further, aware that he was a stick man, a naked figure on the South Downs, seventy-five yards long and holding two straight staves. And while there were some who wished his origins to be more ancient – a mystery figure from Saxon times would be nice – he was probably more recent, a chalk creation of the Stuarts, so a survivor from the sixteenth century.

'Any witnesses to your trip?' asked Tamsin.

'You mean apart from the Long Man?'

Terence enjoyed his joke and Peter smiled warmly.

'We'll be speaking to him as well,' he said.

'It looks like he's cut from the chalk, of course,' said Terence. He did like information, when it didn't concern him.

'Well, he is, isn't he?' said Peter, genuinely interested.

'Originally, yes, but no more, sadly – the distant eye deceives. He's white breeze blocks now. Still, we don't need to tell any-one ... everyone should be allowed their secrets, without fear of persecution. So are we done?'

And they nearly were, but not quite.

'There's just one small matter,' said Tamsin.

'Oh?'

'Who's Benedict?' she said.

'Benedict?'

There was slight horror in his eyes.

'Do you know anyone called Benedict?'

'I don't think so.'

'Well, that's odd, Terence.' The bursar looked quizzical. 'The police searched your room yesterday. And they turned up a letter you'd written – but not sent. Remember it?' She had his attention now. 'Well, it was hardly a letter, more a note really – a note to Benedict, begging to see him.'

Terence shrugged.

'And just his name on the envelope,' said the abbot. 'So it wasn't going by royal mail. An internal letter perhaps?'

'Perhaps they planted it,' said Terence.

'And perhaps you wrote it.'

He looked at them blankly.

'You can see how that might interest us?' said Tamsin. 'Why someone called Benedict might interest us. Is this someone we know?'

Penny arrived distracted,

and explained her lateness.

'They've just found my phone,' she said, slightly breathless with the drama.

'Who found it?' asked Peter, aware of the backstory.

'Well – it was Geoff, I think. It was him who told me, anyway. Found it there this morning – complete mystery.'

'Found it where?' asked Peter.

'Next to the sink in the common room kitchen.' Peter took this in with interest. 'God knows how it got there, it's not a sink I ever use – it's a health risk!'

'I didn't know you'd lost it,' said Tamsin, feeling out of the loop with everyone else. She didn't like not knowing what was going on.

'It disappeared yesterday,' said Penny, now looking at Peter with disapproval. He'd not been helpful last night . . . and it wasn't forgotten. 'I'm sure I had it when you spoke to us all. So perhaps it was someone in the common room . . .'

'Would you like to sit down?' said Tamsin. Peroxide Penny was still standing, looking down on them, which gave her too much power. 'We perhaps have bigger things on our agenda than your phone.'

Peter, however, was fascinated by the phone, particularly the location of its discovery . . . by the sink in the common room, which struck him as odd. Why there? But in the meantime, he'd calm Tamsin's anxious psyche by filling her in.

'Penny reported its disappearance last night,' he said, remembering the unfortunate scene in his bedroom.

'Not that that helped at all.'

'But I'm glad it's turned up, Penny.' Peter smiled as best he could. 'And before you ask, yes, there is an alert out for Jennifer.'

'It doesn't work,' said Penny.

'What doesn't?'

'The phone. Looks like it fell in the sink or something – no life in it.'

'Oh well . . .' said Tamsin, wanting to get on.

'Rice can sometimes do the trick,' said the abbot, who'd once used this method, after dropping his phone in the sea.

'Really?'

It was an angry 'really'.

'Uncooked obviously,' said Peter. 'Stick it in a packet of rice and it may do the trick.'

'I'm more concerned about Jennifer,' she said, sitting down with a sigh. 'I don't think rice will help *her*. Do you, Abbot?'

That put Peter in his place.

'We'll find her,' said Tamsin. 'Or she'll suddenly appear, that's my guess.'

'Suddenly appear from where?'

'I've seen it happen so often. She's been missing, for what – fourteen hours, which isn't a lot.' Though in the circumstances, and this Tamsin wasn't mentioning, it was a great deal and a matter of concern. Like a swan, Tamsin was serene on the surface, but her mind paddled furiously beneath the water. 'You're clearly concerned about Jennifer, Penny. Do you think *she* had reason to be concerned?'

'Not that I know of. Why would she?'

'I don't know.'

'I suppose she was close to the headmaster, perhaps she knew things?'

'Knows things,' corrected Peter.

'Yes, oh God, I'm sorry, that's terrible,' said Penny, blushing a little and flustered. 'My fears run ahead of me.'

'Fears often do,' he said, allowing Penny some recovery after the Freudian slip.

'And I didn't mean to insinuate anything last night, Abbot,' she said, calming a little. 'With regard to you and the boy – Crispin, I mean.'

'Have I missed something?' asked Tamsin.

'You've missed nothing,' said Peter, 'because that's what it was: nothing. Crispin had seen a ghost – he was disturbed and needed to talk.'

'And I was just disturbed . . . about Jennifer. I shouldn't have said what I said.'

'The stressed need a scapegoat, tethered to a post – and there I was.'

Peter was still angry.

'You're good friends, are you – you and Jennifer?' said Tamsin, hurriedly. She wanted away from the scapegoat narrative. Peter had clearly slept on his rage but not exorcized it.

'We're close, yes. Well, we've grown close. I can't begin to say what her death would mean to me – I mean, how it would affect me.'

'Her *death*?' said Tamsin. 'Let's not be hasty here.'

And now for the ammunition casually handed to them in conversation with Terence. What goes round, comes round . . .

'And poor old Terence sobbing in the chapel,' said the abbot.

'Er?' Penny was thrown.

'Must have been disturbing. Why were you there with him?'

'Well, I wasn't with him – I was with Jamie.'

'Oh?'

Peter feigned surprise.

'Yes, I think we both felt we needed some quiet away from the others – and went to the chapel to sit for a while.'

'How very holy.'

She wasn't the sort, surely?

'Clearly Geoff wasn't happy with the head about being – well, moved sideways. Though let's be honest – it was effectively demotion. Jamie had seen straight through Geoff.'

'I'm sure he wasn't happy,' said Tamsin. 'There's not much to celebrate in demotion.'

'So we needed to consider how best to handle that.'

'The two of you?'

'Yes.'

'Did you have some ideas?'

'I'm sorry?'

'How best to handle that?'

'Oh, just pastoral support, really.'

Not the strong hand of either Penny or Jamie, Peter imagined. And so he didn't believe the story.

'You and the head were a bit of a team, were you?' he asked.

'I suppose we were, yes. And it's a very happy memory, our time there together in the chapel – just Jamie and I, sitting alongside each other, another year over. It's a significant piece of work a school year, a journey you travel side by side. And we just sat and gazed at those awful stained-glass windows, full of bearded saints with haloes!'

'The saints don't do it for you?' said Tamsin.

'Do they do it for you?'

'I don't sit in churches.'

'No offence, Abbot, but they're not modelling anything very interesting for my girls. I was saying this to Jamie, actually. Images of strong women would be more helpful. People like you, for instance.' Tamsin took the compliment.

'Any other women come to mind?' asked Peter, always interested in the heroes people chose for themselves.

'Lady Macbeth – again, for her strength of character.'

'Not a familiar figure in church windows.'

'And perhaps that's a shame,' said Penny, carelessly. 'The Reverend Patrick Brontë could tell us a story – he sent his daughters to the Clergy Daughters' School at Cowan Bridge. Two died of tuberculosis after returning home. Emily survived to write *Wuthering Heights* and Charlotte, *Jane Eyre*, her most famous – if not her best – book.'

'Their English department were clearly doing something right – even if the medical team . . .'

'And I've ensured the English department performs with similar distinction here at Stormhaven,' said Penny, with pride. 'And part of that is promoting female writers and characters as independent voices.'

'Quite.'

'But in chapel, all we have is the Virgin Mary bowing her head and whimpering, "Let it be done according to thy will."'

Tamsin could see her point. That wasn't a line she was in danger of using.

'I do believe I can change things here,' said Penny, with Peter noting the saviour complex on display. 'But I'm sure we're all tired right now, saying unfortunate things – it's been a long and demanding term.'

'Indeed,' said Peter. 'But the work you do is remarkable. I can't remember when I last did a day's work.'

'Then you're clearly not a teacher!'

'I wouldn't survive five minutes. So you didn't argue?'

'Argue? With whom?'

'In the chapel.'

'Argue with whom in the chapel?'

She was suddenly flustered.

'With the head.' Penny's face coloured red. Terence must have heard everything. 'It was just a suggestion from someone . . . they said they heard raised voices – particularly yours.' Penny dismissed the claim with her eyebrows and a sorry shake of the head. 'But a mistaken perception,' continued Peter, 'from the sounds of it. Perhaps it was someone else arguing . . . near the chapel?'

Peter did not sound convinced.

'If anything has happened to Jennifer,' said Penny, 'I'll hold you responsible, Abbot.'

Geoff confirmed the phone story.

He'd found it on the side when washing his coffee cup that morning.

'I like to give a lead,' he said.

'A lead?' said Tamsin.

'A communal kitchen can quickly become a messy place if people don't take individual responsibility for washing up.'

'So you always wash your cup?' asked Tamsin, trying to keep mockery out of her voice. What a prig!

'Always,' said Geoff, with some satisfaction. He was Director of Boys, a man with many responsibilities in the school . . . but he also washed his coffee cup. 'You set an example. It's something I try to do.'

'Because some don't?'

'Not everyone, no,' said Geoff, shaking his head with disappointment.

'So who doesn't wash their coffee cup?'

'And they're the murderer, are they?' he replied, with mockery.

'Everything's material,' said Tamsin.

'Though, no doubt, a psychologist would trace their inability to wash the cup back to some childhood trauma – imagined or otherwise!'

Peter noted the anger. Here was a man whose own childhood was a confused and confusing affair, still begging for resolution.

'So who doesn't wash up, Geoff?' said Tamsin. 'Who are the traumatized among us, as you say?'

'Is this really important? I didn't mean this to become—'

'As I said, everything's material.'

Geoff paused – would he play this game? Oh, why not? He'd kept his counsel on the matter for a while now and it hadn't helped. It wasn't as if he was being vindictive, the police wanted to know – and perhaps they had a right to know. He was only telling the truth.

'Bart hardly ever bothers.'

'Bart Betters, Director of Wellbeing?'

Geoff nodded.

'It never occurs to him that wellbeing might start at the sink, with a dirty cup being washed.'

No love lost there, thought Peter. But then who *did* like Bart?

'You'd think the Director of Wellbeing would wash everyone's cup,' said Tamsin, with a good shot at innocence. No one at HQ washed their cups. It was left to the cleaner at the end of the day, the lowest of the low in the feudal police hierarchy. They'd steal other people's yogurts from the fridge; but washing their cup was beneath them.

Geoff grunted in response, he'd said enough on the matter.

'But you had no reason to kill the headmaster yourself, I suppose?' said Tamsin, casually.

'I had no reason at all!' What sort of a question was that? You help the police and this is how they thank you. 'We were shoulder to shoulder leading this place forward.'

'That's a lovely phrase,' said Peter – '"shoulder to shoulder".'

'I took him under my wing when he arrived,' explained Geoff. 'I helped him through those tricky first months, when there weren't many other volunteers, I can assure you. He wasn't a popular man at first.'

'Oh?'

'He arrived in a reverie of negativity towards the place, which isn't always the best way.'

'No,' said Peter.

'He was full of what we were not and how we were failing – and that got people's backs up. But he grew to trust me, confided in me.'

'What did he tell you?'

'All sorts of things.'

'And this weekend past? Any particular issues of concern for him?'

Geoff had had 'a particular issue of concern' . . . but he wouldn't be mentioning that.

'He was worried about Ferdinand.'

'Really?'

Tamsin saw a new road opening up.

'Yes, he said he was in a mess – I don't know what sort of mess, he didn't say.' Geoff pondered for a moment. 'Last thing he said to me, in fact, before the afternoon break.'

'What did he say?'

'He said Ferdinand had been a fool – and he didn't know what to do. A worried man . . . and now he's gone. Still can't believe it.'

'Shoulder to shoulder,' said Peter, allowing Geoff his maudlin moment.

'I've been here a long time, you see. Seen a lot of comings and goings, seen a lot of change – and you can't buy that sort of experience.'

'Though you can demote it,' said Tamsin, like a silver stiletto. 'And that would be very difficult to take, I'd imagine.'

Geoff's face spoke of rising rage.

'Only for a diva,' he said looking pointedly at Tamsin. 'Are we done?'

'No.'

'Well, I am.'

And with that, he got up from his seat and walked out.

'He handled
that question well,'

said Tamsin, smiling.

'Surprised you let him go.'

'He left without resolution – that will hurt him more than staying.'

'Ah, Tamsin chooses the crueller way!'

'Are you revving up for a sermon?'

They sat together in the school waiting room. It was tucked away behind the school reception area, comfortable chairs, occasional tables, with a full set of magazines about the countryside and glossy school brochures. And on the walls hung framed photos of vibrant teenagers – all hope and health with the confidence of the rich. Here they were at the Under-15s national hockey finals; there, in the school production of *Macbeth* – and by the door, a sun-drenched scene of a diving trip to Malta.

'Angry man,' said Peter and then, looking around at the photos to relax the atmosphere, added, 'The children do get up to a lot at this place. Never a dull moment here.'

'Just one lethal one,' said Tamsin, despising the pupils for the opportunities they had. Her teenage years had been a harder road, one less paved with opportunity – and then her phone rang and she took the news with barely a flicker of reaction across her face. 'Make that two lethal moments,' she said. 'Jennifer's dead.'

The grinning teenagers now looked insensitive.

'Where?'

'Tide Mills – found by a dog walker an hour-and-a-half ago.'

'What was she doing at Tide Mills?'

'A history project? How do I know?'

Tamsin could be flippant under stress.

'Everyone was asked to stay in. So what made her leave?' Peter was talking more to himself. But Tamsin was thinking about Chief Inspector Wonder, about a spiralling disaster – and about her insistence on the abbot when perhaps a proper detective would have been better.

'And how?' asked Peter.

'And how what?' There was frustration in her voice.

'How was she killed?'

Tamsin stared at him, irritated by the question. She was suddenly looking at an old man in stupid clothes. He held her gaze. 'Is there something wrong?' he asked.

'Only another murder, when we're supposed to be protecting everyone!'

'And I was here last night, so I'm responsible? Jennifer murdered on my watch. Is that the accusation that's choking you?'

Tamsin's breathing was tight, she needed to calm herself and share the information – this is what she told herself. The therapist had said, 'Sometimes you just need to count to ten, Tamsin, and let the panic pass.' And though the advice grated a little, it was true . . . or true in a way. The abbot was all she had at the moment, and it had to work.

'It's strange,' she said.

'What's strange?'

'The murder.'

'How strange?'

'A blow to the head – but death by asphyxia; her respiratory system broke down.'

Peter absorbed the information. He thought of Mrs Docherty – and Gerry, the gardener. And then he thought of the effect of this news on the common room cabal.

'We need to speak with the others now, as a group,' he said.

'I'd prefer we got on with the interviews.'

'This is going to unsettle them.'

'Good.'

Peter paused. How to sell this to Tamsin?

'Tamsin, you may be a brilliant detective.' He didn't believe this at present; he merely needed to calm the panicking child. 'But if you want to avoid a heady mix of hysteria and delusional assumptions in the interviews to come, you will gather the group together now and settle them down.'

'*Settle them down?* We'll be doing centring exercises next!'

'We'll just be talking with them,' said Peter, without adding the thought, *and by the way, you're sounding ridiculous.*

'They started doing centring exercises at my yoga group – and I was off, out of there in flash.'

'I don't understand the offence,' said Peter. 'But beyond your personal issues – and it's a big beyond, the land of the sane, in fact – we have to do this. We have to meet with the suspects now – and tell them about Jennifer.'

And they did, gathering everyone together in the common room where Tamsin had the task of announcing another death. The room smelled of coffee, years of its aroma soaked into the wooden chairs and panelled walls. Though they hadn't needed gathering. They'd all been there anyway, finding some sort of refuge in each other's company. Well, all apart from Crispin and Holly who were lying in the sun on the grass outside, swatting flies and laughing together.

'Rather sweet, isn't it?' said Penny, watching them. 'The freedom of youth!'

'That's what I envy in teenagers,' said Geoff, 'the gift of excess.' He seemed to have forgotten that he'd recently stormed out of the police interview. *Who cares?* was his feeling . . . perhaps he should try a bit more excess. 'The freedom to be full of themselves,' he said, 'without a thought for others – to go with how they feel, no need to apologize! The head's been killed, smashed on the rocks and there they are, out in the sun, life goes on, swatting flies, having a laugh – too full of their own life to care too much! That's what I envy.'

And then he froze, remembering Cressida, who was reading in the corner. Oh God! He immediately turneds towards her, full of remorseful rage at himself.

'I'm sorry if that sounded – well, insensitive, Cressida.'

But Cressida was smiling.

'I'm sure we share your envy, Geoff. No need to apologize. The gift of excess – we lose it, don't we? Or perhaps we never

113

found it and have some catching up to do! We can learn from those two.'

Then Tamsin and Peter arrived – and once Holly and Crispin had been called in from their idyll on the grass, Tamsin spoke: 'I need to make an announcement. And it's not good news, I'm afraid.' They were all silent, motionless. 'We have just heard that Jennifer Styles is dead – has been found dead in suspicious circumstances.'

'Murdered?' asked Ferdinand.

'It appears so, yes.'

There was an anguished squeal from Penny and incomprehension from everyone else.

'To show an unfelt sorrow is an office which the false man does easy,' said Crispin, with the confidence of one who recently sat English A level. 'Malcolm in *Macbeth*. He says it after the murder of his father, King Duncan. He suspects Macbeth of crocodile tears. Like now – everyone looking sad . . . but there's a false man here somewhere.'

'Or woman,' said Geoff.

It was Cressida who recovered first from Shakespeare's sharp arrival.

'Where was she found?'

'At Tide Mills.'

Another gasp from Penny and Cressida was across to calm her.

'And how did she die?' asked Geoff, 'if we may be allowed to know. Though presumably someone here already knows?'

'I'm afraid we can't say anything more at present – but we . . . the police are treating the death as suspicious.'

'So definitely a murder,' he said quietly. 'Or rather, another murder . . . there really is a psycho sharing this common room with us.' He looked around the room, smiling. 'Well you've got to laugh, haven't you? Laugh – or scream.'

'We're pursuing every lead, but it's true that, at the moment, we don't want anyone to leave this site. You'll stay in the East Wing – for your own security.'

'Or closer to the killer,' said Geoff, 'depending on how you look at it.'

'I'm just worried about Cressida,' said Ferdinand Heep, the chaplain. 'Stuck there at home by herself.'

What he was really thinking was something different. If freedom of movement was a factor, then if anyone had got down to Tide Mills last night, it was most likely to have been her. But he preferred his accusations passive, shrouded in the cloak of concern.

'We are in the East Wing for our protection,' said Peter, 'not for our holding. We each have a window in our room – a window without bars. So that if we wished to open it and leave by it . . . then we could. I checked everyone's door was locked at eleven – but I didn't check everyone was in their room. You could have been at Tide Mills as well as anyone else.'

'Perhaps your checking should have been more thorough,' said Penny, still distraught.

'Yes, perhaps it should have,' said Peter. 'But there are police . . .'

'I knocked on Jennifer's door last night and there was no reply.'

'So you say.'

'You could have done the same with everyone – the killer's room would have been a silent place.'

'That's not a helpful image, guys,' said Bart.

'I cannot change the past, Penny,' said Peter. 'But I can attend to the present and I'm wondering about your phone.'

'My phone?'

'You said Geoff was the first person to see it, by the sink in the kitchen area here.' Peter walked across to the small kitchen area. 'And that was at . . .'

'Nine o'clock this morning,' said Geoff. 'There it was, by the sink. Soaking . . . well, destroyed.'

'Did anyone here put it there?' asked Peter. 'Or see it earlier?' Blank faces.

'Does a phone matter?' asked Terence. 'I mean, really! She's found it, end of story surely? The headmaster's dead – murdered! And now Jennifer!'

'I hear your frustration, Terence. But I'm just thinking that either the phone put itself there last night, after a quick swim in the washing-up bowl – or someone in this room is lying.'

115

'Is the idea that Penny simply left it there so impossible to believe?' said Terence. 'I mean, *really!*'

'Well, she says she didn't,' said Peter. He glanced at Penny who was glaring at Terence. 'And I believe her . . . in this matter.'

'And for obvious reasons, we now ask that everyone hand over their phones,' said Tamsin.

Silence.

'You're not having mine,' said Holly.

'I'm afraid we need everybody's, Holly.'

'No way. It's against my human rights.'

It was always one of the harder aspects of an investigation: asking people to let go of their phones was like asking people to say goodbye to a limb.

'But what am I going to do without it?'

It was a cry of abandonment from the head girl, who could not conceive of a meaningful existence away from the most important relationship in her life.

'We'll get them back soon enough,' said Cressida, in a warm manner. 'We must all just be brave.' And with that she got up, walked forward and placed her phone on the table by Tamsin. Others followed suit, like defeated warriors handing over their weapons to the victorious commander. Holly was the last to let go.

'When do we get them back? It'd better be soon, I need my phone.'

'We'll get them back to you as soon as we possibly can,' said Tamsin.

Holly's trauma made it easier for the adults; they could play the strong and mature role – though inwardly they screamed quite as much as the girl and there was a fresh sense of bereavement in the common room as the phones were placed in a bag.

'So what now?' asked Geoff, feeling a change of subject might be useful. He wasn't happy about losing his phone. It was where he did most of his shopping – well, his more unusual shopping, at least. But best just to get on with things. 'The summer holidays are postponed for another day or five?'

'I think they are, Geoff,' said Peter. He didn't want Tamsin jumping in at this point with a 'You'll stay until I say you can leave!' speech. 'It's a very difficult situation for us all and we're all going to have to dig deep. You're being asked to stay on site, keep as calm as you're able, stay in contact with each other . . . there's strength in the group. Avoid private encounters, though, if you can – and when alone, keep your door and window locked.'

The group assimilated this new set of orders but Ferdinand had a question: 'Why *Jennifer*? Can anyone tell me why Jennifer had to die?'

'And is it so obvious why Jamie had to die?' asked Cressida pointedly.

'Well . . .'

'You're talking as if Jamie's death was quite normal!'

'No, I mean – it's just that, well – Jennifer. Not perhaps my favourite person, but . . .'

'Who *is* your favourite person, Father?' asked Crispin.

'The Virgin Mary,' said Penny, under her breath.

'Or someone closer to home?' asked Crispin, archly.

Where did that confidence come from?

'Let me tell you all why Jennifer died,' said Tamsin, intervening. 'Jennifer died because she knew something.' It was like throwing a rat in the snake pit and watching reactions.

'She knew how to stop anyone getting to Jamie,' said Geoff, jokily . . . but no one laughed. It was reckoned inappropriate, given the circumstances . . . though they all knew the truth of it and had raged often at her behaviour.

'Murder is not a leisure activity,' said Tamsin. 'It has its own dark reasons. And one murder can lead to another, once the awkward track-covering begins. The murderer looks around them and must consider: *Who knows what? And can what they know harm me?* If it can harm them, they may well kill again – killing does get easier, though less assured. Mistakes get made in the cover-up operation.'

She looked around her, seeking panic in one set of eyes.

'Look guys, I'm not finding this very helpful,' said Bart. 'What's the point of spooking everyone?'

'You mean you're scared?' said Penny.

'I'm sure we're all scared,' said Cressida. 'And the truth is, we may not know what we know. Who knows what I've seen without realizing I've seen it?'

This was a further concern for the room to ponder. It's one thing to know you're a target and why ... you can take precautions of sorts. But not to know what you know – or the significance of what you know; to be an innocent amid the evil plans of an anonymous psycho ... well, this was disturbing.

'I think Cressida should move into the East Wing to be with us,' said Ferdinand. 'She'll be safer.'

'I've already spoken with the police about that,' she replied. 'And I'm in my new room already ... just waiting for some fresh sheets to arrive.'

Ferdinand did wonder why she couldn't go and find the sheets for herself, like they'd all had to. There would be some on Matron's Landing – matron always kept a supply there for 'accidents' as she called them. But then Cressida probably thought this beneath her, just like she thought many things beneath her, this was Ferdinand's view ... a rather distant queen of the school. Obviously one must cut the bereaved a little slack, grief can make a good man bad – but to be honest, she'd always been like this, always slightly removed from the school community, which was not ideal ... far from ideal in his book.

'You'll find fresh sheets on Matron's Landing,' he said. 'It's where I found mine.'

Cressida made no response and no eye contact.

Tamsin stepped in. 'So if you do know something, however small, it would be wise to tell us – rather than lie to us.'

'Has anyone lied so far?' asked Holly, with interest.

'People do lie to the police, Holly – it's almost an automatic response.'

'Why?'

'Perhaps they have little secrets of their own to hide; or perhaps they want to protect another, someone who they think – or hope – is innocent.' Holly nodded, thinking about this. 'But it's always unwise, Holly. Protecting those you deem innocent can sometimes make them appear a great deal more guilty, believe me.'

'Well, I'm not protecting anyone!'

'Withholding the truth is not the same as a lie,' said Geoff.

'I'm not sure I agree, Geoff,' said Peter.

'And I'm not sure I'm bothered, Abbot!'

'What was it Edmund Burke said? "For evil to triumph it requires only the good to stay silent."'

Geoff raised his eyebrows in disdain.

'Oh, and does anyone here know a Benedict?' asked Tamsin. 'Or is Benedict one of you?'

The interview with Crispin

was a brief affair. It was gentler for the blue school blazer he still wore – as though he was about to go off for a double science class. But he wasn't – he was a suspect in a murder investigation ... though hardly top of anyone's list. Where was the necessary hatred to be found in him? And when he spoke, he spoke mainly of the ghost he'd seen. Peter learned nothing new, but it gave Tamsin a chance to probe.

'It's not really likely it was a ghost,' she said, declaring her hand. She wasn't prepared to sit here and pretend ghosts existed.

'What else could it have been?' said Crispin firmly. *Most Haunted* was one of his favourite TV shows; he recorded them and watched them back-to-back. He'd even spent a night in the most haunted house in England, Preston Manor in Brighton ... and a ghost was almost inevitable in an old place like this.

'A real person?' suggested Tamsin.

'I don't see how that works – not when there's no one here who looks remotely like the person I saw.' If he'd argued about anything with his friends, it was about the possibility of ghosts – a debate which generally found him in a minority of one. But he was happy with that. The idea of ghosts, the fact of their existence, was something he needed, a source of comfort to him, a sign of something beyond ... and the hope he'd see his mother again. Perhaps she'd come and speak with him? That would be awesome.

So while he'd been shocked last night by the strange apparition, and been glad of the abbot's company, by the morning he was nothing but happy. There are ghosts, they do visit – and he'd told Holly all about it.

'So what did you do on Sunday afternoon?' asked Peter.

'Nothing really. I was on the internet a bit, had a bath. Nothing much.'

'Apart from a visit to the headmaster's house.'

He hadn't been going to mention that. And how they knew, he had no idea. Had he been seen?

'Oh yes.'

'So?'

'I just went to return some stuff Dr Cutting had lent me.'

'What stuff?'

'On my Crippen project. She'd given me something on the Hippocratic oath; I was just returning it.'

'And she was there, was she?'

'Yes.'

'Do you get on well with Dr Cutting?'

'She's been nice to me.'

'Is she nice to everyone?'

'I wouldn't know. And I don't much care. Why would I care?' He was angry.

Whereas Holly, former head girl, was charming in interview. She sat in the blue school tracksuit, with *Stormhaven Towers* in gold across her back. Yet she transcended her clothes in a manner Crispin could not; Crispin was a boy, Holly a woman . . . or almost.

'I've never been interviewed before,' she said winningly, sitting down opposite them, a little giggly.

'Well, it's all quite painless for those who tell the truth,' lied Tamsin – the truth hurt a great deal sometimes. But she wished to be firm, to lay down some markers. Men may stumble over Holly, but she wouldn't be following them. 'Do you have anything you'd like to tell us?'

'I don't think I know anything about the murder. I mean, he was just the headmaster, I didn't really know him.'

'I'm told he liked you.'

Holly shrugged as if to say, 'Well, he was hardly the only one!'

'And we hear you were going to be with friends this week?' said Peter.

'I'm usually with friends in the holidays.'

'Oh?'

'My parents are getting divorced and it's not a place I want to be.' Peter nodded with full comprehension. 'So I make my own plans, always have really. I don't want to be dependent on them in any way at all, if I can help it.'

'And you're a great one for the truth,' said Tamsin. 'We hear that as well.'

'I suppose so,' said Holly, unsure.

'Well, I was thinking of your wish for the school, in one of your review meetings, that it was ...' – she looked down at her notes – '... that it was "a place of truth".'

Holly looked unsettled.

'Yep,' she said, suddenly looking younger ... much younger.

'So do you always tell the truth, Holly?'

She didn't respond.

'It's just that during our meeting with everyone yesterday afternoon, there was a police search of all the rooms currently being used in the East Wing.'

'Oh?'

'We didn't ask permission – but then you don't in murder cases. You have to be quite grown-up about it all, quite brutal. The police, I mean.'

'Yes,' said the head girl.

'And in your room, there was a bit of a surprise waiting for us. Can you guess what it was?'

'No.'

Her worry was evident.

'Certainly not something we'd expect to find in a wardrobe.' Tamsin paused with Holly, looking straight at her. 'That clue isn't helping?'

'No.'

'Then perhaps it's going to be a surprise to you too.'

The ghost had decided

he must be more careful. He was quite sure someone had seen him the night before. He'd heard quiet footsteps and then a gasp in the dark when he turned towards the moonlit window. He suspected it was the little dear, Crispin, who shouldn't have been around, most remiss of him. The boy should have been in bed, all tucked up with his teddy, instead of breaking the curfew. And he did still have a teddy – not a well-known fact about the head boy . . . but one which just made him all the more adorable.

It would be quite wrong, of course, a relationship – and by that he meant one of a sexual nature, which was the only sort he wanted now. There's a certain age-gap between people, a certain difference in their years on earth, which, though quite legal – and often desirable – does sit a little uncomfortably with one's conscience; this was how the ghost felt . . . though his conscience had never been a very clear guide, a rather faltering beacon at best.

But he would return to the corridors tonight . . . such a spillage of tragedy in the place. First there was Jamie's death, the tortured fall towards the rocks – a gasp but no scream. They never screamed as they fell, not those he'd seen; there was simply no time and one's thoughts were elsewhere. And then little Jennifer at Tide Mills. All so unfortunate really . . . but perhaps inevitable, some sort of a judgement on what Stormhaven Towers had become, he thought.

Nathaniel Bleake, the founder of the school, may have been an intolerable bore – forcing good works, God and seriousness down everyone's throat. But at least he wanted the best for the poor, whereas his schools today – well, they had good wishes only for the rich . . . unless the poor happened to be extremely good at cricket.

So he would return tonight and seek a glimpse of the monk detective, which was rather fun. He wasn't against the idea of a monk being a sleuth – good for a monk to be doing something useful for a change. But perhaps not too useful, he wouldn't wish for that. He would have to be watched. And in the meantime, there was enough damage done to scupper the link-up with that Japanese corporation, surely? They'd hardly want the place now for their expensive summer conferences ... the school was damaged goods, too stained with blood for their public relations department.

In his heart of hearts, the ghost probably wished for the collapse of this place and its utter humiliation ...

'So what were they doing there?'

asked Tamsin. She had explained to Holly about the five cloth bags of money found in her wardrobe. The head girl's face had betrayed no emotion other than a frozen quality – a face put up for public view while work went on behind the scenes.

'I don't know,' said Holly. 'Someone must have put them there.'

'Well, that's what we thought. It's the obvious answer – because really, why would you have five bags of money in your room? It just doesn't make sense.' Holly nodded. 'But then the question: if someone else did put them there – why haven't you reported them? That's a query we've had to ponder. It must have been a bit of a shock to find them there – odd arrivals in your wardrobe. Worth a mention to someone, probably . . . only you didn't.'

'I didn't see them. I didn't see the bags. I've had other things on my mind – like a murder you haven't solved.'

Tamsin smiled. She liked the girl's spirit, her desire to attack, the brave words of a condemned woman.

'I don't see a guide dog by your side, Holly – and you don't walk with a white stick . . . so I'm jumping to the conclusion that you're not blind.' Holly did not respond. 'No one could use that wardrobe – and you *do* use that wardrobe – without seeing those bags of money . . . bags of money sitting in the wardrobe of the bedroom you've lived in for the past year.'

Holly felt some readjustment was necessary.

'I did see the bags there.'

'When?'

'Yesterday – but I didn't bother to look inside them.'

'You didn't look inside five large bags that suddenly appeared in your wardrobe?'

'No.'

It was the best answer she could manage, because this was quite scary. It wasn't like school because the woman wouldn't put it down, she kept coming back. 'And you didn't think to mention that someone had broken into your room – or worse, had a key? Will you be asking us to believe in the tooth fairy as well, Holly?'

'The strange thing for me,' said the abbot, changing the tone from bemused ridicule to sympathetic enquiry, 'was how much the bags resembled a church collection. Did you not think that?'

'Oh, well ...'

'I mean, it's a mad idea, I grant you, because why would various church – or perhaps chapel – collections be sitting in your wardrobe?' He made a smilingly puzzled face. 'It makes no sense at all. And perhaps you looked inside, thought the same ... you just couldn't work it out?'

A bridge back to the truth was offered and cautiously Holly placed a foot on it.

'Maybe. Can I talk with the abbot alone, please?' She looked at Tamsin and then Peter. 'I have a confession to make.'

'You can trust DI Shah,' said Peter, not believing his own words. 'And often confession is the best thing to do.'

And now she was crying, tears breaking down her young face in faltering rivulets.

'I'm really sorry!' she mumbled, 'sorry for what I did! I shouldn't have done it.'

Tamsin's phone rang. She got up and answered it, indicating with her free hand that she needed to take the call. She left the room with another wave, which said, 'Carry on with the confession ...'

'It was stupid, really,'

said Holly, in the stillness of the school waiting room.

On the table, her beautiful face smiled out from the cover of the school brochure, all gloss and colour. No one was in any doubt that she'd been an excellent marketing tool for the school . . . not that it had been that cynical, of course. But, well, you don't look a gift horse in the mouth. And Holly's face was a gift . . . a gift for the school publicity which said, 'Attractive and rich – join the club!'

But now the face was struggling, soaked in tears and recalling how it had all started, all this 'nonsense'.

'I was thinking about how I'd survive, mainly,' she said, pushing a blonde hair back from her damp eyes. 'My parents were all over the place at the time – and still are – a complete nightmare. And I didn't want to be with them. Absolutely no way did I want to be with them. But then how would I survive? I had to earn money. I had to be independent.'

'I quite see,' said the abbot. 'Your situation was difficult.'

'Total, like, nightmare.'

'So what did you do?'

'It wasn't what I did – it was what someone else did.'

'Who?'

'They're on the review team, you've met them. And you'll be surprised when you hear who it is.'

'Aconite,' said Tamsin.

'Jennifer was killed by aconite, applied to the head wound after blunt instrument trauma.'

'What blunt instrument?'

Tamsin had returned to the interview room.

'A piece of old concrete – but no prints on it. The body had been there for eight to ten hours.'

She spoke with frustration. You have to move quickly with forensics; something is lost with every hour of delay – and they'd lost too many already. And Peter remembered the conversation in the kitchen with Mrs Docherty that morning . . . and the fate of poor Gerry, the gardener.

'I did suspect aconite,' said Peter, which rather threw Tamsin. 'The manner of death did suggest it. And bleakly appropriate in a school of learning.'

'Why so?'

'It's a poison for the classicists, really.'

'You mean we're looking for someone who speaks Latin and wears a toga? That narrows it down a bit.'

She both did and didn't like it when Peter knew things. At present, she didn't.

'I mean, Roman history tells of its effectiveness,' said Peter. 'Agrippina murdered her husband, the Emperor Claudius, by mixing aconite into a plate of mushrooms.'

'He may just not have liked mushrooms.'

'While the Greek writer Ovid believed the herb came from the slavering mouth of Cerberus, the three-headed dog that guarded the gates of Hell. And one can see why – its effects can look a little like rabies.'

'So Jennifer didn't die happy?'

'Nausea, vomiting and diarrhoea are the initial symptoms.'

'The scene of the crime was messy, I'm told.'

This was making sense.

'It's a poison readily available from the wolfsbane plant,' continued Peter. 'Purple or yellow in flower and so called, as you'll know, because it was used to kill wolves; arrows were tipped with it.' Tamsin did not know this. How could she ever have come across information like that? It was hardly what you would call 'relevant' – until now. 'It's powerful stuff . . . you don't need much if you can get it into the bloodstream. The Aleuts used it to stun whales in Alaska. And it's quickly absorbed through the skin – especially if the skin is broken or if applied to a sensitive area . . .' the abbot paused for a moment '. . . such as the female genitalia.'

Tamsin made a face.

'Do I need to know this?'

'Marcus Caelius accused Calpurnius Bestia of using it to kill his wives in their sleep. The prosecutor spoke of the defendant's finger as the murder weapon.'

'That's quite gross, really. '

'I'm surprised you didn't cover it on the inspectors' course.'

'We focused mainly on the twenty-first century.'

'To your detriment, obviously.'

'Have you finished?'

The abbot shrugged, aware he'd shown unacceptable superiority of knowledge . . . but then the poison had always intrigued him. Tamsin decided on a change of direction, to a place of greater supremacy.

'So you finally got rid of Miss Tearful?'

'Holly? Interesting conversation. We must talk about that.'

'But what a performance! I mean, why not just tell the truth, instead of that absurd . . . ? Well, you heard her.'

'I think you're being a little harsh.'

'I hope so. It's how I get results.'

'But you have to imagine how you'd feel, Tamsin.'

'What are you talking about? Why would I want to imagine that?'

'How you'd feel if you had to recount the most embarrassing experience of your life to some stranger?'

'I wouldn't.'

'Precisely. But the police – you expect people to do just that, and without deviation or emotion.' Tamsin arched her eyebrows. 'We all have embarrassment in our lives, aspects of our past we'd prefer not to recall – given what we did or how we behaved. Who wants to talk about their most shameful experience to anyone, let alone some nameless – and possibly aggressive – police officer, who they don't know if they can trust?'

'It's not about trust.'

'It's all about trust. And you can multiply the shame by ten if you're eighteen years old and life thus far has been about little more than appearance and survival. So Rule No.1 – you lie or cry when the police come knocking.'

Tamsin gave him a 'have-you-quite-finished?' look. Peter contemplated the chair the girl had vacated.

'So what was the confession of Holly Hope-Walker?' she asked.

Father Ferdinand took his seat

in the waiting room. He had the hunched shoulders of one used to leading, but aware roles were now reversed and humbly content with these circumstances.

'If I can help you, Sergeant, you can be sure that I will.'

'Inspector,' said Tamsin and Ferdinand smiled knowingly, having discreetly made his point. He didn't agree with women bishops – a really most unfortunate development; and this policewoman seemed to imagine herself with similar powers, which, with the best will in the world, was not how God intended things to be.

'It is, of course, a great tragedy,' he added – though Ferdinand was the tragedy as far as Tamsin was concerned. So much about him irritated her it was hard to know where to begin. She was irritated by his attack on her status, by his pious words which sounded like a script . . . and by the dog collar he persisted in wearing during the investigation. It marked him out as separate, when really, he was nothing special – just another murder suspect . . . and not a popular one at that.

'Isn't the dog collar just for the pupils, Father Heep – so they know who you are?'

'A calling is for life, Sergeant – not just for term time.'

Heep smiled knowingly. He'd learned to defend himself from such attack. He was like the fish who muddies the water around it by ejecting sand from its mouth, obscuring itself until the threat has gone away. In like manner, Ferdinand had lines he could use until the danger had passed. But the danger hadn't passed yet; Tamsin was a determined predator.

'And part of your *"calling"'* – it was said with disdain – 'is a white piece of plastic round your neck?'

'I can't not be what I am . . . and I'm a priest.'

More sand blown; perhaps they'd leave him alone now.

'Which explains why Jesus wore his dog collar with such pride?'

131

Ferdinand would not even bother to respond to that.

'So are you a good priest?' asked Tamsin, changing tack.

'That's hardly for me to say!'

'Then shall we ask Holly?'

'Holly?'

'Head girl of Stormhaven Towers last year − she might have some insights.'

Ferdinand's heart beat hard, more defence needed . . . more sand in the water.

'Well, you may know where this is leading, Sergeant, but I certainly don't! Has Holly said something? I imagine she must have done. But she can be a rather − well, imaginative girl.'

'She said that you touched her up.' Ferdinand was silent. 'So how imaginative was that? We found the money, you see.'

'What money?'

'The story started two years ago, didn't it?' said Peter. 'This is what Holly says.'

Ferdinand turned to him in disgust and then to Tamsin: 'Does he have to be here?'

'Yes, he does have to be here, Ferdinand.'

'I do have a name,' said Peter.

'He's not even a monk any more − he's just some washed-up nobody, pretending to be . . .'

Peter watched him. The sand-blowing fish now a fish on the end of a line, thrashing about, this way and that. Tamsin cut in: 'So shall I tell you the story? Or will you tell us?'

'There's nothing to tell, I'm afraid.' He grimaced in bemused defiance. 'Holly is presenting a tissue of lies. I don't know what they are, but they appear to have fooled you − just as she fools everyone else, drawing them into her pretty little thrall.'

'You're making her sound like a witch.'

'I'm making her sound like a misguided and deceitful teenager, which is exactly what she is.'

'You find teenagers difficult?'

'Have you not noticed that everyone wants to be Holly's friend?' said Ferdinand. 'Perhaps she took you in as well?' Tamsin paused for a moment, thinking back to their meeting. Had they been suckered by her? Ferdinand continued: 'I have some experience of these things, and there's a pattern — certainly with the allegations of sexual impropriety against celebrities — which I follow closely.'

'Really?'

'Yes, really.'

'A strange hobby, Father.'

'And the truth is — it's the number of witnesses that tends to make the case.' Peter could hear his growing confidence, as if this was a common room discussion he'd had a few times — and perhaps he had. Common rooms across the land lived in fear of the nightmare allegation of sexual impropriety . . . and the suspension that followed, while the investigation was carried out. It was always the beginning of the end, with no way back for the accused. 'Of course we believe you one hundred per cent, Malcolm, you know that — we just have to go through the process, be seen to be taking it seriously. And if you want to use the time to consider other schools — or perhaps another career — then do!'

One spiteful teenager — no shortage of those — and there was your career gone.

'If there are a number of allegations,' continued Ferdinand, 'allegations from more than one child, then it doesn't look good. There's no smoke without fire, as they say.' This, sadly, had been the case with his predecessor at Stormhaven Towers. 'But when there's just one allegation — and from a rather insecure girl from a broken home — then you have to start wondering about the motive. Are they really to be believed over the word of an adult, and not any adult — but the school chaplain?'

Absolutely, thought Tamsin, who'd believe anyone before him. But without the necessary evidence on this occasion, she was struggling. And where was such evidence to be found? One word against another was not a good way to proceed in sexual harassment cases; the chaplain was right. Corroborating evidence was required, evidence that built the story . . . like other victims coming forward. But the ones who might do so in this case — the other pupils — were long gone, driven away in their BMWs and 4×4s and now holidaying in the Alps . . . and with Chief Inspector Wonder already pressing for a result. She could still hear his voice.

'Wrap it up quickly, Shah, for God's sake,' he'd said on the phone earlier. 'Half the Rotary Club seem to have a grandchild at the school, which did not make for an easy lunch today.'

'My sympathies are with you.'

'All sorts of comments over the prawn cocktails! They don't want the name of the school tarnished. "A local jewel" as one of them called it and we have to look after that jewel. I mean, are we sure it wasn't simply two suicides – unfortunate, but hey-ho, life goes on?'

She'd put the phone down soon after, but the pressure was still growing in her head. And now here was Ferdinand posing more questions, when she just wanted answers.

'Wherever Holly got her money, it wasn't from the chapel collection,' said Ferdinand, like a barrister winding up the case for the defence and he left soon after.

'We need that letter,' said Peter.

'If it exists,' said Tamsin, with the air of the defeated. 'Who do you believe?'

Bart Betters was irritating.

He was the last to be interviewed and couldn't keep still. It was painfully apparent in the confined space of the waiting room, where his twitching ankles pushed his knees up and down at some speed. Peter was vexed by the movement, as restless as a monkey; and so he asked him if he could perhaps calm his legs. Bart asked what he meant by that and Peter leaned across and placed his hand on Bart's knee until it stopped its frenetic movement.

'It's just an informal chat, Bart,' said Tamsin, even more irritated than the abbot. 'There's no need to be tense.'

'I'm not tense.'

'Your legs were just a bit restless.'

'My legs? I've done it all my life!'

'Perhaps you've been restless all your life,' said Peter. 'Perhaps your muscles have never dared to relax?'

'Why would I be restless? I've had a great life.'

'I'm very glad,' said Peter, allowing the foolishness for now. The 'great life' narrative would perhaps need questioning at some point, but it could wait.

'I'm just a very active guy,' said Bart. 'I don't like keeping still, too much to do in the world, too much to see — it's like there's a carrot in front of me!'

'What's like a carrot?'

'The future! It's there to be chased, I'm always chasing it. That's wellbeing for you — seeing the carrot up ahead and striving to get there.'

'That's not wellbeing, Bart, that's an illness,' said Peter, who couldn't be doing with this and felt the murder enquiry could wait. 'Have you never learned to be still?'

'*Still?* Why would I be still? Still is dull.' Yes, Peter was afraid he might say that. 'I like to run, as I believe you do, Abbot. Do you run far?'

'Me? Oh well, I manage seven or eight miles a day ... while the world is slowly waking.'

'I prefer the shorter run, the sprint – faster! But I could catch you, Abbot, over any distance – and shoot past you!'

'That's possible. There's the short-haul and the long-haul, Bart – the hare and the tortoise,' said Peter.

'We should try it! I use the barefoot running style, do you?'

'I've read about it.'

'Reading about it doesn't help, Abbot – you need practice not theory! You should join the Stormhaven Striders – it's a great running club, we run together twice a week.'

'I prefer to run alone.'

'No, this would be better for you. You'd enjoy it more.'

That was not a good line to offer Abbot Peter.

'I'm one of their lead runners now,' continued Bart. 'But all ages are welcome, you just find your own level. We have members older than you – and they're learning the barefoot style! You should come down on the ball of the foot rather than the heel – which is, like, the last place you should be placing your weight when running. You should try it.'

'That's a lot of "shoulds",' said Peter, smiling through the pain.

'Just trying to help.'

'Is that why you walk in that odd way?' asked Tamsin.

'I'm sorry?'

'You walk in an odd way. I was just wondering if your barefoot running caused it?'

Bart did look a little effete as he walked, apparently proceeding on tiptoe. But he had a reply: 'From where I'm sitting, it's you who has the odd walk, Inspector. All that heel-crunching! You wouldn't have survived as a cave dweller – absolutely no way. You'd never have caught an animal with all your heel-crunching.'

'Then how fortunate I have a Waitrose nearby – they catch the animals for me.'

'You don't like to be trapped, Bart – is that it?' asked Peter, still dwelling on his restlessness. Bart did seem like a man on the run from something ... never calm, never settled. Beyond the determined smile were hollow eyes ... and now his knee shake had started again. It was as if this small circle of chairs was oppressing him.

'Who *likes* to be trapped?' he asked with a laugh. 'I mean, c'mon, guys!'

'And who likes it when the head thinks you're a waste of space?' said Tamsin, wishing to move on.

'What's that supposed to mean?' Bart was punctured but managed to keep smiling. 'It was nothing like that.'

'What was it like?'

'He didn't understand wellbeing, anyway – he smoked, he drank, that's how he relieved the tension.'

'While your knees go up and down . . . cheaper, I suppose. And, of course, Jamie did have his running machine.'

'You're joking.'

'Not as far as I know.'

Bart pulled an odd face.

'Anyway, I preferred the previous head,' he said. 'He was more understanding. He was old school, sure – but he listened to the advice of others, who told him that wellbeing is where it's at now. A truly visionary leader.'

'You mean he agreed with you,' said Tamsin.

'We were just starting some really, like, creative work when he left. We actually had "Woodland survival" as a core subject at Stormhaven Towers.'

'And yet school numbers were dropping . . . because for better or for worse, not that many people live in woods these days.'

'That's not the point.'

'And certainly not those who can pay thirty thousand pounds a year for their children's education – plus add-ons for exotic school trips. I mean, I'm not an expert or anything, but people like that don't tend to live in tree huts. Where would they park the BMW?'

'More fool them. I once lived in a tree hut for a week in Tuscany. Amazing experience.'

'But back on the ground, Bart, how long do you think you would have lasted in your present post, had Jamie had his way? Until Christmas? One more year tops?'

Bart went on the attack.

137

'So I'm the obvious murderer, am I? You really think I'd tell you these things if I killed him?'

'Everyone's an obvious murderer in my book,' said Tamsin. 'The abbot here – everyone.' Peter looked slightly aggrieved but she'd made her point. 'And you only tell us what you know we'll find out. Isn't that so? The head's issues with your particular post are hardly a secret.' She wouldn't repeat Jamie's comment to Ferdinand that the Director of Wellbeing post was 'just a job for a teacher who can't teach'. But she knew Ferdinand would be a willing source for other such anecdotes, should they be needed ... anything to nobble Bart. And she knew Bart knew this too.

'So where did you go when the head gave everyone two hours off on Sunday afternoon?'

'I went for a run.'

'Anywhere nice?'

'I ran to Loner's Wood beyond Cuckmere Gap. I fancied some dark leafy paths and the rich aroma of rotting bark. It's a special place, you should try it, Abbot ... as long as you don't mind being alone in the dark!'

'And you didn't come back via Stormhaven Head, by any chance?'

'It was hardly on my way.'

'Only a ten-minute diversion, I suppose,' said Peter.

'But not one I took, all right?'

He was eager in his denial.

'On this occasion, perhaps. But you are often up there, I'm told – often seen around Stormhaven Head in your running kit and your rucksack weights. It is very beautiful, I grant you.'

'It's about the history.'

'Oh?'

'It's about feeling connected to the past in some eternal now.'

An eternal now is what this conversation feels like, thought Tamsin, with the sense of one who has gatecrashed a Stormhaven Striders social night.

But Bart wasn't done: 'There were Bronze Age and Iron Age forts there, you know. Think of that! All those years ago, people going about their lives in this place where we now live. Such

138

different lives! Yet the same really, seeking peace and oneness, that sort of thing.'

'Do you feel happier in the past?' asked Peter.

'I think you should honour the past.'

Another 'should', noted Peter.

'Because who's now aware that the Romans settled here, for instance?' asked Bart, now on a roll. 'No one! Stormhaven doesn't remember the Romans. But they took over the place, they were here, looking out on the same horizon that we do ... Italians far from home, longing to get back ... but many never did. They lived out their days in a foreign land – and died in a foreign land. You wouldn't guess what's beneath the Stormhaven Head golf course!'

'A Roman burial ground?' said Peter.

'Well, yes.' Bart would have preferred to surprise his interrogators. 'A very large one. And *most* people here don't know that.'

Tamsin was now thinking fondly of Peter and decided to join in.

'I can't think which is more useless,' said Tamsin. 'A Roman burial ground or a golf course? Both feature the dead, of course. And one other thing, Bart,' she continued, managing the transition without any change of tone, 'how can you afford such an expensive car? I mean, on your wages?'

The smart black Porsche, admired on their arrival, turned out to be owned by the Director of Wellbeing.

'I believe in the Law of Attraction,' said Bart. 'What we are on the inside, we draw to ourselves on the outside.'

'I see.' She didn't. 'So you've been getting in touch with your inner black Porsche, Bart?'

It remained a crime scene,

the usual police tape, closing off the area – though forensics were long gone. And tomorrow, the haunted ruins that were Tide Mills would again be open to the public – open to walkers, to children and to the ghoulish, fascinated by recent death, voyeurs on murder. Some stood around the perimeters even now, trying to get a view, phones and binoculars straining for a sight of blood.

'Don't you find the people of Stormhaven repulsive?' said Tamsin. 'Human hyenas for the morbid.'

'They're hardly unique, Tamsin. It's the history of show business. Remember that public hangings were for centuries the single most popular form of entertainment in England.'

'Among lowlife, perhaps.'

'No, among *all* life. Thomas Hardy, one of our most revered novelists, made great efforts to attend public executions.'

'Really?'

'Really. And he was keen to get a good view apparently. He didn't want to miss out on any of the twisting agony . . . and really, you can only call it "book research" for so long.' Tamsin smiled. 'And I'm told the hanging of two men and a woman in Iran last year has over 784,000 visits on YouTube – whatever that is. Humans like to loiter around death from a place of safety. They flirt with mortality from the comfort of their own armchairs. Or in this case,' he looked at the present watchers, 'from the side of the A259 with their smartphones and Thermos to hand and a short walk from their cars.'

Tamsin and the abbot had come here to get off-site, away from the school and review the day's interviews. The two of them now sat in one of the old workers' cottages, the roof long gone but still retaining the outline of the flint stone walls. Such small rooms, such close living, thought Tamsin. Red poppies, fragile and strong, grew in the concrete soil, delighting in the evening sun and the salt breeze.

'The gardener,' said Peter.

'I'm sorry?'

'Gerry, the gardener. He died last year, while working at the school.'

'What of him?'

'Jennifer wasn't the first employee at Stormhaven Towers to die of aconite poisoning. Gerry did too.'

'How do you know?'

'Mrs Docherty told me.'

'A police informer, is she?'

'In a manner. She's a cleaner there, so she knows everything. She mentioned Gerry when I was collecting my breakfast this morning. And then Wilson kindly found the relevant newspaper cuttings online.'

'Saint bloody Wilson.'

'The roots of the wolfsbane plant – as I'm sure you know – are where the highest level of poison is found – but it's still there in the flower. And this unfortunate fellow had a cut on his hand when he touched one, the pathologist said – so the poison entered his bloodstream quickly and went straight to the heart. He died in the cricket pavilion – that's as far as he got.'

Tamsin wondered whether this digression was a waste of time. She didn't like wasting time. The abbot seemed to be enjoying the meander, but was it taking the case forward?

'It wasn't much reported at the time,' said Peter, 'because, well, it wasn't considered a murder . . . just a tragic accident. He died holding the plant.'

'Why was he holding it?'

'I don't know.'

'And where was it growing?'

'I don't know.'

'Well – where had he been working that morning?'

'No one knows.'

'I'm spotting a pattern.'

'Somewhere on the school premises – but gardeners do their own thing, they go where they will. You have a gardener at the

141

police HQ, I saw him there. But I don't imagine you could tell me much about his daily routine.'

Tamsin couldn't argue. She had never even noticed the gardener. Why would she?

'But here's the fact of interest,' said Peter. 'Someone at Stormhaven Towers grows aconite. And the likelihood is that the grower and the killer are one and the same.'

'Not necessarily.'

'No. But if they're two different people, why didn't the grower come forward when Gerry died?'

'Fear?'

'Possible.'

'Relationship?'

'Possible.'

His idea wasn't as watertight as he'd imagined – Tamsin had spotted the leaks.

'The killer certainly has a streak of the nasty about them,' he said and looked down at the spot where Jennifer was so recently killed. 'She didn't need to die in that slow and humiliating manner. They could have killed her instantly with the concrete slab. But they didn't want to, they wanted to use poison – an unpleasant poison.'

'Is there a nice one?'

They sat for a moment listening to the sea, though Tamsin heard only the bells of panic. She needed to bring this case home.

'Ironic, really,' said Peter.

'What's ironic?'

'The word "aconite" comes from a Greek word which means "without struggle"... when in truth the victim struggles a great deal before death.'

'Have you finished?' said Tamsin. She wasn't really listening, the anxiety drowning the abbot out. 'It's getting late.'

'And one other thing: obviously Ferdinand had told the headmaster something before they broke on Sunday afternoon.' Tamsin nodded in a distant fashion. 'Cressida told us there was a worry on his mind and Geoff confirms that. Was that to do with Holly – or something else that Ferdinand knew?'

'You'd best be getting back to the school.'

'Yes.'

He knew a dismissal when he heard one.

'Keep an eye on them tonight, Abbot. I don't want to be arriving to another murder tomorrow.'

Peter got up and contemplated the tough little poppy bending in the wind, making good from dry rocky soil.

'Give my love to Hove,' he said and, without further pleasantries, started the walk back to Stormhaven Towers.

And the killer.

Peter was deep in Loner's Wood.

He ran a steady pace through the dark and twisted trees, and dismissed the noise at first. The night has sounds all of its own, unheard in the day, and this was surely just another?

On returning from Tide Mills, where Tamsin had behaved badly, he'd sat alone in his room for a while ... but felt the need to get out. He needed to exhaust his body – the best way he knew to clarity of mind. And so in the running kit provided by PC Wilson, he'd set out across the Downs towards Hope Gap and then Cuckmere. He'd run past the famous Smugglers' Cottages, silhouettes on the cliff edge, and then along the grassy path to the Cuckmere Inn offering lunches 'from just £5.50'. He then turned on to the steep and winding Eastbourne road before stepping off into Loner's Wood.

The light was fading and the wood was obscurer still – shadowed and hidden even in daylight, with sky kept out by the thick overhang of oak, sycamore, conifer and ash. As Bart had said, it was a good place to run as long as you didn't mind being alone in the dark. But now Peter was wondering if he was. It was dark – but was he alone?

He reminded himself again, the night had its own conversation, this he knew. It was different in the desert night. There, you heard the rustle of the wind in your clothes, the camels' snuffle and spit – but in between, and beneath a trillion stars, the silence hung heavy, allowing the soul to listen for subtler signs of life, information from the unknown inner regions. But here in England, there was noise. Perhaps a fox was on the prowl or a deer even – he'd seen a deer on Stormhaven golf course; there must be some families around.

But the noise seemed to follow him – he did not leave it behind. And it possessed a thudding human quality ... the quiet pounding of a runner on those soft woodland paths – though whether in front or behind, he couldn't be sure. And so what? So what if another runner was out and about tonight? This was not private land. Why shouldn't they be running here? It was probably a local runner, their paths crossing briefly. And so Peter continued, unsure of his bearings but glad to be out beneath the stars, with nothing to do but put one foot in front of another, to keep going.

Was running spiritual? There was certainly health in it, beyond the merely physical ... this, at least, was Peter's sense. It was the tenacity required, the endurance – the willingness to make the mind and body do things they do not want to do. These were good disciplines ... though he had some way to go before reaching the endurance of the running monks of Mount Hie in Japan. They supposedly achieved enlightenment by completing a thousand marathons in a thousand days.

It wasn't quite as it sounded, however, as Peter had discovered: the thousand days did not have to be consecutive. Indeed, seven years was the normal length for this challenge. And it was also true that each marathon had a number of 'shrine breaks', with the monk pausing for prayer at holy places along the way. It was a different sort of marathon to those he'd endured in the Sahara – such desperate, relentless and dismantling affairs ... not a shrine break in sight, just sun, rock and scrubland.

The spiritual benefit of this practice, according to the Japanese monks, lay in the physical demands which exhausted the mind, the ego and the body, until nothing was left. 'And when you are nothing,' said one of them, 'then something comes up to fill the space.' And this something was the vast consciousness that lay below the surface of their lives, a sense of oneness with the universe ... Peter had known such things.

But in Loner's Wood tonight, a sense of oneness had gone, replaced by a dread sense of two ... a sense of hunter and hunted. Peter was being followed, he was sure of it now – and his heart beat in fear in a place he didn't know. He'd keep on running, this seemed the best action, his mind racing; he'd aim for clearer ground, there must be some ahead. With luck, he'd find the Eastbourne road, wherever that was – he'd quite lost his bearings. There was no setting sun to guide him, just overbearing trees, opaque vision and the different rules of the night.

And then suddenly, there was a noise behind him, approaching fast, the loud pounding of feet close at hand. Peter turned to his right, but it came from the left, a grunt of breath, a hand over his mouth – and laughing. Peter's response was immediate, instinctive. He was at the assaulting arm, gripping the wrist, twisting it with desperate power, making it hurt, pulling it down and round, savage force, back up towards the aggressors shoulder – and then pushing him forward, falling together, another body beneath him as they hit the soft ground.

And then Loner's Wood went quiet.

The ghost stood on Matron's Landing.

He was listening to the night, as often he did. The East Wing of Stormhaven Towers seemed quiet, but this was not the quiet of peace. A fearful silence hung in the dark corridors; a pleading silence which begged the angel of death to pass their door and leave them be, let them live to see the dawn.

But no matter . . . the ghost would walk awhile, enjoy the space of the students departed. The school was so much better with them gone. In a dark cape and black safari hat he reached the Head's Landing where the old grandfather clock ticked and tocked with heavy beat. He moved silently down the wooden staircase, past the portrait of Nathaniel Bleake, the school founder who stood forever at the top of the stairs, pride of place – though ignored in every other way.

'They pay you nothing more than lip service, Nathaniel,' said the ghost.

And he did not speak out of turn. This school had drifted some way from its original vision, like a drugged animal with no memory of the days of its health. He continued down the stairs and let himself out by a side door. Schools have many side doors, doors away from public gaze, for trade, for cleaners, for gardeners and the like . . . and for those who wish to leave without being seen, for whom the main entrance is not appropriate, not doused enough in darkness for their purposes. He would be mindful of the policeman by the gate. He kept close to the walls, running his fingers along flint as he walked, smooth and sharp, the sun long gone in the western sky. 'The day thou gavest Lord is ended,' as he had once sung in the shadowy chapel to his left, in clearer and more certain times.

The ghost noted another policeman hovering around the main entrance; and so he returned inside an alternative way, a small path round the side, a hidden area for the bins and then through another door away from public gaze. He walked silently along the corridor. He shouldn't be here, it was unwise but he couldn't help himself. He stopped by their door and listened. He heard the tap running, smelt soap, heard teeth being cleaned at the end of the day.

And he felt sad, sharp pangs, for that is something they'd once shared – and never would again.

Peter felt for blood

at the side of his head, where he'd taken the hit. He expected blood, the wet feel of the damage done. He'd thudded against a gnarled root in the fall after the attack. Beside him, his attacker rolled in pleasing pain.

'No need for evasive action, Abbot!' Bart lay on the ground, rubbing his wrenched arm. He was angry at the abbot's assault, the sharp twist and wrench, when he'd only been playing. He hadn't meant anything by his midnight jape ... it was just a joke. The abbot had not needed to act as he had, absolutely no way. 'I saw you leave the school – and thought it would be fun to give chase.'

There was no blood as far as Peter could tell ... just fury at this stupid invasion of his solitude.

'An attack from behind, the hand over my mouth – this was not fun,' said Peter. 'It was angry.'

'But I didn't mean anything by it – you're making it more than it was.' Peter got up from the ground; his only desire was to be away from this man. 'I just wanted to give you a bit of scare, Abbot – in Loner's Wood and all that! You know, like we spoke about. You didn't need to assault me.'

'I *did* need to assault you.'

Bart remained on the ground, rubbing his arm.

'You were like a mad man.'

'Fear can make us mad ... but tonight, I hope I was sane,' said Peter. 'It was a move I learned in the desert. Brother Sosimus, as I recall – a monk who'd previously been a policeman in Algiers. And if you want a quiet life, you don't become a policeman in Algiers. It's a defensive move, of course – damage limitation in the face of attack ... your attack.'

'It's a shame you can't take a joke.'

Bart was in some pain and still on the ground. He was wondering if his arm was broken.

'I'm going back to the school now,' said Peter. 'I expect you to as well – there's a curfew after eleven. Otherwise you'll be reported absent and have the police to deal with.'

'I'm so scared!' said Bart, sulkily – like this monk had any power over him!

'And a police caution on your CV to aid further job applications,' added Peter. 'I don't wish for your company on the return journey, however – so do find another way back to the school. And I hope your arm feels better in the morning.'

This wasn't completely true ...

'I said I could catch you,' said Bart. 'I just didn't realize you were a psycho who can't take a bit of fun.'

'You first,' said Peter, inviting Bart to start running. 'I'll leave after you.'

The Director of Wellbeing rose to his feet awkwardly, leaf mould on his hands and face. For a frozen moment, they faced each other in Loner's Wood – but it was Bart, the larger man, who backed down. 'Till next time, Abbot,' he said and then turned away and began the run home. He made off towards a copse that was almost a wood within a wood. Peter let him go. He'd seen the road ahead, a way out of the wood ... and he had a ghost to catch.

It was quiet in the common room,

a gathering of restrained evening chat.

'It does have the feeling of a tomb,' said Geoff as he placed a sweet sherry on the table for Terence. 'We really could be inside one of the pyramids.'

'I wouldn't know,' said Terence crisply. 'I have little experience of tombs.'

'We'll all get there eventually,' said Geoff.

'And if the tomb is like a quiet summer's evening, then perhaps it's not all bad.'

Why be so depressed, Geoff? thought Terence. Really!

'And you call this a quiet summer's evening, Terence?'

The bursar shrugged . . . while across the room, Holly struggled.

Had Holly been with her friends, it would not have been a quiet summer's evening . . . anything but. When Holly and her friends got together, they aimed for a screeching, dancing, vomiting oblivion by midnight . . . a reverie of excess away from the powers-that-be.

'Here's to the Oblivion Girls!' they'd say, 'Love you all and love you forever!' But tonight, the Oblivion Girls seemed a long way away. Holly sat holding an amaretto on ice, bought for her by Penny. It seemed very grown up. Penny was sad, though, and unable to say much. So Holly found herself holding her hand, which was odd, because Mrs Rylands was Director of Girls and part of the Senior Management Team and Holly was – well, what was Holly now? Pupil? Old girl? Child? Adult? Blackmailer? For the first time, she felt slightly ridiculous in her Stormhaven Towers tracksuit, which had always been a home, a place of safety. It was as though that game was finished . . . but she wasn't quite ready to leave the cocoon.

151

'I didn't know her very well,' said Holly. It was Jennifer who Penny mourned and Holly didn't know what to say, because she didn't care a fig about Jennifer, not really; and adults were meant to cheer *her* up, not the other way round.

Penny smiled.

'You must look after Crispin,' she said, in a mother-to-daughter way, looking to where he sat. Crispin was a lonely figure across the common room, staring out of the window at the last embers of the summer's day. He wasn't quite a man among men yet, still soft-skinned . . . and cautious.

'Crispin doesn't need looking after,' said Holly with a dry chuckle. 'He knows more than the rest of us put together.'

'Really? He always seemed a rather shy boy to me.'

'There's not much that Crispin doesn't see.'

'Is that a note of admiration, Holly?'

Penny squinted a little in mock intrigue, as women do in matters of love.

'I'm just saying,' said Holly, primly. She wasn't in love – or even close to it, no way. Crispin meant nothing to her! And Penny once again looked sad.

'You'll get over her,' said Cressida, sitting a couple of seats away, reading. Her move into the East Wing was complete. She'd asked Mrs Docherty to make up her bed and was settled enough. She was even quite enjoying this whole common room thing. It was like being back at university, hanging around doing nothing . . . more carefree days, long left behind. She'd be watching *Countdown* next and eating pot noodles . . . At some point the next day she'd need to get back home to feed the cat – and escape the present company for a while. Pets did have their uses – there was only so much university life she could endure.

'What do you mean, "I'll get over her"?' said Penny, with no attempt to hide her irritation. Was that meant to be helpful or something?

'I'm sorry,' said Cressida, seeing Penny's distress. She even put down her book and removed her glasses. 'I never had much of a bedside manner – always been my weak hand.'

Penny melted a little, aware once again that she wasn't the only one who grieved.

'As long as the diagnosis is correct, doctor.'

'That's where I excel,' said Cressida.

And then Holly spoke up: 'Is it true that when it comes to killing people, doctors are the best?'

Penny flinched at the insensitivity ... but Cressida laughed. It was not so much at the comment itself, as at the capacity of Holly to make it, in these circumstances.

'That's gatecrashingly offensive, Holly – you do know that?' said Penny.

'Oh, I'm sorry!' said Holly. 'I didn't mean ...'

'It's OK,' said Cressida.

'Really?'

'No, really – quite OK.' If truth be known, it almost felt like an act of friendship from the pretty little Holly. 'But why do people obsess about doctors as killers?' asked Cressida, whimsically. 'It's a strange obsession, almost perverted.'

'It's our hope and our powerlessness when faced by the white coat,' said Penny.

'Is that how you feel?'

'There's both awe and fear. We want to submit to this person's expertise – but can we trust them? What if they're bad? Awe and fear ...' And at that moment, Bart walked into the common room, a waft of sweat and running clothes. He held himself awkwardly.

'Lycra man!' said Geoff, generously, pleased for a distraction from Terence, who seemed more distant than usual tonight. 'A drink?'

'Oh, yes, Geoff – thank you.' He looked around at the faces turned towards him. 'Perhaps some tonic water.'

'You all right, old man?' asked Geoff.

'Had a bit of a fall on my run – went down on the shoulder.'

He wasn't hiding his injury but Cressida made no move; she was not at work. She wouldn't be saying, 'Take your top off, you poor fellow, and let's have a proper look at you.'

'Nasty,' said Geoff. 'Sure you don't want something stronger?'

Terence was briefly worried. He was afraid that Geoff's visit to the bar would leave him sitting with Bart, which was not a happy prospect. The two of them had nothing in common – absolutely nothing at all. There were many teachers he had no time for professionally – constantly whining about their hours or contracts. But ultimately, he didn't mind writing the cheques if he thought they were doing a job, and doing it well. Bart, however, was not, not in Terence's reckoning. He was a waste of money – £34,000 per annum that could be much better spent. So yes, the bursar had quietly supported Jamie in moves to make the Director of Wellbeing redundant. Perhaps the money freed up could be spent on a business or sports scholarship?

And Jamie would have seen all this through, had he lived. Bart had been a man on borrowed time at Stormhaven Towers ... though who the fellow was, Terence really had no idea. As far as the bursar was concerned, Bart was something of a caricature, almost fictitious in his ridiculous self-creation, trying too hard to be something, to be useful, to mean something. This was the thing about Bart – beneath all the mindful claptrap and the folk songs from Olde England, you sensed this desperation, a man lonely in the crowd ... a man in the wrong place.

'On second thoughts, I think I'll shower first,' said Bart. 'See you later, guys.'

With a wince and a gasp of pain, he carried his wound from the room.

'So what on earth was that about?' asked Geoff theatrically, when he'd gone.

'I think he just wanted us to know that he'd been running, sir,' said Crispin. 'And that he got hurt.' Well, surely the others must have seen that? The victim who needed a witness ...

Ferdinand was at prayer.

He was bringing the world to God's attention – and it did need his attention, particularly Stormhaven Towers, where moral anarchy ran free.

He knelt alone at the altar in the school chapel, a solitary figure in the cavernous space, all candles and shadows – mainly shadows, which appeared more viscous tonight, more secretive, as if the chapel itself had been drawn into the darkness death brings. Ferdinand had asked in the common room if anyone wished to share in evening prayer with him; but there'd been no takers. They had made the Burundi jokes again about 'Father Desperate', which was all rather childish.

It was a running gag among the faithless – hardly a minority, sad to say. They said that whenever he led a service, Ferdinand always included long prayers for some obscure priest – Father Desperate – in some obscure parish in some obscure country way across the world, like Burundi.

'We've had enough of Burundi for this term, Ferdinand,' Geoff had said. 'I wish Father Desperate all the best, but I'm more worried about my own skin at the moment!' And everyone else had laughed. 'You could of course pray that the school psycho has a heart attack,' he added. But that hadn't gone down so well, only the laughter of the nervous. It reminded them of their fear, which wasn't funny at all.

Not that the chaplain minded being alone in the chapel. He was used to it. What did the others understand anyway? It was disappointing they stayed away, but really – did any of them under-stand spiritual things? Ferdinand gazed heavenwards from the prayer book he held tight. Jesus looked so alone on the cross, there on the cream-plastered wall of the sanctuary . . . and Ferdinand knew the feeling. He'd tried so hard to make the chapel the focal point of the school community . . . but it wasn't easy when neither the head nor the parents were believers in anything but academic results – and the money that good results led to. Shame on them! Oh, the parents would say, 'I just want Oliver to be happy in life.' But in their world, 'happy' meant 'rich', there was no other way. His recent sermon on 'Blessed are the poor' had led to five complaints being made to the head. People felt it wasn't 'aspirational' enough and gave all the wrong messages.

How times had changed from the nineteenth century when the school was founded! And how he hated it sometimes! Nathaniel Bleake wanted a school to educate the children of impoverished clergy – yet now, no clergy on the outside could afford it . . . and no clergy on the inside were listened to!

He prayed for God's way to become clear at Stormhaven Towers. And for the murderer? He didn't know what to pray for the murderer . . .

The abbot stood naked.

After a hot shower, Peter was motionless and unclothed in his room. He must gather himself, still himself – he had a ghost hunt to attend to. He closed his eyes and allowed the vulnerability of this present moment, the fragility of life, a deep sense of unknowing about the future . . . nakedness helped this.

'Who is anyone without clothes?' as he sometimes said. 'If you are someone without clothes, then you are someone indeed!' And he felt it even now, the energy of the stripped soul. But as he stood, he knew another energy as well. He knew the energy of anger which, if uncoupled from ego, was a strong guide. He would dress and step out into the darkness with Brother Anger . . . but first, a simple rite of passage.

It was his practice sometimes, when wishing to focus, to count down from ten to one, slowly. He had learned it from a Buddhist in the desert called Okahito. The poor man had ended up at the monastery by mistake, but chose to stay for six months and proved a very welcome addition to the community.

'You count slowly from ten to one, Abbot.'

'Maths was never my strong hand.'

'Do not limit yourself, Abbot.'

'Quite.'

'To help yourself become still, you visualize each number in your mind before moving onto the next one.'

'Picture the number in my mind, starting with ten?'

'That is right. Perhaps the number will appear written in chalk on a blackboard, perhaps it will appear in flames, perhaps as biro on paper or in flowers – who knows and it doesn't matter how it appears – only that it does.'

'I see.'

'How quickly you reach one will say much about your inner state. When calm, each number will appear quite easily in your visual mind; when anxious, distracted thoughts might obscure the number for a while. But keep going until you get there ... until you get to one.'

The abbot thought of Okahito as he counted down. And tonight, each number appeared quite simply in his mind, with only a slight distraction between three and two – which then appeared in a wall of fire. With the countdown complete, he dressed. He chose trainers over sandals for stealth and paused a moment. He pulled back his curtain and looked out on the starlit sky. Everything was still across the rolling Downs, an idyllic setting ... except for a sick soul at work somewhere within these walls. And he suspected he knew who the sick soul was, just a hunch – a circumstance which surely could only point to one person?

Seventy yards away, across the well-kept lawn, he noted a lone policeman at the school gate. He'd no doubt have a moan in the morning about the experience ... but there were worse shifts than his across the country tonight, armed as he was with a Thermos and sandwiches. His presence had been hugely popular with the suspects.

'There is something reassuring about the bobby on the beat,' Cressida had said, with a wry smile. 'Though whether anyone is actually safer for their presence? Perhaps, like a placebo, he just makes us feel better ...'

But the thin blue line could barely be thinner tonight and while it gave reassurance to the residents, it gave little to Peter. He closed the curtain. It was eleven o'clock, when everyone should be in their rooms. And coming to think of it, perhaps he was the thin blue line tonight rather than the uniformed placebo on the gate.

Enough. He needed to face the pale presence who haunted Stormhaven Towers ...

Peter stepped out into

the silent corridor. He stopped for a moment, adjusting his eyes
to the lack of light, and then closed his door behind him. The
closing of the door was like a Rubicon crossed; and like Caesar,
here was a venture in which he must succeed. He needed to find
the ghost . . . and identify the elusive Benedict. Was the ghost
Benedict? Or was Benedict already known?

The East Wing was dark, lit in parts by occasional night lights.
The floor was shiny red tiles and along the side, various glass
cabinets displaying their wares. They were the holders of history,
the moments applauded down the years at Stormhaven Towers: an
Under-15s Hockey Trophy from 1963, in need of a polish. Peter
wondered if there was anyone alive who remembered the game.
But it was remembered here in the East Wing in a cabinet, set
alongside other cups . . . like the Cuckmere Gap Running Trophy
from 1954. Was the winner still running? Possibly – though perhaps
not with their former zest or speed. And in between the cabinets, the
history continued, rolls of honour carved into the dark-varnished
wood, head boys since 1919 – though gatecrashed by girls of late.
No doubt Holly Hope-Walker would soon be there, alongside
Crispin Caudwell.

And on another board, further along, the House winners of the
Towers Football Trophy since 1899. Did anyone care? They did at
the time, that's for sure, keenly fought – but now? Peter was standing at the top of the staircase, the Head's Landing, where portraits
of old headmasters hung, academic gowns and long sideburns –
serious-minded folk, still glaring down on the scene making sure
no one ran: 'No running in the corridors, Winkworth!' And looking down on them all, at the top of the stairs, was Nathaniel Bleake,
founder of this great beast. There was no academic gown on his
shoulders but the black coat, white shirt and black cravat of a
successful but godly industrialist who does not wish to be too

tall a poppy. Still the sideburns, however, and the serious-minded stare.

Peter felt drawn into another era, different times – and found himself wondering what Okahito would have made of it all. He remembered the Zen painting kit he had brought to the desert – and seemed so determined to show everyone.

'It looks like a normal painting kit,' he'd said, his face filled with mischief.

'It does look rather normal,' Peter had said, perhaps a little disappointed.

'Oh, it is very normal, Abbot Peter! You take your brush, dip it into the water – go on, dip it.' Peter had done as he was told. 'That's right – and then paint an image on the board.'

And Peter, a reluctant artist, had done this, while wondering what exactly was Zen about a bit of painting. He drew an outline of the monastery against a darkening sky and was quite pleased with his creation.

'Your drawing is there before your eyes, is it not?' Peter nodded; he was quite pleased with his efforts. 'But not for long – see.'

And the abbot did see. After a few seconds, he watched his image fading away, the monastery and the darkening sky, in all its glory, fading into nothing . . . nothing. There was now nothing on the board except a big blank. But Okahito was not upset – if anything, he was excited.

'So now you reflect a while, Peter, dip the brush in the water again and paint something else.'

'And that too will disappear?' said Peter, somehow knowing the answer.

'Of course, of course! Why would you wish it to remain?'

'Well . . .'

'It would only hold you back from the present.'

'I can see that, yes. I suppose I'm more concerned for the art world than myself.'

'Ah, those rich people would not be so pleased to see their Picassos and Van Goghs disappearing!'

'Not hugely.'

160

'Forty million pounds that might have helped humanity – gone! You expect me to cry for them? We must invest in the present not the past.'

The message was the impermanence of things, this is what Okahito said . . . and not everyone thought he was mad. One thing was for sure: there'd certainly be no old headmasters on the staircase in the Zen school. They'd have faded long ago.

And then Peter saw the ghost.

Peter stood stock still.

And he could have been in the stocks, so locked was his body at the sight. Back down the corridor, caught by a spillage of light, was a figure with a white face in dark clothing and black safari hat. Or was that just the light? Peter eased himself further into the landing shadows, blessed in hiding by the dark textures of his habit. There was something anonymous about the monks' habit in a monastery, the uniform of shared non-existence, the colour of the stone, the colour of the earth, the refusal to stand out and the abbot hoped it worked here. The ghost seemed to be pondering the bedroom doors, leaning forward and then drawing back. What was he doing? Was he listening at the doors?

There was presently about twenty yards between them, which felt close to a ghost he had no wish to be seen by. And then the ghost turned – turned around and moved forward, moving towards Peter who withdrew further. He tucked himself behind the large grandfather clock, ticking loudly the minutes and the hours and the days and the years of this unfolding school story in which Peter found himself.

And now the ghost was but five yards away, a man in his late fifties, slicked-back hair, salt and pepper grey, smooth-skinned but white as a clown, cream suit beneath the cape, shiny shoes, fastidious – this was Peter's first impression of the ghost . . . he looked fastidious as he pondered Nathaniel Bleake on the wall.

'You give the appearance of certainty, Nathaniel, but I'm sure it wasn't always like that. Certainty is for those with hindsight, wouldn't you say? For those who look back – they invent a certainty that was never there at the time.' The ghost spoke in a refined manner, slightly posh. 'But this shall be the end game, I think, one way or another – and maybe it is better that way. Maybe it had to be this way – that people had to die. Enough died in your factories, Nathaniel.'

The ghost gathered himself again. 'There is a rather pretty inspector here. Did you ever lust, Nathaniel? You probably did, you old rascal. In between your good works. Oh, and a monk. You will never have met a monk, I suspect, different world to yours – but they have survived, in their way. I don't know his quality. We'll see. He may be a paedophile – he may be Sherlock . . . or he may simply be a disappointment, who can say?' The ghost paused and a frown appeared. 'You do not approve of young Benedict, I know, your face says it all. You would prefer him hanged, no doubt – wasn't that the way of malcontents in your day? Perhaps he would prefer to be hanged. But if I go, I will take you with me. Out of kindness. I will take you and the whole school with me . . . out of kindness for a vision abused. Good night, Nathaniel.'

He turned and walked back the way he'd come, back down the corridor, sometimes brushing the walls with his outstretched hands as if listening to the stone with his fingers. Peter stepped out, cautiously. Keeping in the shadows, he followed the ghost down the corridor, for he did not wish to lose him; he wanted to know where he slept . . . if ghosts do sleep. He was glad of the silent tread of his trainers. Should the ghost turn, he would probably be seen, but what choice did he have? The ghost was no ghost but a man, all flesh and blood, caught in some time, some era, that Peter could not quite pinpoint. And then the ghost stopped, outside the abbot's bedroom door – and started beating on it, loudly. And then in a stage whisper, which travelled easily down the corridor: 'I knew it, Abbot! I knew it!'

And then he walked on, in a careless, carefree manner, as if aware he was being watched, playing to the audience a little until he reached Matron's Landing, where suddenly, and quite inexplicably, he disappeared. Peter pulled up in surprise. Where had the ghost gone? He stood still for a moment, waiting for his reappearance. Was this some game or trick? But there was nothing, just the gentle wind in the trees outside, a dog barking across the fields . . . and Peter's beating heart. He walked on, up three steps and onto the landing – Matron's Landing, from where he had collected his fresh sheets. Peter looked around. Only two doors led off the landing and both had been in vision when the ghost had evaporated from view. So where had he gone? There was the large wooden wardrobe, quite unlike any other wardrobe he'd ever seen. It was almost a room in its storage capacity: two large doors and then a separate door to the side – a side cupboard, presumably. And then beside the wardrobe, a curtain. Was this where the ghost had escaped? Peter approached quietly, paused for a moment, then – heart pumping – took hold of the curtain and firmly pulled it back.

It was a cleaning cupboard for brooms, dust pans, furniture polish and bleach. The abbot breathed a sigh of relief and disappointment, closed the curtains and looked around. Again the question: how could he disappear like that? Ghosts walked through walls but this was no ghost, this was human – one requiring a more conventional exit. Peter looked up at the timber-beamed ceiling and then again at the wardrobe. He stepped forward and opened its two large doors but found only what he expected to find – sheets, pillow cases, towels. And, above a shelf to the left, a little sign in red felt tip saying 'emergency pyjamas'. Matron was ready for anything . . .

So where was the ghost? Peter sat down on a fine wooden seat, almost a throne, as one might have found in a Tudor manor – placed at the end of the table, where his Lordship sat to eat, drink and watch the after-dinner fools juggle and jest. Only tonight, Peter was the fool, missing something which was staring him in the face – but what . . . and where?

He thought of Okahito. He counted down from ten to one, visualizing the numbers. The number one, when he reached it, appeared hollowed out, as a narrow gate. A narrow gate . . . Peter looked again at the wardrobe – but he'd checked the wardrobe, the main doors at least. Not the side door, which was a narrow gate – but presumably another cupboard. He would check it – and he felt a fool, for it was quite clearly a wardrobe. But he would check it anyway and wait for 'emergency duvets' or the like to fall on his head. But nothing fell on his head as he opened the side door in the wardrobe. Inside were no shelves but a small windowless porch. Beyond the porch was a curtain, where there should have been the back of the wardrobe. Peter stepped through the door, reached forward, took hold of the curtain and eased it back.

164

He looked into the gloom, seeing nothing. He closed the wardrobe door behind him to allow his eyes to adapt to a world without light. He stood now in an enclosed space, three feet square, a cave of his own choosing. He listened to his breathing, stepped forward and out of the gloom there appeared a staircase ... a small wooden staircase.

I think I would have preferred Narnia, he thought. But he shuffled quietly forward – he could hardly go back – and placed a foot on the bottom step. Was it solid? It seemed solid enough and so began the climb, one creaking step after another, slowly upwards until ahead of him, he could see a door ... a door, perhaps seven or eight steps away. Where was he now? Matron's Landing and the smell of fresh linen seemed a long way back, another country, as he reached the top. Would he knock at this strange portal – or push it open and enter? He knocked, three firm strikes and the response was almost immediate.

'Come!' said the voice ... and so Peter stepped inside.

'What kept you?'

asked the ghost, with slight puzzlement. He sat in a room of satin and silk; a room of greys, whites and the occasional pink in a picture, flower or vase. 'My name is Benedict,' he said standing up to shake Peter's hand. 'Benedict Bleake. Can you see the likeness?'

'Peter,' said the abbot, because he couldn't think of what else to say. The light was suddenly bright and the surroundings ornate, with the smell of patchouli.

'Please, have a seat,' said Benedict – the ghost's white make-up still in evidence ... like a clown who hasn't had time to wash. 'You will share a whisky with me?'

'Thank you,' said Peter, aware that his arrival was no surprise.

'Ice?'

It felt like a test of his manhood.

'No ice,' he said.

'I do not approve of making things easy,' said Benedict, handing Peter a glass of Scotch. 'We must never make things easy for the young. Struggle is good. But you passed the little test ... eventually! Had I known how long you'd be, though, I'd have washed off the make-up. Just a little fun, of course ... the rumour of a ghost suits me, deflects attention.'

'I had heard of you,' said Peter, settling a little and enjoying the inner warmth of the whisky.

'You'd heard of the ghost, no doubt.'

'No, the flesh-and-blood version.'

'Oh? Well, there can be only one blabbermouth responsible – the terrible Terence!' Peter didn't respond. 'I saw you by the clock, by the way. The grandfather clock – you were hiding there when I was chatting with the boss.'

Peter acknowledged the news with a silent look of 'Oh, really?'

'You stood out like a sore thumb, my dear.'

This was humiliating news, despite Benedict's bonhomie – or perhaps because of it. There was a growing sense he was this man's evening entertainment, an upgrade on the soap operas available.

'The monk behind the clock!' said Benedict, with delight. 'Sounds like the name of a children's book, doesn't it?' Peter nodded. 'The monk behind the clock! How strange, I thought. And how delicious!'

'Well, I didn't come here to be delicious, Benedict.'

He was struggling for control of the situation, like a man trying to pull down a vast balloon blowing wildly in the wind.

'I know, I know! And that's what makes it all the more delicious! You came as "Abbot Earnest", intent on finding the murderer.'

'Or murderers.'

'Quite, quite, nothing can be ruled out – not by you at least.'

'And by you?'

Benedict smiled and his white face cracked a little.

'The monk behind the clock,' he said, still amused. 'There's a line I never thought I'd say!' The bonhomie was beginning to fade, however, the energy of welcome dissipating. 'You do know that you're the first to climb those stairs – apart from myself – for the last ten years?'

'Really?'

'Well, that's not quite true – we have had one visitor recently.'

'Terence?'

'This is not a kiss–and–tell, Peter! Civilized folk discuss ideas – not people.'

'Ideas don't commit murder.'

'Well, you say that, Abbot – but of course that's precisely what ideas do. Ideas are always committing murder! They place the thoughts in people's heads which become murder. It's the ideas that really wield the knife. Or, in this case, make that push' – he enacted a push – 'or rub the poison into the wound.'

'You're very well-informed,' said Peter.

'Thank you!'

'Almost revealingly so.'

'Thank you again!'

They both took a further sip of the whisky.

'So what do you do here, Benedict? In the school, I mean – and this is a magnificent room, by the way.'

'It's called taste, I suppose,' he said, getting up from his seat and striking a pose by the mantelpiece. 'And what do I do here? Well, I live here, it's my home – my birthright, so to speak.'

'You mean, because of your relationship with the founder?'

Was he understanding this correctly?

'Since my great-great-great-great-whatever grandfather founded the school, there has always been a place for a member of the family ... however much the school may dislike the idea.'

'They don't want you here?'

'They hate it! Positively *hate* it! I'm as popular as a slug at the Chelsea Flower Show! They probably want my lovely rooms for some awful IT unit – or staff accommodation.'

'But they can't have it ... because it's your birthright.'

'I was fortunate enough to make a tidy sum of money early in life, working for a rather large company. Complete luck, of course. Making money is all about luck. And I was able to leave rather royally – an indecent pay-off really – and run my own little business from home. Medical supplies, certain drugs sold under licence, Eastern Europe mainly. And when poor Uncle Colin died – most unfortunate, and still something of a mystery – this delightful accommodation became available. All very suitable ... I heard my forefathers calling me in the night.' Peter smiled. 'So welcome to the virtual offices of "BenBleake Cures"!'

The abbot pondered the authenticity of Benedict's delight – and found his mind read rather easily.

'Of course, I hate this place,' he said. 'But I love it as well. I love its past – and hate its present. Is that ambivalent enough for you? Like a man who loves his wife as she was – but not as she is. A little like Jamie, really.'

Was that true?

'And could the hate make you kill?' asked Peter.

Benedict looked at him surprised, bemused ... as though Peter was an idiot.

'Can we keep the conversation sensible, Abbot? I don't have energy for the ridiculous.'

Peter smiled, he couldn't help it, almost a laugh really – and changed tack.

'Do you know any of the school staff?' he asked.

'The staff? Why would I wish to know any of them? They don't even know I'm here. It's not public knowledge, you know – indeed, it's blessedly secret, as you discovered in trying to find me. The side door – my door – is usually locked. It was only left open for you. And of course there's a back stairs, the servants stairs, out of the building – so I can move quite freely. And if anyone asks who I am, I say I'm a schools inspector – I have a little identity card, great fun it is. They're always most polite after that.'

'It's a slightly leaky secret.'

'Meaning?'

'Terence knows you're here.'

'He's the bursar – so of course he would.'

'Because?'

'He was a bit of a busybody on my arrival, as people sometimes are ... makes them feel worthwhile for a moment, making their mark. And Terence, bless him, wasn't keen on my rent-free status, which is apparently still recorded each year in the books – like some niggling slight the school must live with. So yes, we met – but it was all sorted quite amicably.'

'He backed down.'

'I simply showed him the deeds, Abbot; it wasn't a discussion after that. Another little pen-wielding bastard overestimating his cleverness.'

'Do you meet many of those?'

'I have done in my time ... only doing his job, of course, so no hard feelings.'

'I can see,' said Peter, attempting sarcasm. But it was a wasted attempt. Benedict was too smooth and sure for anything like that to stick. 'So who would want to kill Jamie?'

'Who would *want* to? Or who *did*? The first list might be a little longer.'

'Do you know who killed Jamie?'

'Of course I know!' He had Peter's attention. 'Do you really think I don't know everything that happens in this place?'

169

'How would you know?'

'I listen to the walls, Abbot, listen with my hands, speak with the corridors after dark – a building cannot lie any more than the human body can lie. And I pass it all on.'

'To who?'

'To Nathaniel, of course, as I believe you heard tonight; a man who had the grace to found this place – though he heartily regrets it now, no doubt.'

'He's told you.'

'Look in his sad face and tell me it isn't so. Stand on those stairs and look in his face! He becomes more traumatized by the year, watching his child in the hands of such cultural pirates. They live under such terrible pressure, of course.'

'Who?'

'The staff – such pressure to perform! I really do feel sorry for the dears. No, really! I mean, they're all quite spineless, so they deserve whatever they get. But staff – well, staff in a school should be encouraged to *be*, not *perform*.'

'How very mystical.'

'It's not mystical, my dear, it's common sense. Otherwise what sort of model do they offer? The school baptizes the rat race with these Johnny-come-lately parents muscling in on privilege – all very distasteful, flashing their cash and their large 4x4s. They really are the most repulsive of souls . . .'

'Privilege should be kept for the privileged?'

'Private education, Abbot, is for those who wish their children taken off their hands. That's the truth of the matter. One can hardly expect such parents to be especially interested in their offspring – apart from as some extension of their entitlement-encrusted egos.'

Peter was taken aback by the force of the rage. He spoke with a passion which suggested more than mere love of debate.

'And are you such a child – or such a father?'

'Do you know something, Abbot?' Peter's eyebrows rose in expectation. 'The staff here must reply to parents within six hours of receiving a complaint or a query. Six hours! Or to put it another way, they must *bow and grovel* within six hours of receiving

a complaint . . . or face the consequences! There are a lot of cas-
ualties, you know.'

'And HR?'

Benedict laughed in derision.

'The purpose of HR in Stormhaven Towers is to sack the right
people at the right time, with minimum disruption and come-back.'

'You do not have a high opinion of HR here.'

'Thirty grand per annum buys you a very servile management,
my friend – one whose only question to the parents is this: "At
what temperature would you like your staff roasted?"'

Benedict looked smug, satisfied with his performance . . . as if all
had been said and there was nothing to add. But there was much
to add from where Peter sat.

'So you do know the killer?'

'Do I know the killer?'

And now he looked sad.

'Unfortunately, they're having an affair with an undesirable,' he
said.

'An undesirable?'

'Well, desirable perhaps, attractive in a manner – but unwise,
shall we say. And it's made things rather messy. So sad . . .'

'So who is the killer?' asked Peter.

'I think that's enough for tonight, Abbot. But so good to meet
you at last!'

ACT TWO

They sat, each with
a strong coffee

in hand. The early morning light danced through the window; it was six o'clock. They'd agreed to rise with the lark to review the case . . . though conversation was struggling to flow.

'Stupid o'clock,' said Tamsin, who'd not had time to put her face on. She felt undressed . . . but it was only the abbot. She didn't dress for the abbot; she dressed for a more hostile world. And there'd be time for make-up before meeting the suspects at eight thirty in the common room. 'And you smell like a brewery.'

'Like a distillery – if we're to be accurate. There was no beer involved.'

'Are you losing focus, Abbot?'

'I'm sorry?'

'You're getting paid for this, remember.'

'Not as much as you.'

'That's because I'm doing all the work.' Peter's eyebrows arched in surprise. 'While you develop a habit for drinking alone – a slippery slope, that one.'

'I drank with the ghost,' he said quietly.

'The ghost?'

'Benedict.'

'Benedict?' Tamsin's reaction was worth the wait. She was awake now. 'So who the hell *is* this Benedict?'

'Benedict lives here,' said Peter calmly and proceeded, with a certain pleasure, to fill her in on the results of his ghost hunt, the place of Benedict Bleake at Stormhaven Towers and the mixed feelings he had for the place. 'Oh, and another thing: he knows the killer.'

'He knows the killer? You mean he knows who the killer is?'

'He thinks he does.'

'And you believe him?'

'Possibly.'

'Sounds like Benedict Bleake's got you deep in his pocket.'

'Better to be in the pocket of a giant than in the mind of a fool.'

'And what's that supposed to mean?'

Abbot Peter didn't know exactly, he'd just made it up – but there was something there, some truth beyond routine self-protection from the irritable aggression of Tamsin. She was never at her best when catching up, when not in the position of 'informational lead'. Peter was informational lead this morning, while Tamsin was catching up and finding it difficult. She liked to be in control.

'He's agreed to meet us this afternoon,' said Peter.

'Well, we *are* honoured!' said Tamsin, layering on the sarcasm. 'And it's his call, of course. After all, it's only a murder inquiry – so who are we to demand a meeting with some no-mark member of the public.'

'He was supposed to be out of the country today, on a business trip. He was flying to Budapest.'

'You can tell him he stays here until I say he can go.'

'He speaks of an affair taking place, Tamsin.'

'An affair?'

'Here, before our eyes. Have you seen an affair? Women are meant to see these things.'

'If it's there, I will. If it's there . . .'

'Someone's having an affair with an "undesirable", he said – an affair that became murder.'

Tamsin snorted a little, amused air pushed through the nose, signalling disdain: 'Has it ever struck you, Abbot, that the reason he might know the murderer, is that he and they are one and the same?'

It was the gardener,
Mr Thomas,

who told them about the car, a little before the school clock struck eight. There was a red hatchback parked awkwardly off the road, just beyond the school gates. It was driven into the hedge and the boot hatch was open ... but there was no visible damage to the vehicle.

'I ain't touched nothing,' said the gardener as they approached the vehicle. 'So I don't know if he's alive.'

'Someone's in there?'

'I think as much.'

'Well, who's in there?'

Peter and Tamsin walked side-by-side across the school lawns and onto the gravel driveway.

'Do you know the driver?' Tamsin pressed.

'I can't say I know him, no,' said Mr Thomas. He'd been at the school for less than a year and kept himself to himself. He preferred plants to people, less trouble. And while they'd never found the aconite that had killed his predecessor, he remained wary of the flower. Some had been injured just smelling it, it was well known.

'So it could be anybody?' she said, irritated. This probably had nothing to do with the school – it could simply be an RTA for Traffic to deal with. She had bigger fish to fry.

'I just thought you might like to look, what with the murders. I mean, it may be nothing ...'

'Of course we'd like to look, Mr Thomas,' said Peter. 'We all need each other's eyes right now. Especially gardeners' eyes – because gardeners see everything.'

'I saw a strange one on Sunday afternoon,' he said. 'And that's a fact.'

'A strange what?' said Peter.

'Thought she was a woman, I did – at first, like.'

'Who?'

'But it turned out to be a man! Lucky I didn't kiss 'er, eh?'

They were close to the vehicle, almost able to see in. Tamsin gloved her hands in rubber, and peered through the open driver's window. And then pulled back.

'Bad?' asked Peter.

'Bad,' said Tamsin, who then moved forward towards the car window again.

'One adult male,' she said, carefully opening the door. The driver was still in the driver's seat – in a manner. But his upper body was elsewhere, wrenched across to where a passenger would have been, twisted and face down. Feeling sick, Tamsin reached forward and took the pulse from the arm hanging down from the seat . . . he was dead. Well, of course he was dead! There was a tight noose round his traumatized neck – and a rope which Tamsin traced out through the car boot to where she could now see Peter standing, by a tree.

'A sad use of an oak tree,' said Peter.

'So it's suicide?' she said, extracting herself from the car and joining the abbot.

The former monk contemplated the scene before him. It didn't seem complicated.

'He tied the rope round the tree, returned to the car, noosed it round his neck – and then drove at speed away from the tree.' Tamsin looked disapproving, like one handed a dirty nappy. She shook her head as she imagined the brief but messy drama so recently played out in this quiet rural idyll.

'He's still warm,' she added.

'But not warm enough, sadly. We had a similar death in the desert, a Bedouin boy – only he tied himself to a camel and rode him with a passion – until his neck broke. He flew off the back of the camel like one dragged, the animal careering forward.'

'Could there have been someone else in the car?'

She didn't have time for the desert.

'To what purpose?'

'Assisted dying? I don't know – but we can't assume.' She wasn't interested in Peter's opinion, not on this matter. 'We'll wait for forensics,' she said firmly, waving to the approaching police cars. It was SOCO's turn to pick over the tragedy, with the science of everything at their fingertips – except the science of 'Why?'

Why would Terence Standing, the bursar of Stormhaven Towers, wish to kill himself – and in this manner?

With the handover made,

a surprisingly quick affair – clearly the first job of the day – Tamsin and the abbot walked back towards the school.

'You take me to the nicest of places,' said Peter.

'I don't know why you're grumbling. There can hardly be a more scenic setting in all England than this.'

She didn't need grumbling now.

'But it's also the valley of death,' said Peter. 'These Sussex-flint walls are getting more bloodstained by the day.'

'You're surprisingly squeamish, aren't you? But there's good news.'

'Really?'

'One less suspect.'

Peter winced.

'That's reassuring only to the police, Tamsin. You need to decentre a little.' Tamsin snorted a little. 'This particular event is going to shock people.'

'I wouldn't be so sure. No one likes a bursar in my experience.'

And Tamsin thought people who killed themselves were stupid, anyway; she couldn't manage sympathy.

'He looked at peace,' said Peter.

'You think?'

'Such an anxious soul in life with those darting eyes . . . peace becomes him. He lost it somewhere along the way.' Tamsin looked blank – the dead were just the dead to her. 'But the question is: why would Terence wish to kill himself – and why now?'

'Am I missing something here?' she asked.

'You do have form, Tamsin.'

'I'm presuming that we haven't just lost a suspect; but that we've found our murderer,' she said confidently. 'Well, aren't you presuming that? Or are you still swaying in the wind, up there on the fence?' Peter chuckled as Tamsin shook her head. 'He's the murderer, no question. And I resent his escape from the due processes of justice.'

'One of the less delightful escapes,' said Peter, remembering the yanked body across the car seat, the deep incision of the rope on his soft neck. The white corpse had the look of a dead pig about it. 'And anyway, what more due process could there be? He's effectively hanged himself, carried out the death penalty on the state's behalf . . . though as I say, I'm not sure I walk with you in your assumption.'

'You mean you don't agree that Terence was the killer?' Peter's face was non-committal. 'Don't disregard the obvious, Abbot.'

'My obvious appears to be different to yours.'

'So what broke him if it wasn't guilt?'

'Oh, it was guilt, I think – but not the guilt of a murderer.'

'Oh?'

'He was sobbing in the chapel, when he's not the type to sob . . . and certainly not about his mother. So what broke him?'

'He knew what he was about to do.'

'Anticipatory guilt? No, Judas sobbed after the betrayal – not before. I was thinking more about his relationship with Benedict. Remember the desperate note?' Tamsin listened. 'Well, what could be worse for a gay-bashing fundamentalist than to discover he's gay? He'll have to bash himself now and that could drive anyone to suicide. Consider the forces against him – the anger of God, persecution from the pulpit, dismissal from the congregation, ostracized in the street by former friends – deep shame! And shame is a violent friend when stirred . . . and I think it was stirred . . . I think someone was stirring quite hard.'

Tamsin, seasoned detective, shook her head.

'That's a speech that gives circumstantial evidence a bad name.'

'I suspect it's also true.'

They'd reached the stone arch of the school entrance. They could still see the off-road car, coated figures swarming around it like white bees in spilt red wine, busy with their tasks, each with their role, working wordlessly towards a particular end: an understanding of the last few minutes of the life of Terence Standing.

'So I'll handle this meeting, all right?' said Tamsin, pushing her dark hair back from her face. It was eight thirty now and time for a bleak meet and greet in the common room. Peter thought she was particularly attractive in the wind ... but wouldn't be saying. Instead, he simply nodded and they turned left down the long corridor of notice boards, team photos and abandoned school books, somehow left behind for the summer, not part of anyone's holiday plans. They walked in silence towards the common room where the murderer and friends awaited them.

While Tamsin spoke,

Peter watched. He watched as Tamsin told the assembled cast of the tragic death of Terence Standing. He'd met them only forty-eight hours earlier, though it felt like a lifetime . . . as though these people had always been around in his life. Depressed Geoff, ambitious Penny, hard Cressida, repressed Ferdinand, desperate Bart, controlled Benedict, intriguing Holly, hidden Crispin. Who here was pulling such furious and vindictive strings?

Peroxide Penny, Director of Girls, had been particularly upset about the death of Jennifer at Tide Mills. Next to her was Cressida Cutting, widow of the headmaster pushed from Stormhaven Head. The statistics at least said that she was the killer: 'It's always the family.' And then there was Geoff Ogilvie, early fifties and widening round the girth, though persisting with squash, all thrash and perspiration. He was Director of Boys . . . though facing demotion had Jamie lived. Beside him, Father Ferdinand Heep, the mannered school chaplain who firmly denied any indiscretion with Holly Hope-Walker, the head girl, who swore it was true. 'A very vivid imagination,' Ferdinand had said of her. And two seats away, the ginger hair of Bart Betters – the restless body-stretching Director of Wellbeing and a recent irritation to Peter in Loner's Wood. Further round, and minding his own business, mousy-haired Crispin Caudwell, the head boy, son of a car salesman, a quiet soul – but cautious? Peter wasn't sure . . . there was something rather bold about him. And, of course, the new arrival to the group, Benedict Bleake – smiling at the mystery which surrounded him.

'Who the hell is *he*?' asked Geoff, when Benedict appeared in the doorway, five minutes after Tamsin and Peter. Benedict had placed himself at the back.

'He lives here,' said Peter to bemused looks all round. 'You may have seen him around.'

Benedict looked faintly embarrassed – but only faintly. For a recluse, he did not seem to mind the attention.

'He's a schools inspector,' said Penny. 'I remember him now.'

'A white lie, I'm afraid,' said Benedict, with self-deprecating charm. 'Though I do inspect the school in my own little way. I apologize for my deception, though, and wholeheartedly because I hold the truth most dear, value it highly ... generally speaking.'

'That's the ghost!' said Crispin, a little disturbed.

'Again, not strictly true,' said Benedict. 'Though, of course, I'm sorry if I scared anyone. I believe I had the abbot hiding behind the grandfather clock around midnight!'

There was laughter at that, including from Tamsin, who looked at him quizzically.

'I'm Benedict Bleake, by the way,' he said. 'And that's Bleake with an "e", so happier than it sounds – distant relation of the great Nathaniel.'

There was some surprise in the room.

'And who's "the great Nathaniel"?' asked Bart, in a slightly dismissive tone. He didn't like this intruder. He wasn't part of things.

'He founded this place,' said Benedict, instant chill replacing charm. 'Though it was a rather different school in those days ... not the whore of the rich.' It was spoken in a matter-of-fact way as something self-evident. But the words offended the gathering, stilled them ... how quickly the atmosphere had changed.

'Did anyone speak with Terence this morning?' asked Tamsin.

There was no response.

'Well, I did, I suppose,' said Cressida.

'You suppose?'

'We were both making a cup of tea in the kitchen here.'

'At what time?'

'Around six thirty.'

'And how did he seem?'

'His normal self. I mean, what do you want me to say? One doesn't wish to speak ill but one never felt close to Terence. He was always polite enough – but never what you'd call warm.'

And I'd say the same of you, Doctor, thought Tamsin with admiration.

184

'We walked back down the corridor together, and then parted when we got to his room.'

'He went inside with his tea – and you didn't see him again?'

'Correct.'

There was a silence in the room. Was that it? Morning niceties, a cup of tea and then – well ...

'What did you speak about,' asked Peter, leaning forward in his seat to up the pressure a little.

'Oh, I hardly remember,' said Cressida, as if the question was ridiculous. 'It was early and I'm an owl not a lark.'

She hoped for some comic effect here; for supportive grunts from other owls who couldn't remember anything until midday ... despite teaching three lessons before. But no grunts came, no affirming smiles – because somehow Terence deserved more, this was the feeling. *You may be more an owl than a lark but these were his last words on earth, for God's sake! What did he say?*

'I'm aware it was early, Cressida, but it was also this morning, so *recent* ... you must remember something.'

Perhaps she genuinely doesn't remember, thought Peter; perhaps she only ever pretends to listen to anyone. Who knows whether the doctor is listening in the surgery? One or two questions, quick diagnosis, then let's get to the end game as quickly as possible: the prescription. That's all they want, that's all they've come for – and then they'll leave, pathetically happy and feeling better already.

'He asked me if I believed in heaven,' she said to some shocked reaction.

'A question even an owl might remember,' said Peter.

'Well, I was a bit surprised, yes – and because I didn't know what to say, I said "Why do you ask?" And he said it didn't matter, and asked me where the sugar was kept, which was obviously not true – I mean, him saying that it didn't matter. But then, you know, if he doesn't want to talk about it ...'

And more particularly, if you don't want to talk about it, thought Peter, before Cressida added: 'Well, what would you have said, Ferdinand?'

'Me? I would have said, "Of course there's a heaven!"'

185

'Well, that's your job, isn't it – to offer some light at the end of the tunnel. It isn't my job.'

'The light is also my belief, Cressida.'

'Really? Then why don't we see it?'

She was angry. She felt too much self-righteousness in the room, as if everyone else would have been this wonderful counsellor, easing Terence away from his suicidal thoughts. Now she remembered why she'd had nothing to do with the common room mob before Jamie's death. Or only to hold a glass of champagne with them on special occasions, end-of-term things, 'drinks at the headmaster's' – thank God for outside caterers.

'We'll need to speak to you all again,' said Tamsin, 'so if you could stay in or around the common room for the rest of the morning, we'd be grateful.'

'Can we go to our rooms?' asked Crispin.

'Not with Holly!' said Penny, 'unless there's an adult present.'

'We are adults,' said Crispin, fixing her with a look. 'And from what I hear, you never had an adult present with your gay friend.'

There was a stunned silence in the common room, all eyes focused on the Director of Girls. Penny was blushing, though whether in rage, embarrassment or shock was hard to tell. Tamsin intervened.

'Yes, you can all go to your rooms – as long as you've signed up for an interview slot. In the meantime, keep your doors locked . . . and don't go to sleep please, or we might imagine you're dead.'

She didn't wish to leave them in any way settled.

The hours between

ten and midday that Tuesday were taken up with further interviews, starting with Penny. She'd recently been the victim of aggressive innuendo by none other than the cautious and usually silent Crispin. His father, as Penny well knew, was a mere second-hand car salesman, if a rather moneyed one – with new offices in Düsseldorf and Qatar. No one was quite sure if there was a mother around; he certainly spoke more of his father, if he spoke of them at all. There was a rumour his mother had died of cancer, but one didn't like to ask and it was his father who came to things, school events . . . when he could leave the curved delights of the showroom office.

'So what are we to make of Crispin's comment?'

Penny feigned incomprehension.

'Back there, in the common room,' said Tamsin, clarifying.

'I have absolutely no idea. You'll have to ask him.'

'Well, I'm sure we will.'

'I was just having a joke. We've always thought there was some-thing between Holly and Crispin, so I was trying to lighten the atmosphere. It was just fun – and suddenly he explodes! Typical teenager – his father is a second-hand-car salesman.'

'Well, he didn't really explode, Penny,' said Peter. 'He made an observation.'

'An observation? You call relational smut an observation? You're as bad as the teenagers, Abbot.'

'I have never imagined otherwise. The teenager in me has never quite been calmed, even if I wish it were otherwise. But in the meantime, you reject the suggestion?'

'Of course I reject it! I'm just amazed we're even talking about it.'

'We could hardly not talk about it – your face did go very red.'

Penny decided to rise above this ludicrous line of enquiry; she'd keep silence on the matter, maintaining a face of relaxed unconcern which said, 'Is that the best you can do?'

'And, Penny, just put a matter to bed for us – because we have wondered a little.' Tamsin paused. 'We have this photo, you see – we found it in Jennifer's room.' Peter watched Penny's reaction . . . there was immediate interest.

'What photo?' she asked, her voice less confident.

'I've got it here somewhere,' said Tamsin, knowing exactly where it was but not eager to find it too quickly. She rummaged through her file of notes, finding it, leaving it, building the drama, as Penny leaned forward, eyes on the file.

'Ah, here it is,' said Tamsin. 'Knew it was there somewhere, and I'm sure it will mean nothing. But I couldn't help thinking, well – you take a look.'

She handed Penny a photo of two girls, ten or eleven, in front of a ruined house, either side of an older man, but too frail for his age. There was something broken about him, but smiling through the rain, smiling for the camera, he could at least do that. Penny stared at the photo, and then put it aside.

'The girl on the left must be Jennifer,' said Tamsin, 'with her father presumably – but the girl on the right? A friend, presumably – and I couldn't help but feel there's something of you about her, Penny. Tell me I'm mad.'

'You're not mad – simply mistaken.'

'And I'm no expert . . . but that must be Tide Mills – where the picture was taken.'

'Well, it could be, yes – I mean, I don't know the place well . . .'

'Oh, it's definitely Tide Mills,' said Tamsin. 'I've had cause to be there a few times recently. And obviously a special place for Jennifer. Perhaps that's why she was there when she was killed, returning to an old haunt.' Penny nodded slowly. She seemed to be about to speak and then merely sighed. 'We're trying to trace her father,' said Tamsin.

'Well, good luck with that!' said Penny. 'And in the meantime, I see the snail is left untroubled, proceeding unnoticed, feeding off the terrain.'

'The snail?'

'Geoff's world was about to fall in before Jamie was killed. You do know that?'

'We're not short of motives in this investigation,' said Peter. 'But they're shared around, a democracy of reasons for the death of the headmaster. And Geoff was hardly alone in fearing the sack.'

'He used to be married, you know.'

'Who?'

'Geoff. I knew his wife well. And one day, quite out of the blue, total surprise, she asked him for a divorce.'

'So you didn't know her that well.'

Penny ignored the comment.

'But since that day,' she continued, 'since that moment, she says, he has not spoken a word to her. Not a word . . . solicitor's letters, separate lives until she moved out of the school accommodation. She said she'd seen something.'

'Seen something?'

'She didn't say any more – despite me asking. "I don't want him hurt," she said. She still loved him! So whatever it was she saw, it stayed a secret.'

'All very interesting, Penny – but dysfunctional relationships are not a crime,' said Tamsin. 'There isn't enough gaol space.'

'The snail proceeds quietly, that's all I say. Discreet in his move-ments – but you don't want to get on the wrong side of him. Whatever there once was between you, he'll eat it.'

Holly had the letter.

She had kept the letter which Ferdinand had written – or the one he'd denied having written, claiming the whole matter was just another fantasy of a teenage girl. But if the letter was real, and not some wicked phoney, the fantasy was now in the 'true crime' section.

'It wasn't that we didn't believe you,' said Tamsin.

'No,' said Holly.

'We just needed to see it. An investigation has to be evidence-led because when there's no evidence, there's only conjecture as far as a court is concerned. The abbot here, he likes conjecture, far from the moorings of fact. But the police and the courts work differently.'

'This won't go to court, will it?' asked Holly.

'We're here to solve a murder, Holly – well, two murders ... maybe three. What's happened to a few school collections is disappointing, particularly for the charities – but not top of our list.'

'It was terrible what happened to Mr Standing,' she said.

'Indeed, very sad. You can't help us there, I suppose?'

'No, no,' said Holly, as if that was a ridiculous idea. 'It's not like the bursar does assemblies or anything ... or makes us late-night hot chocolate! I'd never seen him before this weekend.'

'So let's see the letter.'

Holly handed it over slowly and with reluctance, for she lost as much as she gained in this transaction. The letter proved she was telling the truth; but would also incriminate her. It would make more real and more public her deceit of these past few years, when she wished it less real and more secret. She'd kept the letter because it was the guarantee of more money from Ferdinand. It was evidence, and to that degree, a friend ... but not a kind friend. It was a friend she'd needed but not one she liked.

'What will happen to me?' she asked.

'So this is a forgery, is it?'

said Tamsin, with casual disdain. 'By the expert forger, Holly.'

She showed the letter to the chaplain – or rather a duplicate, courtesy of the school photocopier.

'Do take it – this is a copy. You won't damage the evidence.'

Bleak recognition broke across Ferdinand's face, his body crumbling a little, like a balloon figure deflated. The tight and shiny exterior shell of his body was now a soft and sunken thing ... although, in a way, these difficult words – they were almost a relief, for a second or two. He needed to regain control.

'It was a moment of madness – that's all it was,' he said, firmly. This whole thing needed a tight lid placed on it.

'All *what* was?'

Ferdinand was angry. He'd offered the truth to the police and how did they respond? They simply demanded more – and they demanded it now! This was unacceptable as far as Ferdinand was concerned. Much too pushy! Who did they think they were talking to? Though he hated himself as well, surrounded by pictures of youthful success on the walls, large colour pictures ... while all he felt was the sweat of failed middle age, the wretched collapse of something.

'I may have touched her in the wrong way on one occasion.' Silence ... neither Tamsin nor Peter interrupted and Ferdinand hoped that was enough. It wasn't enough.

'You *may* have touched her?' said Tamsin.

'It wasn't rape or anything!'

A slight pause.

'Do you want our applause?' asked Tamsin. '*Chaplain doesn't quite rape sixteen-year-old schoolgirl!* There's a feel-good story to restore confidence in the Church!'

'I'm just saying. There are degrees in these matters.'

'You certainly seem to have one.'

191

'And she led me on. I mean, she knew what she was doing. She's not so innocent, you know!'

'Excuse me!' Now Tamsin was angry, loud bells ringing in her head. 'The school chaplain was led on by a sixteen-year-old girl? Was this part of your calling from God – or private work?'

'I grant you, it was a mistake.'

'That is some way short of an apology.'

'Well, I think I've paid for it, haven't I? Quite literally!'

'It wasn't your money,' said Peter. 'Unless you're paid from the chapel collections.'

'Holly says you placed your hand on her inner thigh,' said Tamsin, like an examining counsel. 'Is that so?'

'Maybe.'

'And she then says that when she didn't move, probably in shock, you pushed it further.' Peter watched a man drowning, fighting for air, fighting for life ... but drowning. 'Quite a way further.'

'A minx,' said Father Heep to himself.

Tamsin kept calm, an extraordinary act of self-control.

'And then she did pull back and said "What are you doing?"' Ferdinand looked at her intently. 'Do you remember any of that, Reverend?'

'I apologized straight away, really – I mean, it was something and nothing.'

'More something than nothing,' said Peter. 'It was the crucifixion of trust.'

'And I begged her forgiveness – it wasn't as if I denied it. I could have denied it!'

'That's true,' said the abbot. 'I mean, Peter denied Jesus three times when he was arrested, so it's not unknown among the faithful – and Peter went on to get a halo.'

Ferdinand wasn't listening, he was back there, back in time, reluctantly revisiting a scene he'd tried so hard to forget.

'But she just got up and left the room – without saying anything else.'

'A minx, as you say,' said Tamsin.

'She just left me there, left me to stew.'

'How very insensitive ... as if it was her task to look after *you* in the situation! Were you a self-pitying child ... or has it come late in life?'

Ferdinand's face darkened.

'And the following day' – the recall was painful for him – 'the following day, the letter arrived with her demands.'

'Her demands?'

'If she was to stay quiet and not speak of the "attack". I mean, it wasn't an attack – not a real attack, no one would seriously call that an attack! But that's what she called it.'

'And what did you do?'

Ferdinand sighed.

'I made a big mistake.'

'Another one?'

'I wrote her a letter ... the letter you now possess. I simply asked her to let the matter be.'

'Something of a begging letter, Ferdinand – quite desperate, really.'

'Asking, begging – she had my career in her hands! You do know that the last chaplain had to leave because of – well, the usual.'

'The usual?'

'It's not easy.'

'Apparently not. So Holly began enjoying the chapel collections – collections which, in theory, were destined for various charities ... but which ended up in her wardrobe.'

'She didn't get all the collections.'

He would defend his integrity.

'No?'

'Oh no! We sent money after the earthquake, I was very insistent about that – made myself very clear. Well, as clear as I could, given that she still had the letter. And there have been other occasions, definitely, when we gave generously.'

'To someone other than Holly, you mean?'

'She particularly liked to collect on Old Boys Days or special school celebrations when there were more adults at the service, governors, parents – with deeper pockets, notes rather than coins. She liked notes.'

'Who doesn't? And this term?'

'She has had most of the collections this term. She said she needed to save, that her family situation was difficult.'

'And the grateful letters from charities on the chapel notice-board?' asked the abbot.

'I do those myself . . . on the computer. It isn't hard . . . really.'

There was almost pride in his voice, which riled Peter.

'And just so there's no confusion, Father – this is the same Holly who yesterday you treated with such scant regard.' Ferdinand shrugged. 'Claiming she had made these things up, concocted the accusations from her excitable teenage imagination.' Ferdinand remained silent; it didn't sound good when put like that. But you do what you must do to survive, this was Ferdinand's thought. 'And I actually believed you,' said Peter. 'I believed you, Ferdinand . . . or I was on my way to believing you, as the adult, as the chaplain.'

There was silence between them in the school waiting room, born again as an interview room. And if silence can be described, given a character, it was an exhausted silence which simply acknow-ledged the spectacular mess and ensuing contortions that a single moment of indiscretion – of ancient longing and desire acted upon – had created in the life of Father Ferdinand Heep, the school chaplain at Stormhaven Towers. They'd reached the bottom of the abyss and there was no further to fall.

'So when did Jamie find out?' asked Peter.

'They call you "Spanker Geoff",

Mr Ogilvie. Is there any particular reason for that?'

They knew the answer and so did Mr Ogilvie ... though he wasn't disposed to tell them.

'It seems you lost your temper on one occasion,' said Tamsin.

'I didn't lose my temper. I merely said to one of the boys – a particularly irritating fellow – that I wished we'd met twenty years ago, when I could have given him a good spanking.'

'You *merely said*?'

'I may have raised my voice a little.'

'You mean you shouted.'

Geoff would not be intimidated by this woman.

'Teachers held a few cards when I started out in the trade – but they don't hold any now. You can't hate the children like you once could.'

'The good old days, eh?'

'Parents are "consumers" now – and I'm a PR executive for the school who happens to teach chemistry. Everything's changed, believe me. No different from the police, really. People used to respect you lot too, a cuff round the ear wasn't the crime of the century ... and then this sick obsession with accountability took hold.'

Angry, thought Peter.

'Would you like to have been head?' asked Tamsin.

'Doesn't everyone want to be head?'

'I'll check with the gardeners, but ...'

'Of course I wanted to be head – and if not here, somewhere else. But I've been too loyal, haven't I? Too bloody loyal! Not thought of myself enough – I've worked for the school, for the team, my first mistake! And now? What is there for me now? Fifteen more years of the same old thing with a poncey title that means nothing? God help me!'

'Perhaps they'll make you the new headmaster?' said Tamsin, setting the trap. 'That's what Jamie would have wanted, surely – his right-hand man to succeed him?'

How honest was 'Spanker' going to be?

'Jamie was demoting me,' said Geoff, calmly – almost with relief. Tamsin acted suitably surprised. 'Yes, he told me on Saturday, bless him, so that was a good start to the summer.'

'That must have been a shock,' said Peter.

'"Just a change of portfolio, Geoff," he said, as the knife went in. "We just need to be grown-up about this," he said, meaning, "Please agree with me and don't be angry." He didn't react well to anger, Jamie.'

'And were you angry?'

'I could keep my senior master's house, which softened the blow – as he knew it would. Well, I'll never live anywhere so nice again, no chance . . . whereas he will, of course . . . or he *would* have. Jamie and Cressida were not short of cash – and Cressida certainly won't be, with the life insurance falling like financial manna from heaven.'

'I'm not sure she needs it.'

'But it is usually the family who kill, isn't it? I mean, Cressida is the murderer, isn't she?'

'You were talking about your demotion,' said Peter, which prompted a wry smile from Geoff.

'Jamie was dreaming up some a fancy new job title like *Director of School Development* – as meaningless as *Director of Wellbeing* in my book. Beware the fancy title bestowed by Jamie – it means he's about to castrate you . . . lipstick on a pig from where I was sitting.'

'That must have made you angry.'

'I'm angry all the time, Abbot . . . all the time. I could pull the skies down on a vast number of people. But I don't. There's a kind man in me somewhere.'

'These people are a joke,'

said Crispin, leaning forward towards his interrogators. He'd decided to enjoy the interview, enjoy the game. 'My dad sent me here because he wanted me to be more like "these people"... that's what he called them, "these people". "A different class," he'd say – but there's no different class here.'

'The rich aren't so different?'

'Apart from Cressida, obviously.'

'Dr Cutting?'

'*She's* class!'

This was not the admiration they were expecting. Indeed, their thoughts had been in another direction before the boy arrived for interview.

'So how about Holly and Crispin?' Peter had said, speculatively.

'Holly and Crispin?'

What was the abbot talking about?

'A love-pact to kill all their old teachers.'

'I hardly think there's anything there.'

'Penny does.'

'That was just a joke.'

'Nothing's just a joke.'

'Holly with Crispin?' said Tamsin, amazed. 'He's not in her league. She's a head-turner – some women are.'

Tamsin spoke as a fellow member of the club, and one who knew the awe and the hate that came with the package.

'Or maybe Holly isn't in *his* league,' said Peter. He didn't deny Tamsin's words but pondered the girl's substance. 'Did you see how he challenged Penny in the common room? There's an assurance about him, almost as if he's growing into this, waking up. It's like he's not alone in that room – but I'm not sure his partner is Holly.'

'Well, she's not just a pretty face, is she? Holly's a seasoned blackmailer, remember, making good use of an abused moment.

Note that she didn't report him. She found a more profitable way to punish him. Holly Hope-Walker is a ruthless girl, who's been hanging the chaplain out to dry for a couple of years.'

Peter had smiled.

'Quite a lethal cocktail, those two!'

But here in the interview, it was Cressida and not Holly who was the focus of Crispin's admiration. She was declared 'class!'

'How is she class, exactly?' asked Peter.

'Oh well, you know,' said Crispin, looking around for adult words. 'Impressive woman, impressive career.'

'You fancy her,' said Tamsin, cutting to the chase – but leaving the chase there. She had no wish to explore the subterranean fantasies of a teenage boy towards an older and unobtainable woman. Crispin went red and said, 'No way!'

'And there's nothing between you and Holly, of course – as you made clear in the meeting.'

It was somewhere between a statement and a question.

'Have women got nothing better to do than invent love stories?' said Crispin.

'Pretty girl, though,' said Tamsin. 'And here you are, thrown together in the strangest of circumstances. You must be laughing as you watch the adults disgrace themselves in various ways. How the mighty are fallen!'

Crispin remained silent as did Tamsin and the abbot . . . until silence became uncomfortable for the former head boy.

'There's a story about Spanker.'

'Mr Ogilvie?'

'Yes.'

'A true story?' asked the abbot.

'Apparently he asked a fifth-year boy what he was going to do when he grew up.'

Crispin had their attention and liked it. He'd never felt adult attention until recently, and not wishing to lose it now, he finished the story.

'The boy said to him, "I don't know, sir. How about you?"'

Peter smiled but Tamsin didn't. She felt the tale was aimed at her, and she was right, for Crispin looked at her as he delivered the punchline.

'No one here thinks the teachers are mighty,' he said dismissively. 'They haven't got far to fall, no distance at all.'

Tamsin decided to attack back.

'So if it isn't Holly, then it suddenly gets much more complicated, Crispin ... and a bit messier, really.' The abbot watched the net closing. He did not wish Crispin hurt, he liked the boy. But they did need to capture the truth. 'Wouldn't you say, Crispin?'

'Wouldn't I say what?' He was confused.

'Well, if it wasn't Holly with you, which is what we presumed – stupidly, as you've explained – then who were you with in your room last night?' Crispin looked blank, a canvas of nothing, except the faint wash of fear. 'Because you were with someone, weren't you?'

'So why are you here exactly?'

asked Tamsin.

Benedict, formerly the ghost, sat looking slightly smug in the interview room, almost as if he were interviewing them. There was no sign now on his face of the white paint he used when he wandered the corridors at night.

'Such oppressive pictures, don't you think?' he'd said on his arrival, looking around at the photos of youthful success on the walls. 'Everyone so busy with achievement.'

'And so young,' said Peter.

'Oh, I don't think I wish my youth back. No, really.'

'But isn't that what the school is about, Benedict?' queried Tamsin.

'I'm sorry?'

'Well, isn't that why people pay the money they do – so their children achieve?'

Tamsin had no qualms about achievement. She woke every day to achieve – what else was there but some terrifying hollow of nothingness?

'It kills you in the end,' said Benedict. 'As a way of life.'

'Did it kill you?'

There was nothing in his manner which suggested fear of this interrogation. And really, why would there be?

'I mean, you have achieved quite a lot,' said Tamsin. 'Financially, at least. Background checks show you to be worth somewhere between six and eight million pounds.'

Benedict smiled as one struck by an amusing thought.

'These things are rather meaningless, don't you think? They've never excited me much. Numbers on a screen, figures on a page – there's an unreality about them, I always feel. Better the wayside flower, in my opinion. As the poem says, "What is this life if, full of care, we have no time to stand and stare."'

'But for one so wealthy, the question does remain: what are you doing here? Why does a man who could live anywhere, choose for himself a little room in a minor public school accessed by a wardrobe and a rickety staircase?'

'There's more to life than a big house?'

'But what exactly?' asked Tamsin. 'Apart from the wayside flower, of course – which you must tire of eventually.'

It was a genuine question from Tamsin.

'The wonderful world of education!'

'But you hate the school.'

'I dislike aspects of the school ... but a school is many aspects and there's much that I'm profoundly attached to.'

'And what sort of an aspect was Jamie?'

Benedict thought long and hard, smiling along with the game ... a game you sensed he was rather enjoying.

'An energetic aspect. Yes, Jamie saw which way the tide was turning. A good business man – and to be fair, he ran a good business.'

'There's something faint about the praise.'

'A school is not a business,' he said politely but firmly.

'And he didn't mind you being here?'

'I'm not sure he had a choice – so whether he minded or not was quite immaterial.'

'You didn't converse?' asked Tamsin.

'We didn't "converse", as you put it, no.' Tamsin did wonder why she'd used that word ... not usually in her vocabulary. Perhaps being in a school was contagious, with seventeenth-century language being one of the symptoms. 'He'll have been aware of my views – and made sure he never had to hear any of them!'

'And Terence?' asked Peter. A seagull swooped past the open window, screaming loudly. It was that time of year, the gulls frightened for their fledglings making tentative first flights from the nest.

'What about him?'

'Did you ever discuss anything other than rental payments?'

'Poor Terence,' he said, shaking his head.

'Why *poor*?'

201

'Well, whereas my God is delighted I'm gay, Terence's God was absolutely furious – really very angry. As would have been his pastor and Church friends. Eternity was too short for the punishment due to him. So, of course, I stopped the relationship when I saw the self-disgust and terror at work in him. Rather gracious of me.'

Tamsin and Peter remembered the letter found in Terence's room, begging for the chance to see Benedict again.

'He took that rejection hard?'

'Apparently,' said Benedict, with a sadness that sent Tamsin back to the slumped figure in the car, red tie askew, garrotted by a rope round a tree and an accelerating vehicle. 'When you're hated for simply being what you are, and for something one has no control over, then life is difficult. I couldn't have saved Terence from that. Well, no one could have saved Terence from his God.'

Peter nodded, not wishing to appear heartless; but he had to ask, because really, the question had not been answered by Benedict, not in a believable way.

'So again, Benedict – why exactly are you here?'

'I do believe I've answered that question; there's only so many ways of saying the same thing. So let me give you another – as you are about to see him. It's more of a puzzle really: Bart, Italy and a rucksack on a rope – spot the connection!'

Bart did not wish to
be interviewed,

this was quite clear.

'Come stai?' said Tamsin.

'Bene, grazie,' said Bart. 'Now, can we get on with whatever it is you want to get on with?'

'Italy,' said Tamsin. 'What is it with you and Italy, Bart?' He looked taken aback. 'I mean, you're an Italian speaker, who owns a Porsche, feels for the first-century Roman émigrés and holidays in tree huts in Tuscany. Why do I not think Bart Betters is your real name?'

Bart looked at them.

'This has nothing to do with anything.'

'Our decision, I suppose.'

'I was born in Italy, so what? Don't tell me you were born in England,' he said, looking at the dark hair and olive skin of Tamsin.

'The difference is – well, one of the differences – I'm not a suspect in a murder case, who's withholding information.'

'Sorry – did I miss the moment when you asked for my place of birth?'

It was clever but awkward, delivered with jumpy, angry eyes.

'It's just that – contrary to what you told us – you were at Stormhaven Head on Sunday afternoon, when Jamie fell to his death.'

'That just isn't true. Who told you?'

'Some runners.'

'What runners?'

'I visited the Stormhaven Striders last night. Some fit folk there, eh?'

'Ultra-marathon runners, some of them. We're training for the fifty-miler from Worthing to Eastbourne along the South Downs Way.'

'Really?' said Tamsin in a manner that denoted no interest at all. 'No wonder they were looking apprehensive. And it was a bit of a long-shot – but I just wanted to know if any of them were up there around the time of Jamie's death. Worth a try, surely? And clearly I interrupted a lot of body worship, so they weren't delighted to see me – but being law-abiding folk and mostly middle-aged, male and bored in their marriages, they gave me five minutes.'

'Males don't like being stereotyped any more than women.'

'Women know when men are looking at them, Bart.' He grunted derision but Tamsin was unconcerned. 'And then one of them – one of the two women present – told me she'd seen you up there, with your weights rucksack. You, Bart! She said you were looking around like Burglar Bill on a night job – or perhaps Burglar Guglielmo in your case.'

Bart raised his eyebrows.

'So I was up there, so what?' he said, with self-righteous incredulity. 'I was on my way back from the Long Man of Wilmington. What of it?'

'What of it, Bart? You said you weren't.'

'I wasn't at the place of the murder.'

'How would you know that?'

'I would have seen something.'

'You do know that lying to the police, wasting police time, obstructing a police inquiry – these are all fairly career-finishing charges, certainly in education.' Bart looked affronted. 'I mean, there may be openings in the underworld – as long as you don't rattle on about wellbeing too often. I think that might get on their nerves.'

Bart's knee had stopped bouncing.

'I didn't kill Jamie, that's a fact, right?'

'It's hard to spot the facts with you, Bart, amid such a crowd of lies. It's a bit like Where's Wally?'

'But if I say I was there, it looks like I did kill him!' There was desperation in his voice, the whine of a frightened little boy, fearing the shame. 'Why would anyone tell the truth in my situation?'

'How about trying it, anyway?' said Peter quietly. 'The truth does set us free – even if it can feel like an ice shower at the time.'

Bart went quiet, silent eyes, lost eyes, contemplating a bleak terrain in the distance. He sighed, and almost shook as he did so.

'We're all skewered on dilemmas,' said Peter, reassuringly. 'We're all making uncomfortable choices. The inspector here can be rather aggressive.' He looked at Tamsin, who was unperturbed. Aggression was a compliment not an insult. 'But that's only because she has demons of her own, things unresolved which she transfers onto others.' Now Tamsin was perturbed. What the hell was Peter going on about? 'So you see, there are no good people or bad people here. Just people skewered on dilemmas, trying to do their best, as I'm sure you are. But we do need the truth, Bart. And not a word out of place – disinformation, misinformation, withheld informa-tion – or you'll be abandoned by all who are good, which is not a place I wish for you.'

Peter's words were prescient. Being exiled from the front room to the staircase had been a terrible punishment for Bart when young. A deep terror of abandonment remained. And so it was that Bart told them his story. And when he left, the abbot and Tamsin sat in silence for a moment, wondering what to make of it all.

'Well, there's a tale,' said Tamsin, still unsure.

'And a true one, I feel,' said Peter. 'Though that was truth at its most odd . . . and he gives me an idea.'

Tamsin's phone rang. It was quickly out of her bag. 'Moron alert,' she said to Peter. 'It's Chief Inspector Wonder.'

She answered: 'Hello, Chief Inspector. All good, I hope?'

'You interview Cressida,'

said Tamsin. 'I'll go and talk him out of it.'

'I'm not confident,' said Peter.

'He's panicking – I'll calm him down.'

Wonder had been in a flap on the phone, mindful of his reputation in a high-profile murder enquiry.

'This isn't some homeless man with mental issues, knifed in a churchyard, Tamsin!' He quickly added that it was sad, of course, when such events occurred. 'But it happens at that level of society: everyone reads about it on Sunday, shakes their head . . . and then moves on. But this is different – this is the head of a famous public school, pushed over a cliff, for God's sake! And Jamie King was a high-flier – unfortunate phrase in the circumstances, obviously – and there are rich people involved, large bank accounts and a sense of entitlement, you know the sort.' But Tamsin wasn't allowed a word. 'People with power are looking on aghast at the value of their investment in their children's education: "What the hell is Wonder doing about my investment, eh?"'

'You're hearing that question?'

'I'm hearing it in my sleep, Tamsin! And when one murder becomes two – the head's PA, no less, battered and poisoned down at Tide Mills – then I'm truly worried. I mean, what's going on there?'

'I can explain.'

'And so I'm thinking, what the hell's Shah playing at with her tame monk? And then the last straw, the third murder – the bursar this time.'

'It wasn't murder.'

'The bursar, for God's sake! Not just a cleaner or a gardener!'

'About the gardener . . .'

'Not a good trinity, Shah: the headmaster, the head's PA and the bursar!'

'The bursar was suicide.'

'And it may be a suicide, Shah, but does the watching world give a fig? You know how it looks. It looks like bloody Midsomer!'

'Is that good?' asked Peter, as Tamsin recounted the call.

'No, it's bad,' said Tamsin.

'Bad in what way?'

'It's getting out of control, Abbot.'

'What is?'

'The case – it's not working out.' She sighed. 'It's not good enough, things will have to change. Operationally, I mean.'

Somewhere along the way – at some point in Tamsin's telling – it had begun to sound like an accusation against Peter. Well, it *was* an accusation against Peter, with Tamsin eaten up by Wonder's words. The murders, the suicide, the slow progress – Tamsin had to blame someone.

'Hold him off until the morning, Tamsin – and we'll have our killer. I think so.'

'You *think* so?'

She smiled condescendingly, she couldn't help herself. The man opposite her suddenly appeared old and frail. Perhaps Wonder had a point. Would it be better if the abbot got back to the public library – or whatever it was old people did with their mornings? It had possibly been a case too far for him and she'd need to cover her back.

'It's over, Abbot.' It was suddenly settled in her mind.

'What?'

'We tried and failed. Or rather, you failed – as far as he's concerned. He's going to bring in two more experienced detectives to work with me.'

'OK.' It wasn't OK. 'So you're giving up on me.'

'I'll try to dissuade him. I mean, Wonder is a runt, he doesn't tell me what to do. But ...'

But he would tell Tamsin what to do, Peter knew this. He knew what it was to be a man in a panic, stumbling blind and terrified in the face of some imagined but all-consuming monster. It was not the moment for rational decisions. Wonder would not have made this call if he were open to debate. Panic is the climate for nothing but irrational and disastrous certainty – and the certainty now would be the dismissal of Peter. And sadly, Tamsin would agree with him, he knew his niece; and not because she agreed with Wonder – she'd never agree with Wonder, even in paradise. But she'd agree because, in the end, it was her own skin that mattered to her ... and Wonder's panic would transfer. For Tamsin, when a partnership could not park itself on Success Street, then it was the partnership, not the journey, which must be abandoned.

'Just do your best,' he said to Tamsin, who looked slightly hollow-eyed. 'You haven't put a foot wrong in the case, not in my opinion, so no cause for head-bowed apology. Sacrifice me, do what you have to do – I'm sure you will, this is your career, not mine. But whatever you do, hold him off until the morning. Give me until the morning.'

'By which time you'll have the murderer?' said Tamsin, with a cruel laugh. Why did he have to make this so difficult with his pretend kindness, as if he didn't care? Why didn't he just rage at her? 'Maybe Wonder's right for once,' she said, gathering her things. 'You're doing your best, Uncle, I know you are – but, well – you're not police.'

'No,' said Peter, feeling angry. And that's why I'm going to succeed, he thought.

The abbot felt surprisingly dangerous.

Cressida approached Peter,

as he watched Tamsin drive away from the school.

'Police cutbacks?' she said. 'And then there was one?'

'A call from above, she'll be back soon enough.' He didn't add that she'd return in the morning with two detectives who would make him redundant. It might have sounded bitter. 'But it does mean I have the privilege of interviewing you alone.'

'I was going to ask about that,' said Cressida. 'I'm in favour mode, actually, wondering if we could speak at my house?'

'I don't see any reason why not.'

'I need to get back to feed the cat – and, to be frank, to get away from everyone.'

'Quite.'

'And if you're there, you can monitor my movements, make sure all is above board – and no one can say I'm sneaking off to plan further carnage.'

'Bluff and double-bluff,' said Peter. 'It's all so exhausting. Another poke about your house and I might find the murder weapon.'

'Strange though it may seem, Abbot, though I am your doctor, I'm not your killer.'

'A bold claim.'

'But until the sick – though clever – soul is dragged from the undergrowth, exposed to the light and led away into custodial oblivion, we must all have our movements monitored, mustn't we? I think that would be best practice.'

And so now they sat in her well-organized kitchen. Cressida busied herself with making coffee from a machine that was some way beyond Peter's powers of comprehension. He was still delighted by a personal kettle. Perhaps he'd have stayed in the desert longer had he owned a kettle.

'They're very easy to use,' she said on seeing Peter's wonderment.

'I'll take your word for it. The aroma is particularly winning.'

209

And then he paused. Through the door of the utility room, Peter saw Jamie's old running machine, sad for lack of use.

'You don't want to buy it, do you?' said Cressida. 'It's very good for burning fats.'

'I prefer the outdoors.'

'There's no wind or ice indoors. That's what Jamie used to say.'

'And no sense of creation either. Perhaps you should keep it for yourself.'

'You must be joking.'

'It doesn't appeal?'

'My job is to tell *others* to take more exercise – not do it myself.'

'I see,' said Peter.

'After all, I'm a consultant, aren't I?' She was now putting some cat food in the bright red bowl as a ginger tom strolled in. 'And a consultant – as I'm sure you're aware – is someone who tells other people to do things they'd never dream of doing themselves.' Peter smiled and sipped a little of his splendid coffee, dark and strong. 'I have been known to swim,' she added, 'when I can find an empty pool or warm sea – which rules out Stormhaven obviously. And I'll play Scrabble, if forced. But nothing that involves sweat – I'm not keen on sweat. I found it distasteful at school – PE was quite dreadful. And I've never been drawn to it since.'

'You don't appear to be a woman in grief,' said Peter. Cressida looked a little shocked. 'Or haven't you got there yet?'

She moved into explanatory mode: 'My reading tells me there's no formula for grief, that each individual handles the grief journey in their own way.'

'Spoken like a book.'

'Perhaps I need to speak like a book. Perhaps that's where I am on my journey.'

She put the red bowl down for the cat, which started to lick and pick with delicate relish. The abbot watched the feeding, thinking of Hafiz. Hafiz was the seagull who lived on his roof and came to his kitchen door for meals. And if the door wasn't open, he'd bang on it with his beak until it was. Frequently, Peter had answered the front door, only to discover the visitor was round the back . . . and feathered.

Hafiz, who took his food seriously, would not have been happy at the abbot's recent absence; he'd have been willing the end of this investigation even more than Peter. But there was good news for Hafiz: whatever the next twenty-four hours held, he should be back to give him tea tomorrow.

'I just can't manage sadness, I'm afraid, Abbot. I don't believe that's a crime.'

'I don't believe it is.'

'We've slept in separate bedrooms for a while – to give each other space.' She laughed a little at her words. 'I used to mock people who said that. It's what you say when a relationship is dying but don't like the word.'

'I wouldn't know. I've always slept in a separate bedroom.'

'Maybe you're the lucky one.'

'Maybe.'

'And maybe I will be sad, Abbot – who can say? I don't really approve of sadness ... all a bit self-pitying, when really, what have I got to complain about?'

'Your husband has been murdered.'

'Perhaps I'm still in shock and the tears and rage all lie in the future, further down the path. Or maybe the terrible truth is that I simply don't care that much – and never will.'

'You were here all Sunday afternoon, you say.'

'I was, yes – fortunately. I can see I might need an alibi.'

'And you rang Jamie, I believe – after he'd gone out – from the landline here.'

'You've accessed my phone records?'

'Not personally. But they do back up your story. Why did you ring him?'

'We didn't part on the best of terms. I ignored him. Maybe I felt a twinge of guilt.'

'So who's the murderer?'

'You ask me? I have absolutely no idea. I'm a doctor not a detective.' She thought for a moment, familiar with being an expert, whose opinion was valued. 'You'd have thought the first two deaths were by the same hand – though different means. If it was a simple

211

push, it must have been someone who Jamie knew well, to get so close. And I hear Jennifer was aconite poisoning.'

'How did you know that?'

'If you wish to keep a secret, don't work in a school. The tentacles of this place are everywhere. A policeman knows a cleaner. A forensics expert is a parent . . .'

'Well, it's true.'

'And I can't lie – I wish I'd been there in a way, though hemlock would have been my choice.'

'Oh?'

'I've always wanted to watch someone die of hemlock poisoning. But don't quote me . . . I wouldn't want it in our patient brochure.'

'Each to their own.'

'Like Socrates, of course, who did just that – and who must be a hero of yours, Abbot.'

'Am I so transparent?'

'You're just the maladjusted sort he attracts, those with an inability to succeed.'

'Thank you.'

'But what an intriguing conversation it must have been as they watched him die . . . as the poison gradually worked its way up the great man's body. He must have spoken such deep things to his killers with death so close.'

'They might just have discussed the weather,' said Peter and Cressida laughed.

'Whereas I have to watch them live,' she said, with disappointment. 'A great deal less interesting, believe me. We celebrate living longer, but really, most people's lives would be better shorter. They spend old age complaining anyway. So do I really do them a favour when I bring them back from death's door . . . rather than hastening them through?'

'Their recovery is a disappointment only to you, perhaps.'

'Well, the flawed healer must be allowed.'

'Consider yourself allowed.'

'A doctor friend of mine is in prison for fraudulently accessing patients' bank accounts and syphoning off large amounts of money.'

'It's called private health care.'

'Clever, really. Once he had someone's bank details for payment of one treatment or other, he'd make other visits there as well, "after hours", so to speak – and he did earn a great deal of money this way, causing huge upset.'

'Not good.'

'Yet many miss him, they can't wait for him to get out. And why? Because he was a genius with allergies ... and there aren't many of those people around.'

'And you're fascinated by poison?'

'Show me a doctor who isn't, Abbot. It's the flip side of healing. The study of that which kills is the same as the study of that which restores. And so, of course, it's fascinating. To see how life is taken, is to see how life is saved.'

'So what about Terence?'

It was time to get less theoretical.

'Terence?'

'What are your views on his death?'

'Am I being paid for this consultation?'

'No – you don't need more money.'

Cressida looked suitably shocked.

'Well, he was murdered by religion, obviously.'

'Religion?'

'Religion makes most people unhappy in my experience. It's meant to make us less fearful, but generally makes us more so. I mean, I'm not a psychiatrist ...'

'Any particular reason why it might make Terence unhappy?'

'I can't think of one – unless he was cooking the books, the flawed bursar. But in my experience, religion doesn't need a particular reason. It's an open-ended ticket to guilt and self-hatred.'

'Quite.' He couldn't argue ... history wouldn't allow him to. 'Well, I won't keep you, Cressida. You may wish for some solitude before returning to the fray.'

And with that, he was on his feet, making his way from the well-appointed kitchen to the large oak front door. But before he left, above the shoe rack, he noticed the small digital screen, revealing 'mileage' to be '1389 miles'.

'What "mileage" is this?' he asked, intrigued.

'Oh, that was Jamie's. He loved gadgets. Don't ask me how it works but it's linked to the running machine. It was to keep him on his toes, he said. Every time he left the house, he was reminded how much he'd done – or hadn't done. Sad to say, in his life, he was more aware of what he hadn't done, than what he had.'

'A sad thought,' said Peter. 'I'll find his killer.'

'Three murders
in forty-eight hours,'

said Wonder, by way of explanation. Tamsin had declared this an
'unnecessary meeting' but that was ridiculous. How could Shah,
an intelligent woman, not see that this was a necessary meeting?
Any enquiry would be questioned at this point – even if there
wasn't an abbot involved.

'Two murders, one suicide.'

Tamsin was sitting opposite her boss in a skirt which finished
above the knee by several inches. Wonder was relieved the desk
cut her off at the waist; it kept his gaze more professional.

'Three deaths, though, Tamsin. You get my point.' It was a hot
day and he was sweating a little.

'And the first murder was committed before we arrived,' added
Tamsin. 'So that's one murder, one suicide – these things happen
when you stir the water.'

'You talk as though it's inevitable, Tamsin, as though it's some
outworking of – oh, I don't know – karma or something, for which
you have no responsibility.'

'I don't.'

'What – you don't think it's inevitable? Or you don't bear any
responsibility?'

'The latter.'

She remembered the abbot's words: no need for apology, she'd
handled the case well. She remembered also, with less comfort, his
prediction of betrayal – though it was hardly that. She'd make sure
he was paid, which was the main thing . . . and nothing need be
public. He'd probably be glad to be off the case, anyway. He could
get back home and feed his pet seagull, Harold, or whatever it was.
She was doing him a favour.

'And I'm happy for him to be replaced,' she said . . . and Wonder
was shocked.

215

'What – the abbot?'

'Yes. I'm aware he'll need to be replaced. He hasn't done as well as he might.'

'Tell me about it.'

'So let's do the right thing. Is that all?'

'Nothing personal, of course,' said Wonder, trying to smooth things out in his moment of triumph. 'We gave the fellow a try ...'

'I understand.'

Though it *was* personal. Wonder had not forgiven the abbot for jumping him into accepting his role in the case ... all that guff about stripagrams and 'frontier men'. Well, the tide had turned now. The swell that had brought the abbot to shore was now taking him well out to sea. 'We'll have him off the case,' he said. 'It will be quietly done, no fuss or anything – and you'll work with Detective Sergeants Shaw and Jones.'

'Shaw and Jones?'

'Yes. It's decided.'

'They're idiots.'

'They're professionals, Tamsin. And they're your last chance on the case. We can leave the abbot there tonight, with Pearson and Wilson minding the place – good boys those two. But you'll need to brief Shaw and Jones immediately. I want them brought right up to date with this car crash of an investigation.' Yes, that was pretty harsh, Wonder knew that – but then he had the power now ... the power to knock this cocky officer off her bloody perch. He should do it more often. 'And then tomorrow you go in and sort this mess out.'

'I'll do that.'

'And if I don't have the killer's head on a plate – I'll have yours!'

*

Tamsin rang Peter shortly after. She explained how there was nothing she could have done, how she'd pleaded with the chief inspector ... but how his mind was made up. She'd see him at nine o'clock for the handover, but that if he wished to sneak away privately, that could be arranged – a police car would take him back to his house. No hard feelings, she hoped, it just hadn't worked out.

'I'll see you tomorrow morning at nine,' said Peter and ended the call. He put the phone on the bed in his small student room – and turned off the sound. He had no need of Tamsin tonight. But he wouldn't be sneaking away.

He looked out of the window. The orange sun was setting over Newhaven to the west. Were the abbot at home, he'd be watching it sink into the sea, that slow silent easing of fire into the water. But he wasn't at home – he was at Stormhaven Towers, a school aching with murder and deceit; and he had work to do before the sun rose again on the white cliffs.

'Bring on the darkness,' he said quietly to himself as he left the room. 'And let there be light.'

ACT THREE

ACT THREE

The abbot was
an embarrassment.

He was behaving like an attention-seeking vicar at a parish party, when the alcohol has flowed and he suddenly believes he's amusing.

'I think the abbot may have overindulged a little,' said Penny. 'He's noisier than usual – and lacking in holiness!'

'I preferred him as the strong silent type,' said Cressida. 'Tonight, he's just another fool.'

Penny and Cressida had grown close over these last two days . . . this was Geoff's take, at least, as he sat with them in the common room that evening, not wholly at ease. Competent women did unnerve him, no question; and when there were two of them together in unspoken alliance – he was a mixture of bullishness and fear. They even held the same drink, G&Ts, with lemon – the last surviving lemon, before the new fruit and vegetable order in September.

'That's the trouble when you're not a proper drinker,' said Geoff, finishing his beer and looking over his shoulder at the embarrassing abbot. 'When you *do* drink . . .'

'I wouldn't mind, but he's supposed to be the lawkeeper round here!' added Ferdinand, shaking his head with wry amusement. He'd been floating in the common room, not quite with anyone or any particular group – but now stepping into this conversation. He was hardly unhappy at the abbot's fall from grace.

The suspects at Stormhaven Towers had gathered together in the common room after the evening meal. It had been cold meats and salad this evening, with boiled potatoes. Dessert had been ice cream, which echoed the previous two nights – but without the fresh fruit, which appeared to have run out. They ate in the school dining room, eight souls in a hall designed to hold four hundred and with its own grandeur: wood-panelled walls, pictures of the eminent . . . and by God, there'd been some grand nights there down the years – candlelit Christmases, end-of-year beanfeasts, Old Stormhavian bunfights. It was usually a space full of chatter and happy consumption – school food was absurdly good these days. Long gone were the likes of Dotheboys Hall, described in *Nicholas Nickleby*, where the boys were given brimstone and treacle as medicine – recommended by Mrs Squeers, the headmaster's wife, in the belief it spoiled the children's appetites, making breakfast and dinner much cheaper affairs. Times had changed – these days, the school canteen was a positive restaurant.

But the chef, Ollie, was here under duress, reluctantly postponing his caravan holiday at Winchelsea beach. And to make it worse, he was watched over by police which was uncomfortable. Ollie had a prison record himself. It was a long time ago and financial fraud – computer-screen stuff – nothing that threatened the pupils. And it hadn't been all bad. Prison had given him the chance to retrain as a chef, and he hadn't liked working for the council anyway. But you don't forget the process of detection, the interviews, the charge sheets, the smell of the holding cell, the smug officers, the damning police testimonies in court. You're never again on their side.

So, Ollie was a turbulent cook and it showed in the food he produced. Cold meat and salad was the chef's ultimate revenge . . . which made alcohol all the more attractive to the residents. Once coffee – instant, not ground – had been served, a long evening lay ahead for the remaining staff and pupils of Stormhaven Towers; they needed liquid support . . . including Abbot Peter, who'd apparently been on G&Ts all evening.

'Not really a drink for a man,' had been Geoff's comment to Benedict, before glancing down and seeing this was also Benedict's choice.

'Well, each to their own,' he'd replied, with a smile fresh from the glaciers of Antarctica.

Holly and Crispin sat staring into space, while Bart read a book – after a long conversation with the abbot. Everyone had wondered what they were talking about, because really, what do you talk about with an abbot for an extended period of time? After initial

222

pleasantries, what is there to be said other than: 'So how was your monastery?'

And then, suddenly, the abbot's embarrassing speech.

'I do know the murderer,' said Peter, stepping uncertainly out to the front. 'No, really I do – I know who they are!' And all conversation stopped, as he delivered his cringeworthy oration. He chose the place where Jamie would stand for the weekly briefing on Monday mornings, with Geoff and Penny alongside him, in their senior management roles. But tonight, Peter stood flanked by no one – and there's none lonelier than an emotionally charged drunk. 'The police haven't a clue,' he proclaimed loudly. 'Halfwits, the lot of them!' The abbot pondered his half-empty G&T – or was it half-full? What did it matter? He finished it off with a flourish.

'No one offer him another,' said Penny, firmly.

'But I'll have my moment of glory – they won't deny me that,' he continued. 'I'll have it here, tomorrow morning, at nine.' He spoke in tones of slurred triumph. 'Tomorrow, at nine, the hour of reckoning – when all will be very much revealed! And the police – the police can learn and listen . . . or rather, listen and learn.' The abbot then stumbled towards the door, aiming straight but unable to stay fully within the navigational beacons of chairs and tables. 'It is someone in this room, by the way.' He now turned around. 'Oh yes, someone in this room! I knew it almost straight away. You made a mistake with the phone.'

He looked around at the faces. Penny eyeing him as if he was mad; Cressida, cold assessment; Benedict, slight concern; Geoff, amusement; Crispin, fear; Holly, worry; Ferdinand, professional disdain; and Bart, blank. 'So don't be alone with anyone tonight . . . but yourself. You can only be with yourself. If you hate yourself, as most people do, then it's going to be tough – but that's life, isn't it, campers! Life's a beach . . . particularly in the Sahara – and then you die!' Ferdinand tut-tutted.

'We really don't have to listen to this, Abbot,' said Penny. 'Take yourself to bed, you sad little man.'

'Was that an offer, Penny?' asked Peter, leering at Penny and then stumbling towards the door. On the way, he tried to take

Penny's hand to kiss it, but she pulled it away in disgust. 'Well, that's not very nice!'

'You're a disgrace,' said Penny.

'Believe me, I'm even bored with myself!' he added. 'So I'm off on a run to Loner's Wood. It'll suit me.' Bart smiled. 'I deserve it, a good run – it's how I and my genius relax.' He started to run on the spot to show his fitness, but the habit didn't help and he tripped over a chair.

Holly held her hand over her mouth in shocked amusement. This was certainly unexpected entertainment for everyone. Peter picked himself up slowly, rubbing his shin. He became serious, as the drunk sometimes does, lecturing others about their lives.

'But for you,' he said, 'the curfew starts at eight and must be obeyed without exception. You must all lock your doors, lock your windows . . . let no one beguile you like the serpent beguiled Eve in the Garden of Eden. Not a good day, that one. So keep yourself to yourself until morning comes, and – as long as you're not the murderer – sweet dreams!'

He staggered from the common room, with a final stumble by the door.

'So what did you make of that?' said Ferdinand to Penny in the shocked silence that followed.

Peter set off slowly

towards Loner's Wood. He'd changed from his habit into the running clothes purchased by PC Wilson – back in the days when Tamsin had wanted him on the case and seduced him with new running gear. He'd been able to ask for privileges then, his bargaining position strong. Now things had changed, and privilege quickly removed. He felt like an outgoing cabinet minister – status, pay and chauffeur-driven car lost in a moment.

It was panic that had led to the betrayal; and now he was sidelined, removed from the case. Somewhere along the line, Peter had been found guilty of 'not being a policeman', a difficult charge to refute. And really, if Wonder or Tamsin were the icons on offer, he had no wish to refute it. He was angry at being the scapegoat for the fractured outcomes of the case; and the anger gave him energy, like a force through his body; though it might get him killed . . . for anger does this too.

The new sports gear was a bonus for Peter; he'd never run in such luxury. Previously, he'd worn long shorts, last modelled by nineteenth-century archaeologists excavating the Pharaohs' tombs; while his shirt had been an old rugby top from school, a faded and frayed affair. But now his body was hugged by rather tighter, more colourful gear – and lighter. He'd previously regarded it as slightly effete when he'd seen such clothing on other runners – an almost obscene display of the body's contours. But such lightness and ease of movement now warmed his heart and quickened his pace, years of judgement melting away. Perhaps Peter could grow to love the obscenity – and certainly tonight he wished to be seen. Well, he did and he didn't . . . his courage came and went as he pondered the hours ahead.

*

The evening light was beginning to fade with a cloudy sky above and a south-westerly behind him. He'd picked up the path at Splash

Point after which the climb becomes steep to Stormhaven Head, where Jamie had fallen. To his right was the site of the cliff chapel, long gone and probably very small – but once used as a hermitage by another recluse, also called Peter. Peter the Hermit had received royal protection in 1272, possibly for providing some service to the area, such as lookout duties. No one saw like a hermit saw and the sea needed watching in those days, with those French, the neighbours from hell.

Nine centuries on, however, royal protection was removed. The abbot was alone with the grassy path at the start of the chalk-white Seven Sisters. He ran at first with the empty golf course on his left, giving way to fields and grazing sheep, the ewes still mindful of their young. They were lambs no more, with spring long gone. But here they were, parents still bent on the survival of their offspring, gathering them close as Peter came near.

It was hard to say who his own parents had been. His biological father was the Armenian mystic and teacher G. I. Gurdjieff. He'd had a brief liaison with one of his pupils, Yorii Khan, as gurus sometimes do. But Yorii was not ready for a child and offered Peter up for adoption. And so young Peter, nine months old, moved from a commune in southern Spain to Eltham in south London, where he was brought up by Mr and Mrs Payne, who felt they should have a child but who, despite several attempts at sex, had so far failed to conceive one.

The idea of a child was perhaps more important for the Paynes than the child itself. Peter did not remember childhood as a happy time . . . it was a thin line between protection and suffocation. He remembered his childhood bedroom, a bland room, in a bland house in a bland road. What would he do now if allowed back? And what would he say to the boy who once slept there, gasping for life, hoping against hope for something better? His adopted parents had changed his name from Peter to Graham, the same name as Mrs Payne's father, who was dying of cancer at the time. Abbot Peter grew up as Graham Payne.

He was educated at a minor public school in mid-Sussex, which Mr Payne, a civil servant, had attended and where he'd been 'very happy, I think'. (Feelings were always expressed as thoughts by

Mr Payne. They were safer as thoughts – more distant things.) But young Graham had not been happy, and though head boy at the time, was expelled for organizing a sit-down protest in the school chapel – the more disruptive as it was halfway through a Founder's Day service. So he'd been glad to get to St Edmund Hall in Oxford where he read history. The expulsion from school had seemed to make him more interesting to the college selection panel, as if anarchy was a sure sign of intelligence – though Peter knew it was merely the shaking fist of rage.

There in the city of dreaming spires and perspiring dreams, he discovered a different sort of unhappiness, a sense of tedium at the game being played out. But he completed his degree – he was a completer – before mental breakdown . . . or whatever it was called then, an inability to proceed. He was placed in a London psychiatric unit for four months, halfway up Highgate Hill. Through his window, he could see Dick Whittington's cat on the road, immortalized in metal. And significant events occurred in that place. It was there he had the religious experience – these things are best not talked about, an experience of beauty – which led eventually to the monastery It was also there on Highgate Hill that he decided to return to his birth name of Peter; and there that he fell in love with a nurse called Rosemary.

This was not a matter he could celebrate, despite some vista being opened in his soul. (Perhaps he would celebrate it one day, but for now it was just a wound.) Nurse Rosemary could not reciprocate his feelings, though sometimes gave the suggestion that she might . . . enough at least to stir the dream.

But the door, with hindsight, had only ever been closed, and when the end came – an unspoken affair, never quite expressed, a slow fade – Peter took it badly. It was the end of the world and the collapse of all things. It was only after five years in the desert that he could speak of his rejection with some sense of thanks, seeing that Rosemary was exactly like his mother, and not what he needed at all.

But these were long ago things and faraway – so much sand between then and now; and it was another man who ran along the cliffs tonight, the sea light fading. He ran with increasing fear, a tightness round his heart – because while he'd made his plans, they were creaky support – frequently stamped on and splintered by life. He could be at home now ... he could be sitting at home with a whisky – he did not need to be out here tonight, bait for a killer of cold savagery.

But for some reason, he had to walk into the fire ... just as he always had. Just as he'd organized the protest in the chapel ... and just as he'd run into Stormhaven's cold sea in January, screaming. He had to face the danger – taken there by deep will, as if to test the human spirit, beyond the anaesthetized life of pretty words and rational solutions. He screamed at the sky tonight, he shouted as he ran, for reasons way beyond the murderous snarling of Stormhaven Towers where a killer had broken loose, like a cannon careering across the deck of a crowded boat.

He could turn back. He could always turn back and if he was to do so, here at Cuckmere Inn was the place to turn ... but he didn't turn. He ran on, along the rough pavement and then over the Eastbourne road.

Why did the chicken cross the road?

Because he wanted to get to Loner's Wood, where he'd meet the killer of Jamie King, Jennifer Stiles – and, in a way, Terence Standing.

The woods were dark as he entered; and they'd get darker still before morning came.

Stormhaven Towers was closing down

for the night. The ground-floor rooms – the last residences of a school year extended by murder – were individually lit and curtained. It was eight and PC Wilson checked to see that the common room was empty and the lights turned out. He stood alone in the dark, intrigued. It smelled of alcohol and teachers ... they had a stale, tweedy smell all of their own, and one which still made Wilson nervous. Instinctively, he began to pick up the used glasses, scattered on tables – he'd worked in a bar for two years while he'd wondered what to do with his life. He still didn't know the answer, but at least he was paid for not knowing and given the security of a uniform.

Outside in the corridor, two women were talking. These were Penny Rylands, Director of Girls, and Cressida Cutting, the headmaster's widow. Penny was suggesting a drink in her room, and Cressida replying, with a giggle, that she didn't think that was allowed, was it?

'And of course you only do what you're allowed, Cressida!'

And then they laughed and Wilson went out into the corridor. Standing as firmly as he was able, he suggested that they remain alone tonight, to stay safe from the killer. This was harder than it might have been – him telling them what to do. He felt like the pupil here and they the teachers. And anyway, he'd always felt inferior to these kinds of women, the smart, confident ones.

Penny reacted angrily to the idiot constable, but Cressida said he was only doing his job – though it would have been nice to meet up. And so the two women parted company after some extended chat to put the policeboy in his place. Both knew what needed to be done this evening and first on Penny's list was some gardening ... flowers didn't look after themselves, while Cressida must pay a visit to a bedroom three down from hers.

Meanwhile, Holly and Crispin sat together in his room – Holly on the bed, Crispin in the chair. They were whispering, not wishing to draw attention to themselves, should any policeman come snooping. 'You'd better not be the murderer, Crispin!' said Holly, with only a little fear.

Ferdinand, two doors down, sat on his bed with his prayer book, wishing he was in the chapel. He opened his curtains to witness the glory of evening sky, but there, quite suddenly, was a policeman looking in. Quite ridiculous! So he closed the curtains quickly. 'God spare us from the long nose of the law,' he muttered.

It was hard to pray in this small, characterless room – so cramped compared to the high arches of the chapel, though whether there was a God to pray to, he did sometimes wonder. He castigated himself endlessly for such faithless thoughts, but – well, he'd scarcely been led to the Promised Land these past few years. Life had been relentlessly hard for the chaplain and you had to wonder why this was so. You can only blame everyone else for so long . . . you must get to God eventually.

Benedict, meanwhile, sat in his upper room . . . pondering. He held a whisky in his hand – a rather better malt than the common room swill. He rolled it gently against the side of the glass. It possessed a luminous transparency unavailable to his life at present. He had wished to make things better – that had been his intention in coming here. But he hadn't made things better, this was quite clear now. Had he in fact made things worse? Whatever the truth, he needed to end this matter tonight. He put down the whisky, got up from his chair and exchanged slippers for shoes . . . while downstairs, in his smaller room, Geoff pondered the holdall beneath his bed. He was looking for comfort, and this was where he usually turned. He bent down, pulled the holdall out, lifted it onto his bed. A thousand times he'd tried to throw this suitcase and its contents away . . . and a thousand times he'd failed. He clicked the lock open and contemplated the contents.

Further down the corridor, two doors away, Bart put on his running shoes. He knew exactly what he had to do and was excited to be doing it.

Peter was deep into the wood

when he heard the footsteps – expected and dreaded. They were somewhere behind him in the deepening night. He'd found a track of soft soil – springy beneath the feet, like a cushion – and made a circuit of it, perhaps half a mile in length. He was at the start of the third lap when he sensed company. For a while, the visitor seemed to run alongside his own path, but now they were behind – or at least he thought they were behind, because sound does bounce around trees; it arrives from one place when it started from another. But Peter had company in Loner's Wood, he knew that – and he doubted it meant him well.

In the faint distance, the sound of a lorry, even a flash of headlights through the branches, as it made its late way to the Newhaven ferry. And then silence again, except for the steps behind, light, plodding but persistent. They were tracking Peter as he approached the quarry site, 'Danger' signs all around. He'd keep a steady pace along the leafy path, night vision good – lost in the headlights but recovered now ... though he missed the log in his way, jumping at the last minute, tripping, falling, lying still – and listening beyond his breath.

Silence. The woods were silent again. It would be nice to hear the nightingale now, that haunting beauty. The 'baa, baa' of the sheep in the distance calmed him. And then a barking dog, guarding a farm perhaps?

He got to his feet. There were no steps in the woodland around, and he could see nothing, peering through the gloom. Perhaps he should wait here – just wait. But no, he felt too vulnerable, a sitting duck. What good was paralysis now? How could caution help his cause? So he started to run again, one foot in front of the other along the woodland floor – and then they returned, almost immediately, the steps behind, the hunter and the hunted, playing out some game. He'd keep steady on the path, they seemed to want him further into the wood, they were not in a hurry, he was the pacesetter – the other feet, whoever they belonged to, were happy to wait. They moved him on, like a sheepdog on the Downs, chasing, harrying, guiding from behind. Silence again . . . or was it silence? Peter stopped to listen – this was mad, he was going home.

'Fair thee well, most foul!' he said, for he'd decided to go home, a noble retreat, which, in the circumstances, everyone would understand. He hoped he'd forgive himself in the morning . . . when the hand came across his mouth, out of nowhere, out of the dry leaves and the bracken, a hand across his mouth, holding a cloth.

A sweet smell . . . and then nothing.

Peter wasn't answering his phone,

which irritated Tamsin. She wanted to explain the role of Jones and Shaw, just in case they met during the handover and to review the case so far, to get his final thoughts on where they were with the investigation. But if Peter didn't want to talk, then that was his lookout – Tamsin wouldn't be losing any sleep.

And really, what else could she have done with Wonder? She could have refused to continue with the case under the conditions Wonder suggested, that had been an option. And perhaps she could have supported Peter a little more. But to what end? It would have been stupid in the circumstances . . . and not something Peter would want, she was quite sure of that. It would have been some meaningless stand on principle – principle without purpose, which would have helped no one. It was ridiculous of Peter to call it betrayal, which he hadn't as such, but that's probably what he was thinking. Tamsin was no Judas – and why wasn't he answering the phone? It was just so childish.

She sat flicking through the TV channels, in search of something half-decent, and reflected on her afternoon meeting with her new colleagues, Detective Sergeants Jones and Shaw. Wonder had instructed her to 'bring them up to speed' on the case and this she had attempted, despite initial provocation.

'I hear it's been a bit of a car crash,' Jones had said as they'd sat down to talk about the case . . . which hadn't been a good start. And from there on, they'd struggled to regard DI Shah as their senior officer . . . struggled to get past her looks, to be honest, so stupid things came out of their mouths. She was bloody attractive obviously, everyone knew that. It had been a subject they'd touched on before the meeting, before DI Shah had arrived.

'Is she with someone?' asked Jones, as if he had a chance.

'How would I know?' said Shaw.

'Apparently the chief inspector had a shot at her at Mick Norman's leaving do a couple of years ago. That's what I was told.'

'The chief inspector and Shah?'

'Apparently he got a bit gropey.'

'Embarrassing.'

'Which explains why she gets all the best jobs, you see – she's got him over a barrel.'

'Way hey!'

But now they were sitting with her, as work colleagues; they were the fresh blood on a murder enquiry, so to speak. Her skirt was definitely above the knee and she was briefing them, a detective inspector and two detective sergeants, about to start work on the Stormhaven Towers case.

'Jamie King was the headmaster of Stormhaven Towers,' she said briskly.

'More like Toff Towers!'

'Could you shut up, Shaw?' suggested Tamsin.

'Yes, ma'am.'

'He was pushed over the edge of Stormhaven Head on Sunday afternoon. And on Tuesday morning, the body of Jennifer Stiles, his school PA, was found at Tide Mills. You know Tide Mills? The weird ruins of a mill village by the sea.'

'Been there, ma'am,' said Jones. 'Good blackberry picking.'

'I'll remember that for when I'm retired and friendless, Jones. But until then, let's stay with the murder.' Jones nodded. 'Jennifer was concussed by a blow from a concrete slab – but killed by aconite poisoning. Either of you gardeners?'

They smiled conspiratorially, to indicate they were not gardeners, no way! Why would fit young men be gardeners? Jones played rugby in Stormhaven's First XV.

'It's from the wolfsbane plant, quite common in England. She was murdered on Monday evening between eight and midnight. And then on Wednesday – yesterday – the bursar, Terence Standing, committed suicide by tying a rope round a tree, a noose round his neck and then driving away from the tree at high speed with the noose still attached. And if you ever wish to do likewise, Jones, please feel free. Any questions so far?'

'What about suspects?' asked Shaw, subdued. Tamsin Shah did subdue people.

'There are eight suspects,' she said. 'And I suggest you take notes – if you can write. We'll be reinterviewing them all tomorrow – we start with a clean slate. But there are things we know already. They were all members of the Management Review Team, meeting at the end of the school year. The two exceptions are the headmaster's wife, Cressida Cutting, and Benedict Bleake, a man who lives beyond the wardrobe on Matron's Landing.' Jones and Shaw attempted professional detachment but their faces could not hide their dismay. 'It's a private school, remember,' said Tamsin, as if this explained everything. Only in a private school do people live beyond the wardrobe on Matron's Landing. 'And they have a chaplain called Ferdinand Heep, who touched up one of the girls: Holly.'

'That's disgusting! How old was she?'

'She's eighteen now – but sixteen at the time.'

'Oh.'

That didn't seem so bad.

'Holly then proceeded to blackmail him out of the Sunday collections.' Jones and Shaw listened intently. 'And would you believe it, she's on the review team as well, because she was head girl last year.'

Jones and Shaw were looking forward to meeting her.

'She's pretty and dangerous,' said Tamsin.

Jones and Shaw had given up professional detachment, their minds too busy. Interesting case, this one! It beat the break-in at the newsagent's last week.

'And then there's Crispin,' continued Tamsin. 'He's the head boy, who fancies Cressida, the head's wife – or rather, the head's widow. But dresses his lust as admiration – ring any bells?' Jones and Shaw looked straight ahead of them. 'He may also like Holly, we're not sure. Geoff Ogilvie is Director of Boys, but he's a loser, a man on the slide – he's called '"Spanker" Geoff and there's a volcano of a temper somewhere in there.'

'It was probably him,' said Shaw.

'Penny Rylands is Director of Girls, ambitious, secretive. A close friend of the murdered Jennifer Stiles; very upset by her death. Got that?'

Jones and Shaw were busy writing; they hadn't really got any of it.

'And Bart Betters is Director of Wellbeing.'

Jones put down his pen as one defeated by the exam question. 'Director of Wellbeing? What's wellbeing?' he asked.

'It's being well, Jones. You wouldn't understand.'

'There's a lot of directors in the school,' said Shaw.

'There are. It's a label that makes people feel important. It means you can pay them less.'

'Are there any teachers?'

'None that could have got either of you any qualifications.' Shaw had done quite well at school, before the A level disappointments. 'Whereas Cressida Cutting has a lot of qualifications, she's a doctor ...'

'So she knows about poisons, ma'am,' said Jones, keen to impress.

'It had crossed our minds,' said Tamsin, drily. She was still fuming over the investigation being called a 'car crash'. 'Cressida does have a cast-iron alibi. A phone call which rules her out from the crime scene. But cast-iron alibis should always make one more suspicious, eh?'

They nodded at the obvious sagacity of this comment.

'While Benedict Bleake is related to the nineteenth-century founder of the school, Nathaniel Bleake.'

'Nathaniel!' Shaw said, laughing. He didn't know any Nathaniels and found it a funny name.

'This means he can live at the school, free of charge,' said Tamsin. 'Nice work if you can get it.'

'He's the wardrobe feller?'

'Indeed. And one of them – one of that eight – is the killer. There may be two. We have been told of an affair but precisely who's with whom is hard to say – and it may not be reliable information. I want you there at nine tomorrow morning, don't be—'

Her phone rang. It was PC Goss from the search team. They'd been going though people's rooms at the school again. She'd ordered a second search after recent developments.

'Anything missed, Goss? Anything new?'

Even Tamsin was surprised by his answer; she wouldn't have imagined that. But with the story told, she ended the call quickly.

'Well, don't get too excited, boys, but we have a new lead.' Jones and Shaw were unmistakably excited. 'PC Goss has just discovered a case of women's clothing and various wigs under the bed of one of our male suspects — Geoff Ogilvie, Director of Boys. They missed it first time round, don't know how.'

'Unlike Gossy to miss a bit of skirt!'

'Very good, Jones. And it probably isn't important, beyond entertainment value, but we will bear it in mind.'

Jones and Shaw — still smirking — were then dismissed. And they were quite sweet really, the two of them . . . as long as one remembered they were little boys, of course. Tamsin found herself thinking this — she must be getting soft — as she lay in bed that night, wishing she could speak with Peter. The truth was, sweet or otherwise, she didn't want to work with two little boys on the case; they were unfit for purpose. She wanted to work with the abbot, she knew that now. She didn't feel good about herself between her cool, fresh indigo sheets, and maybe that's why she couldn't sleep, though it was the abbot's fault — if the investigation was a car crash, it was the abbot's fault.

And he was also to blame for having a tantrum tonight, refusing to answer the phone.

She lay on her back in a quiet road in Hove, a recent arrival and still some way from home . . . she eventually found a troubled sleep.

The face was no surprise,

as Abbot Peter returned slowly to conscious thought in the darkness of Loner's Wood. It appeared suddenly, in the cold, clear moonlight, freed from the obscuring cloud.

'It's time for your drink, Abbot,' she said.

'What drink?'

Was she offering help?

'Hemlock time.'

She wasn't offering help.

'What are you doing, Cressida?' he said. 'I'm here to meet the killer – not you.'

Cressida smiled.

'I think we both know that isn't true, Peter.'

'I know nothing of the sort! For goodness sake, untie me – we don't have much time!'

'You knew as soon as you saw the mileage counter by my front door,' said Cressida calmly . . . and Peter remembered the moment well. 'I saw your face as you noticed the figure. You knew I'd put in some additional miles since your last visit with Shah. You were interested in it when you left.'

'It may have caught my eye.'

'But then all the miles were mine, Jamie never used it – hated it being in the house!'

Peter accepted the situation. He'd feign ignorance no more.

'I knew it before then, Cressida,' he said, for clarification – and out of pride. 'Though confirmation is always reassuring – and yes, the mileage was confirmation.'

And now where the hell was Bart? This is what Peter was thinking . . . he should be here, though perhaps he was waiting. The abbot's hands and feet were tied with cord, he was going nowhere. But Bart should be here, he should have intervened – well, that had been the plan. Who better as his protector in Loner's Wood than a runner and woodland survival specialist? He'd no doubt be along shortly. Perhaps he was watching them even now, waiting his moment . . . yet this was the moment: Cressida had the hemlock in her hand. She'd made a drink of it in a child's drinking bottle.

'Oh, and just so you don't wait up, Abbot – Bart is indisposed,' she said.

'Bart?' He tried to sound calm.

'Yes, he's asleep on his bed, I imagine. Out cold.' Peter felt as a man winded, collapsing plans crushing his body, his head screaming . . . but he remained still and silent. 'Well, it's been a trying time for us all, Abbot, he must be tired.'

'No doubt.' Did she know?

'I heard your conversation, you see, your clever conspiracy.' She did know. 'So we shared a nightcap, Bart and I. He believed I was one of the good guys, in on the plan.' Abbot Peter listened with dull horror. Here was a killer who had outplanned him with some ease. His saviour was asleep in the school, three miles away, lost to all but his dreams until daybreak. 'And now, two birds with one poisonous stone,' she said.

'Are we bypassing the Hippocratic oath, Doctor?'

'It's the Hippocratic oath,'

said Crispin, like an expert slightly bored of their knowledge. 'And no, I don't mind you nosing round my room.'

Holly had found the sheet on the side.

'Where did you get it?' she asked.

'Why?'

'Just asking.'

'It's for my project.'

'So where did you get it?'

'Dr Cutting gave it to me.'

'Dr Cutting?'

'So?'

'Your totally favourite person!'

'She's not my favourite person.'

'Do you love her or something?'

'She just helped me with my project.'

'"She just helped me with my project",' echoed Holly, mimicking him in a lovesick manner.

And the truth was, Cressida had helped him with his project – but had also left him overwhelmed and unable to say no to anything. So he'd made the phone call she'd asked him to make, after leaving the key in the flowerpot. It had been strange being in the head's house alone that Sunday afternoon, quite exciting. And there was probably a good reason for her request, and perhaps she'd come back, this is what he'd been thinking, and . . .

'It's a bit ancient,' said Holly, looking at the sheet. 'Listen to this.'

'I've read it. I sort of had to.'

'No, but listen: "I swear by Apollo Physician and Asclepius and Hygieia and Panacea and all the gods and goddesses, making them my witnesses, that I will fulfil according to my ability and judgement this oath and this covenant." Who's Hygieia, for God's sake?'

'The god of soap dispensers.'

'But who believes in that now?'

'It was written in the fifth century BC, Holly.'

And Holly was captivated, despite its age. '"To hold him who has taught me this art as equal to my parents and to live my life in partnership with him, and if he is in need of money to give him a share of mine, and to regard his offspring as equal to my brothers in male lineage and to teach them this art – if they desire to learn it – without fee and covenant."'

'Doctors had respect for their teachers in those days.'

'How pompous and old are you sounding?'

'I'm just saying.'

And then Holly was reading again. '"I will apply dietetic measures for the benefit of the sick according to my ability and judgement; I will keep them from harm and injustice. I will neither give a deadly drug to anybody who asked for it, nor will I make a suggestion to this effect. Similarly I will not give to a woman an abortive remedy. In purity and holiness I will guard my life and my art."' Holly appeared moved. 'I suppose it does make you look at Dr Cutting differently.'

Crispin nodded and she read on: '"Whatever houses I may visit, I will come for the benefit of the sick, remaining free of all intentional injustice, of all mischief and in particular of sexual relations with both female and male persons, be they free or slaves." Or children.'

'Children?'

'I added that. Perhaps clergy should sign up to the Hippocratic oath as well.'

'Why do you say that?'

'It doesn't matter. Well, it does matter. I'll tell you. It's embarrassing.'

'What's embarrassing?'

'Just let me get to the end of this,' said Holly.

'Is this the bit about gossip?'

'"What I may see or hear in the course of the treatment, or even outside of the treatment in regard to the life of men, which on no account one must spread abroad, I will keep to myself, holding such things shameful to be spoken about." And finally: "If

I fulfil this oath and do not violate it, may it be granted to me to enjoy life and art, being honoured with fame among all men for all time to come; if I transgress it and swear falsely, may the opposite of all this be my lot."'

They sat in silence for a moment.

'Respect for Cressida,' said Holly.

'Right,' said Crispin and, feeling uncomfortable, asked: 'So what is it that's so embarrassing?'

Could she tell him? Was it wise?

'Two advantages,'

said Cressida.

She held the hemlock close to his lips as moonlight broke through again, a chill light on her face.

'First, I bring your private inquiry to a standstill, before your great reveal tomorrow. Because that's the one thing I believed about your show tonight – that you really had cracked the case . . . and really hadn't told the police.'

'I wouldn't be so sure.'

'A risk I'll take. And second, Peter, I get to talk to Socrates as he slowly dies . . . well – a stand-in for the great man. You don't mind being a stand-in, do you?' Peter felt the tree root against his back, the soft woodland soil beneath his head. He flexed his arms and legs, his movement limited. 'No offence, Abbot, but I was always disappointed when I read in the theatre programme that a stand-in was taking one of the parts. I'd paid my money – I wanted the best!'

'Quite,' said Peter.

'Still, you'll be very good, Peter, I have no doubt. And the police won't touch me after you've gone. They don't have your eyes or your unfortunate feel for people. And Tamsin likes me too much, anyway, sees in me a kindred spirit. I sense grudging admiration . . . she hates everyone at the school just as I do.'

'But *why*, Cressida?' Peter had to keep her talking . . . and killers did like the 'Why?' of their deeds. The ego loves to explain, to rationalize and justify, to drool over its smart behaviour . . . the last laugh and all that . . . the ego just loves the last laugh. 'Why all this – when you had everything?'

Cressida smiled knowingly.

'Oh, we can have that very interesting discussion once you've drunk the hemlock, Abbot. But I'd say this,' and suddenly there was rebuke in her voice, 'you should be careful about judging someone's life from the outside, really you should – especially when claiming they "have everything".'

'But you do.'

That riled Cressida.

'How on earth would you know what I have?' She almost spat the words. 'It's always quite different on the inside, believe me.' She calmed again and Peter lay still. 'I do want to reassure you, however – putting my doctor's hat on for a moment – that it's all quite painless. I've said it before in the surgery, haven't I?'

'You have.'

'And I was always right?'

'You were generally right, Doctor. No complaints so far.'

'It's all about trust when it comes to healing.'

'And killing?'

She didn't answer, she was looking for a tissue. And it was such a schoolboy question anyway, rushing headlong towards the drama of the kill. She wanted an adult conversation.

'So what's going to be quite painless?'

'Oh, the hemlock, Peter – well, the technical name is *Conium maculatum*, of course. But this isn't some medical conference, thank God! So we'll just call it hemlock and note that it's distinguished as a poison by its action of killing from the outside in – from the extremities inwards. Quite unique!' She was genuinely excited. 'It moves inwards slowly ... well, you'll be able to describe it to me. You will do that, won't you? As numbness of your extremities becomes paralysis of your lungs ... which will be your peaceful end.'

'My inability to breathe?'

Peter listened as one in a dream, needing a plan – but without a plan in the silent wood.

'It has no effect on the brain, though,' said Cressida. 'This is the wonder of hemlock ... enabling us to enjoy a most interesting conversation for the next couple of hours, quite alone in Loner's Wood. It's not busy at this time of night, as you'll have noticed. And then I'll need to get back.'

'You were always the runner.'

Cressida laughed.

'School champion – I would have beaten you whenever we met. I mean, before you got old.'

'It's how you got to Stormhaven Head on Sunday afternoon.'

'That knowledge will die with you.'

'Possibly – though possibly not. You left the school in disguise, dressed as a man. Mr Thomas, the gardener, saw you. So that was your first mistake – there were others to follow.'

He hoped she might enquire about them.

'This is just white noise to me,' she said.

'He said, "I thought it was a woman – but then realized it was a man." I trusted his first instinct.'

'And look at the good it's done you, Peter, lying here facing death. The prize for your remarkable intuition is hemlock.'

'Will you kill him as well?'

'You imagine I fear a gardener?'

'Lower down the food chain, I suppose.'

'He doesn't know what he knows. And that's why Jennifer had to die – she did. I saw her realize what she knew, there in the common room. She remembered where she lost her phone.' Peter listened to his breathing; it was important to stay sane. 'Still, a good life, I hope, Abbot. What was it Auden said? Something about letting your last thinks be thanks? I'm sure he said it better – after all, he's the poet, not me – but a rather wonderful idea ... one of Jamie's favourites as well, strangely. We must hope that's what he felt as he fell – thanks.'

'That may be optimistic.'

'Will your last thinks all be thanks, Peter?'

'And you stole Penny's phone for twenty-four hours ...'

'... borrowed, please!'

'... to lure Jennifer to Tide Mills, by text presumably. And all because you thought she knew?'

'She was also a Grade A bitch. She was forever keeping me away from Jamie, putting a screen between us. "He's not presently available, Mrs King." She always called me Mrs King. "Can I get him to call you back?" She impersonated Jennifer savagely. 'She never did get him to call me back.'

'Perhaps he didn't want to call you back.'

And the thought of that merely made Cressida hate Jennifer more.

'But more pressingly – and that was an unfortunate remark, Abbot – I'd used her phone to lure Jamie to the cliff edge. I texted him from the front room when he was in the study that afternoon. He thought it was her, of course – well, why wouldn't he? People always believe texts, trust the hand that sends it. And it was all suitably dramatic: she was going to kill herself, throw herself from the cliff! And Jamie being Jamie – well, he had to go to the rescue!' She paused a moment. 'I don't know if he was in love with her. But if I couldn't have Jamie, no one else was having him – certainly not Jennifer.'

She hesitated, a moment of sadness, deflation. 'Only when he arrived there, of course, there was just me, standing distraught, a maiden in distress, one might say.' And she remembered the conversation, went back there now to Stormhaven Head – their final conversation after fourteen years of relatively happy marriage.

'Why are you here, Cressida?' Jamie had been amazed to see her, standing on the cliff edge. He hadn't recognized her at first in the odd running hat which changed her appearance quite dramatically. But he was disappointed as well as surprised. He'd wanted to save the day without anyone's help. Jamie was quite binary in that regard. Either he saved Jennifer or someone else did, his work or another's – it shouldn't be shared. But Cressida had been convincing in the moment.

'She called me shortly after you'd left, Jamie. Jennifer often confided in me.'

'Really?'

He walked towards her.

'Such a dear, sweet woman,' said Cressida.

That had surprised him, to hear those words. Jennifer had not hidden the fact that she did not believe Cressida was a proper wife to him – couldn't even share his surname, which surely spoke volumes. Jennifer had said it on more than one occasion, 'She's not a proper wife, Jamie – speaking as a friend, of course.' But now here was Cressida trying to save her. So where was Jennifer?

'Jamie, this is terrible, just awful!' said Cressida, standing like Florence Nightingale on the cliff top, desperate in her running gear. She noted they were alone on the cliff for now ... only distant figures on the golf course, no walkers with a view. 'I ran here as fast as I could, but ...'

'You mean she ... did she ... did she do it?'

Cressida remembered Jamie's face, so full of concern. Perhaps he should have been more concerned for his wife, she thought.

'I saw her jump, Jamie, it was just too awful. But I mean, why would she do that?'

'You saw her jump?'

'I saw her jump — now look at her! Tell me that's not her!'

She was hysterical, quite out of character. But he'd be strong. He'd stepped forward to look over the edge, to take control. She said, 'Be careful, dear,' and then nudged him forward, hardly a push at all, hardly a murder at all. She hadn't touched him so gently for years ...

'And Terence?' asked Peter,

gazing up into the swaying branches overhead.

'Terence?' Cressida spoke as if he was long forgotten and quite unimportant. 'Terence took his own life, Abbot.'

'Without encouragement from you, I suppose?'

'And now it's time for your drink.'

'You didn't help him towards the rope?'

'And excuse the bottle. It's a kiddy's bottle which somehow seems inappropriate. But it's just so we don't spill any.'

'You're too clever, Cressida – I mean, for it to be a coincidence.'

She smiled with pride in the moonlight, her face still glistening with sweat from the run.

'I may have dropped him the odd note about his homosexuality being exposed. I *may* have. His awful God knew already, of course, and was choking in heavenly disgust! But no one at the school knew ...no one at school knew their Bible-bashing gay-bashing bursar was, well, gay as May! That would have been a fine shaming...he couldn't have coped at all. His meticulous love of order and detail hid a very anxious soul, rather ill-equipped for this difficult world.'

'And so you simply made it more difficult.' She shrugged, a half-smile. 'Do you like yourself, Cressida?'

'I'm not a monster, you know.'

'No one is a monster.'

'Though really, that was a rather excessive response from the poor boy. I mean the rope and the car business.'

'But why pick on him?'

'I didn't know how much he knew, given his "special relationship" with Benedict. Now drink up, Abbot.'

'Benedict? How did you know ...?'

Cressida moved the bottle firmly towards Peter's mouth, like mother to child, nurse to patient – but he refused it, turning his head away.

'Doctor can make this much more painful,' she said and pushed the bottle against his mouth. 'I'm giving you this the nice way, Peter, a sweet goodbye to life. Most people would be grateful.' With a heave of his bound body, at the last second, he rolled away, face down now in the earth with a mouthful of leaves. She pulled him back, with all her strength, slapped him across the face, held his head once again, her fingers pressing his jaw, and said 'Drink!' as she tried to force the nozzle into his mouth. He opened his mouth for a moment and spat out the leaf mould towards her. She pulled back.

'OK,' she said, 'we'll do it another way, we'll make you scream – and then you'll be glad to drink.' And in the half-light, Peter saw her take out a syringe from her bag and then a needle. She withdrew also a small bottle, pricked it with the needle and drew its substance into the syringe. 'Not quite as hygienic as the surgery, but we'll survive. Well, you know what I mean.' She paused for a moment, still and pale like some statue in an Italian garden. 'Do you know the last sermon I heard in that godforsaken chapel, Abbot?'

'Tell me,' said Peter.

'I mean, I'm sorry to talk shop, you must be sick of sermons – but it just struck me.' The moon's glare caught the needle, a thin glint of murder in the dark. 'It was about Christ in the Garden of Gethsemane, cornered by those with a desire to execute him. Recognize the feeling?'

'At least Judas wasn't his doctor.'

'Oh, don't be so prim, Peter – please! There are no pills for self-pity. And really, what's so great about a doctor? It's just a label. It carries no promise of virtue with it. It has suited me to heal people – reputation, money . . . but that doesn't mean I'm good! Healers can be flawed, remember.'

'I think you're good.'

'Don't be stupid.'

'No, whenever I've caught a murderer . . .'

'. . . only you haven't caught me. I've caught you.'

'. . . I've always liked them. I've always liked the murderer, admired their adventurous plunge into excess. And I like you, Cressida.'

'Don't be stupid . . . a stupid thing to say.'

'But true. You seem flustered.'

She'd lowered the needle for a moment, but then lifted it again as if ready to prick the skin. But first, some verbal needle.

'And then the sermon moved on from Gethsemane,' she said, 'to the second betrayal of Jesus, by his close friend Peter. Remember that one, Abbot?' The abbot saw only the needle, dripping a little. 'Well, of course you do! "Before the cock crows, you shall deny me three times." And again I'm thinking – that's so you.'

'You've lost me.'

'DI Shah, I mean. She is a friend, isn't she? I sense a closeness.' Peter stayed silent. 'Oh, you aren't in love with her, are you? Peter, Peter! She's way too young . . . that's bordering on the abusive.' And then in a quieter voice. 'But whatever you have together, I'm afraid she's betrayed you.'

Now Peter's mind was busy again. Where was this going?

'Fiction is a very crowded market, Cressida. I'd guide you towards the self-help section.'

'This isn't fiction, Abbot. Fiction has never interested me. Why waste time with other people's fantasies? No, I complained about your behaviour today to the police . . . spoke to Chief Inspector Wonder.'

'An experience that should be on everyone's bucket list.'

'Well, it seems I was pushing at something of an open door! It transpires that you've been taken off the case, with DI Shah in full agreement – full agreement – as he made very clear! It was her suggestion! "Before the cock crows three times . . ." Now let's find a nice big vein.'

Her fingers moved easily over his bare arm, his soft receptive flesh – and then she lurched forward . . . full forward, as if hit or pushed, thrown across the abbot's chest, the syringe sent flying. Peter felt the force, gasping for breath, before she was dragged back across him, arms waving, pulled by an unseen figure, head in a balaclava, grunting with the strain, another blow – and then the stunned Cressida dealt with, her hands tied behind her back, her shoes removed.

'I'm sorry, dear,' muttered the figure, 'but you were always rather fast – and you can't be now.' It then came over to Peter, knelt down beside him and untied his cords. Thank God for Bart – so something woke him up!

'Feel better?' he asked.

But it wasn't Bart.

'Much better,' said Peter, only half-believing the voice.

The figure now stood up and removed the balaclava.

'Father!' said Cressida in the moonlight. 'What are you doing here?'

Wonder was feeling good

about today . . . very good indeed.

'Call it territory reclaimed,' he'd said to himself in the shaving mirror that morning.

And above all else, this was a victory for Wonder over DI bloody Shah. It had been a difficult eighteen months since the unfortunate incident at Mick Norman's leaving bash. And it had been nothing, really – it wasn't as if he was serious, just the drink talking. And who in his position wouldn't have tried it on a little? As his old mate Darryl used to say, 'She only has to say no.' Which she had done – like the fridge that she was.

And somewhere in his body the remembrance of the encounter remained. Mick's embarrassing leaving speech, then the music blaring, the alcohol flowing and Shah telling him that she was going home – and him not wanting her to leave. He'd wanted her to stay, wanted them to dance . . . or whatever.

'You do know that you're a good cop, Tamsin,' he'd shouted.

The music was too loud for talking but she heard clearly enough.

'Yes, thank you.'

'Bloody good cop.'

And she was thinking: why do men get like this when drunk?

'And a bloody attractive cop to boot,' he'd continued. 'Shouldn't say it but there we are!'

Oh dear.

'And it's not just the wine talking, Tamsin,' and now as he held her arm, she was acutely aware this was the first time he'd touched her body. 'It's the truth talking! You have no right to be so bloody good and so bloody attractive. And if I was a younger man . . .'

'And not married—'

'—we're not close, my wife and I.'

'Good night, Chief Inspector,' she said, easing herself free. She needed to get out.

'Er, yes, good night, Shah — or whatever you call yourself.'

His hands and lips moved towards her in a vague lunge but one she avoided with an evasive spin . . . and then she left, walked out at speed.

'Fridge,' muttered Wonder as John Lennon's 'Jealous Guy' played across the room and he thought, we could have been dancing to that.

*

But this morning, that was all left behind, ancient bloody history. Wonder was a man back in charge, his authority re-established. She wouldn't be taking any liberties in the future: 'Territory definitely reclaimed!' was the mood music of the day. And so a clean white shirt from the drawer — swanky place, Stormhaven Towers, they'd see him at his best. Then a quick polish of his pips and perhaps an extra squirt of aftershave . . . smack it on strong, Cecil! Because Cecil Wonder was turning things around and he'd be taking his new team to Stormhaven Towers himself, this he'd decided. He'd oversee the handover of the case personally. He'd be a visible presence to make a statement to the watching world and the statement was this: 'Wonder's in charge, Wonder's calling the shots now — and thank God Wonder's on the case!'

At twenty past eight, they all met at the Lewes police headquarters and drove from there to Stormhaven. In the driving seat was the chief inspector, a symbol of the new order of things. In the back of the car were Jones and Shaw, shaved and polished for such a grand assignment. And in the front of the car, feeling slightly sick, was Tamsin. Jones had tried to make it up to her before leaving, not wishing to be at odds with his DI — frightened of her, in a way. And he wanted to work with her again, that would be pretty decent.

'I think I may have got off on the wrong foot with you yesterday, ma'am,' he'd said as they waited for the car.

'Do you have a right one, Jones?'

Tamsin did not want this conversation.

'It was just that when I referred to the investigation as a "car crash", I was referring, of course, to the abbot fellow, not you.'

253

'Really?'

'Yeah – we understand from the chief inspector that he wasn't quite up to the mark. An old man out of his depth – to put it politely!' Tamsin had looked at him blankly. 'Just wanted to clear up that little misunderstanding, ma'am – the "car crash" wasn't you – it was the abbot.'

Tamsin had said nothing and got into the car.

'Good morning, everyone!'

said Chief Inspector Wonder in his heartiest manner. He could handle public speaking, could always get the punters on his side, even in a tricky situation like the one before him now. Assembled in the common room were the suspects, all looking rather withdrawn and none more so than Bart, who was struggling to keep his eyes open. He said to Geoff that he couldn't understand it, that he hadn't had that much to drink and Geoff had said, 'You're just a lightweight, Bart!'

'It's like I've been drugged.'

'You have. It's called alcohol.'

'And thank you for gathering so promptly this morning,' continued Wonder. 'The early bird catches the worm, as they say.'

'I don't see many worms caught so far,' said Penny.

'That's going to change, believe me!'

'But the second mouse gets the cheese,' said Geoff, who was not an early morning man.

'Er, quite,' said Wonder, who had to press on. 'And I'm here to announce the fact that I'm bringing in a new investigation team this morning.' He looked for a reaction but found none. 'A new team to continue the work in the school – hopefully bringing it to the quick conclusion we all want.' He looked at Tamsin. 'I know you all must be eager to get away, and believe me, we do not wish to detain you for a moment longer than is necessary.' He could have done with a little more enthusiasm. After all, he was the knight in shining armour here. 'You know DI Shah of course, and she'll continue to head-up the investigation. But she'll be assisted now by Detective Sergeants Jones and Shaw, both very meticulous officers – and perhaps more suited to this sort of work than the, er, abbot fellow.'

'What's to become of the abbot?' asked Penny.

'He's finished,' said Wonder succinctly.

'How do you mean?'

'Well, he will no longer be involved in the case. In this case – or any other case.' Put that on record, thought Wonder, public record.

'And where's Cressida?' asked Penny, worried.

People looked around and noticed her absence for the first time.

'Could someone go and find her?' said Wonder. 'Jones?'

Jones sprang into action as the common room door opened and all eyes looked round. There was Cressida standing in the doorway, still in her running gear, hands tied behind her back, dead-eyed and pale. If she'd slept, there was no evidence of the fact.

'She's here,' said a voice in the shadows.

It was a voice they knew.

'No need to concern yourself, Jones,' said the abbot. 'I went and found her.' Peter now emerged from behind the prisoner with PC Wilson beside him. 'And the excellent PC Wilson here has helped her stay found. While you all slept, he has been a most excellent guard.'

'Cressida, what happened?' Penny was up immediately, but Benedict calmed her. She sat back down as the widow walked forward. The abbot and Wilson guided her to a seat. She sat down between the two.

'Top copper, this one!' volunteered Wilson to no one and everyone. What's Wilson saying? thought Wonder. Is he talking about me?

'Well, now we're all here,' said Wonder, reclaiming control, 'I'll hand over to the new investigation team to get started with the handover ...'

'No need, sir,' said Wilson.

'I beg your pardon?'

Why was Wilson getting involved? Had he forgotten who was in charge here?

'The investigation's over, sir! We sorted it last night – me and the abbot.'

'And Benedict,' said Peter quietly, like a prompt in a school play.

'And Mr Bleake, yeah.'

256

Wonder's clean shirt was becoming infused with sweat once again – and so early in the day ... particularly unfortunate as he wasn't wearing a jacket.

'I can explain,' said the abbot.

'No, let me explain,' said Benedict, standing. 'As the representative of the Bleake family today – and father of ... the murderer, Cressida Cutting, née Bleake.'

Jones stepped in. Let the amateurism be halted here.

'I think you'll find she has an alibi for the murder of Jamie King, mate. Cast iron.' He referred to his notes, ostentatiously. 'Having made a call from home at the precise time the headmaster was killed. Now, if you'd like the serious investigation to begin ...'

This was his chance to make his mark with the chief inspector. And he was going to take it.

'Crispin?' said Peter ... and all eyes turned towards the former head boy, who was blushing. 'Help us now – and I'm sure all will be well.'

Crispin looked at Cressida – but she didn't return his gaze. He then looked at Holly who returned it in full.

'I made the call,' he said, his voice steady and clear.

'You *what*?' asked Penny.

'I made it. Cressida asked me to make a call from her home, when she was out ... and I made it.'

'But why on earth?' said Geoff, who'd known Crispin since he was seven, a small boy in shorts in the prep school, such a nervous little fellow.

'Dr Cutting asked me if I might help her out.'

'Help her out?'

'Of a tricky situation. I didn't know what, didn't need to know ... at the time.'

Benedict was on his feet again: 'I am a witness to the confession of Cressida, by the way – the confession in which she admitted to the murders of her husband, Jamie King, and Jennifer Stiles.'

'You bitch!' shouted Penny. 'You killed my sister!'

And now Cressida laughed, sudden life in her face.

'The secret team, Jennifer and Penny, the hidden sisters of Stormhaven Towers trying to get you the headship!' There was shock all around her. 'How you harassed Jamie about him moving on. "In your own time, of course, Jamie – but when the call comes from on high . . ."' Again, the savage mimic.

'Somewhat wasted as a doctor!' said Ferdinand to no one in particular. 'The mimicry is quite excellent!'

'But it wasn't secret from me,' said Cressida. 'I'm an expert with family photos, I always know who's who. And all because your pathetic father was broken by this place.'

'You bitch!'

Cressida wanted to explain, or rather, to humiliate: 'Penny's dear daddy was expelled from Stormhaven Towers! Did none of you know that? Oh yes, the sad man was expelled from here. And then – being the inadequate he was – he turned to crime and drink. It's a joke!' Cressida was hysterical, no one had seen her like this. And Penny was up again in anger but Sergeant Shaw used effective restraint. Were all private schools like this?

'Nothing personal, though, not with Jennifer,' continued the doctor, who was some way past caring, a furious ego at play. 'Jennifer was collateral damage. I just needed her phone for a while, I took it over tea, and all was fine – until she remembered where she lost it. And so I arranged a meeting between the two of you at Tide Mills, using *your* phone this time, Penny – Tide Mills where you used to play together. I knew she'd come.' Despair and sadness broke Penny's face, past anger now. 'She just *knew* the text must be from you. *I need help. Meet me at Tide Mills at 8.* You'll be reassured to know that your sister was very prompt. She'd clearly do anything for you.'

Stunned silence.

'Cressida, dear,' said Benedict, 'you don't have to speak now.'

'And I don't have to listen to you and your rules any longer.'

'I came here to help you, Cressida . . . clearly I failed.'

'You – help me? You could never help me! You're the cause, not the cure! You sold my pony!'

This was news to everyone. Was this really about a pony?

'We talked about that at the time,' said Benedict. He remembered the pony. 'It was difficult but we all agreed . . .'

'I never agreed.'

'Your mother and I . . .'

'It was the only creature I'd ever loved or felt loved by.'

Cressida had never sounded so raw – or so young.

'You needed to concentrate on your studies.'

'And I did, Father, I did!'

'You did.'

'And haven't I done well? Proud of me, I hope!'

Benedict breathed deeply.

'I could see the affair growing in your mind – but I couldn't stop it.' His voice weakened, as if losing the power to speak. He was talking to himself.

Benedict sat down. But Peter wasn't finished: 'And while Terence undoubtedly killed himself, poor soul, he was encouraged by Cressida here.'

'He wasn't an embezzler, surely?' said Penny.

'No,' said Peter. 'He didn't embezzle funds – he merely found himself crucified by a forbidden love.'

'Forbidden by whom?'

'Terence was gay.'

'Absolutely not!' said Ferdinand. 'I won't countenance the name of a good man being . . .'

'He had a brief relationship with Benedict,' continued the abbot calmly. 'But he couldn't cope with the self-hate and when Cressida threatened exposure, well . . . Chief Inspector?'

Wonder was poleaxed.

'It does look like there have been some advancements in the case since yesterday,' he said.

'That rather undersells the achievement, Chief Inspector,' said Benedict. 'It's solved . . . the case is closed.'

'A little premature, perhaps . . .'

'As PC Wilson said, we have a "top copper" here,' continued Benedict as he looked with both warmth and sadness towards Peter. Without Peter, his daughter would surely have got away with it, she was clever – she would not have been caught, never. But did he wish his daughter her freedom? When was the right time for one's child to face the music and take responsibility for things done? Benedict had created a successful business; but whether he had done so well with his family . . .

'We all get lucky sometimes!' said Wonder, in a bluff sort of way.

'No,' said Benedict, who had no love for this pompous officer of the law. 'He got clever, Chief Inspector, and he got brave. While you slept last night, snoring in Mrs Wonder's ear, this abbot lured the killer out into the woods.'

Tamsin looked questioningly across to Peter, a hint of mirth, their first eye contact since her return. The abbot mouthed 'later'.

'He was acting like he was drunk!' said Holly, excitedly. 'He was saying how rubbish the police were – and how he so knew who the killer was, and like, how he was going to announce the killer today!'

The abbot looked suitably abashed, as an actor must when his performance is praised.

'Look, I'm so sorry, Abbot,' said Bart, leaning forward. 'I was meant to protect you. I don't know what happened.'

'You were drugged,' said Peter. 'And I was the fool, not you. She read my hand too easily.'

'I genuinely thought you were being a complete prat!' said Holly merrily. 'And, like, we did "playing drunk" in drama. It's not as easy as you think!'

'You became the shark bait,' said Crispin, who was now holding hands with Holly. 'Bloody amazing.'

'Well, the shark bait would not be here but for Benedict,' said Peter. 'Without Benedict, the shark would have won – death by hemlock.'

Faces now turned towards Benedict Bleake, who tried to play the whole thing down.

'I merely saw the trap being laid,' he said. 'After all, I noted the abbot drinking nothing stronger than tonic water all night – with a lemon, to give the appearance of gin.' There was some consternation, as if this was cheating in some way. 'But I also knew who would fall into his trap – who would have to push the boundaries further still.' He sighed. 'I went to Loner's Wood to be with my daughter upon her arrest, nothing more. The saving of Abbot Peter was not my intention. And since virtue is all about intention, there was no virtue at all.' Ferdinand nodded. 'But I am glad to have done so, in a manner. I respect the abbot's power of being nothing but sane ... quite rare, in my experience.'

Tamsin then spoke, quietly and calmly: 'Clearly I'll need to have contact addresses for you all. We'll also need to take statements from each of you before you go. But with that done – and we'll work to make sure this is all done as soon as possible – then you are free to leave and start your summer holiday.'

'What about our phones?' asked Holly, instantly, for here was a more pressing matter than any holiday ... or murder.

'*With* your phones,' said Tamsin and there were cheers and a sweep of relief across the room.

'Hallelujah!' shouted Geoff, both fists in the air, and everybody laughed – apart from Ferdinand who started to cry. It was Crispin who said, 'You don't need to cry, sir,' but Ferdinand didn't reply.

Tamsin continued, now standing in front of Wonder – perhaps unwittingly, who can say? But he was cut off from the audience. 'And I'm sure it's only right to say that we're all grateful to Abbot Peter for bringing this case to such a swift conclusion.' There were mutters of approval, 'hear, hear!' and the like. 'My only contribution – small but telling – was to bring him in on the case in the first place.' She smiled awkwardly at Peter and then turning round, smiled at Wonder ... in triumph. 'We've worked well together in the past, the abbot and I. And perhaps we will do again?'

And the other question on Tamsin's mind was this: with whom was Cressida having the affair?

Wonder had left the scene.

He'd driven away from Stormhaven Towers with Jones, Shaw and Dr Cutting, who had been placed under arrest. 'I'm arresting you for the murders of Jamie King and Jennifer Stiles,' said Jones, with a trace of regret. 'You do not have to say anything, but it may harm your defence if you do not mention when questioned something which you later rely on in court. Anything you do say . . .' Cressida wasn't listening to the boy. And there wasn't much talk in the car on the journey back to Lewes. Wonder remained in the driving seat but it seemed to count for less. His day was a strange ruin given the successful outcome of the investigation; while for Jones and Shaw, there was a terrible sense of anticlimax. Cressida Cutting remained silent. She had no time for these people, had nothing to say to them. Prison didn't frighten her. It might even be quite interesting. She'd still be a doctor and everyone loved a doctor . . . especially the prison officers.

*

Back at Stormhaven Towers, the atmosphere in the common room was less elated than might be expected with murders solved and eight weeks of holiday beckoning.

'Sometimes you don't know the stress you carry until someone takes it away,' said Penny to Peter. The former murder suspects were relaxing with coffee and chocolate bars which the abbot had brought from his room. Further supplies had thoughtfully been delivered by Wilson, from the local newsagent's. Wilson was thinking that one day he might like to run a hotel by the sea.

'And was Cressida right about your father?' asked Peter.

'Yes, he died of liver failure four years ago. Both Jennifer and I, we wanted to come back here to the scene of the crime and redeem it in some way, reclaim it for the family.'

'The crime?'

'They expelled him for groping a minor, when he himself was a minor . . . he never recovered. I mean, he was young, he was just growing up, unboundaried – he wasn't gay, for a start!' She paused, her anger cooling. 'Though Jennifer did become slightly too close to Jamie. I mean, she never said as much – but I sensed a change.'

'And now, Penny?'

'Oh, I'll apply for the headship.'

'The school hasn't hurt you enough?'

Penny's eyes watered a little.

'Nothing is bad in itself, Abbot – if that doesn't sound too much like a fridge magnet.'

'It does sound a little like a fridge magnet.'

'I mean, I'm no great fan of the chapel here – certainly not as delivered by the chaplain. But I keep coming back to the word *redemption*. I don't know exactly what it means – but I do believe that graves are for the planting of flowers. I like flowers.'

'Just be careful which flowers you grow. Avoid wolfsbane where possible . . .'

*

'We will be pressing charges,' said Tamsin to Ferdinand, an isolated figure . . . though Crispin and Holly had sat with him for a while. Holly had even apologized for the trouble she'd caused him – an apology which Ferdinand had accepted with a nod. 'It'll be up to the CPS as to whether they take it further.'

'But the matter is dealt with, surely – finished?' he'd said.

'How exactly is it finished?'

'Well, it was so long ago – and Holly has apologized to me, just now, you can ask her. She apologized for the trouble she's caused me. That says something surely?'

Tamsin paused . . . in shock.

'Why is she apologizing for you abusing her?' she asked.

'The blame has hardly been one way!'

'Answer my question.'

'It was just a moment,' said Ferdinand.

'It's always just a moment, Reverend. Prisons are full of moments. But my question remains: why is the child apologizing to the adult for the adult's crime?'

Ferdinand's eyes were hollow.

*

It was warm, the sun taking hold through the common room windows, spilling across the wood-tiled floor. Holly took off her Stormhaven Towers sweat top, revealing a turquoise shirt underneath. It was the last remaining piece of school clothing she'd been wearing.

'That looked a bit symbolic,' said Geoff.

'Sir?'

'A farewell to the uniform, Holly – a farewell to the school. Out of here and good riddance, eh?'

This hadn't crossed Holly's mind.

'Well, I suppose we all have to leave sometime – sir.'

'I think it's *Geoff* now, Holly – or Mr Ogilvie ... or whatever other name seems appropriate in the real world. Or to avoid any names at all, simply cross over the road when you see me coming, and walk by on the other side of the street! It's traditional among ex-pupils.'

Holly thought that seemed a lonely remark and she felt sorry for him.

'Are you happy here?' Crispin paused. 'Geoff?'

Crispin too had dispensed with uniform this morning, appearing now in jeans and a loose-fitting red jumper.

'Happy? That's pushing it a bit, Crispin. I was happy once, when I was starting out. But you don't want to hear this.'

'I do, sir – *Geoff.*'

'Well, you've got ambition then, the promise of everything good waiting for you in the future. All you have to do is get out there and seize it! But somewhere along the line – well, I became what Jamie King would call "the passed-over and the pissed-off!" – he had a way with words. And now I'm asking myself, "Can I do this for another fifteen years, as they move the pension age ever closer to eternity?" And the answer is, "I don't know." So am I happy,

Crispin? I'm looking forward to a walking holiday in the south of France. Does that count?'

'Sounds good to me, Geoff.'

*

'I believe the bones are Roman,' said Bart, 'and I want them checked – but not in England.'

He'd already told Tamsin and Peter of his discovery – or rather, that of a friend of his who claimed to have found another Roman burial site in Loner's Wood. And it was these bones that had brought Bart to Stormhaven Head on the afternoon of the murder. He'd been lowering them over the cliff to a designated spot for collection by boat.

'If the bones are checked in England they'll stay in England.'

'Is that so bad?'

'They deserve to go home – home to Italy. Ten skeletons have already made it home.'

'Where a museum is paying you rather handsomely?'

'They also believe in the cause – the return of Italians to Italy!'

'And how about you, Bart?'

'Me?'

'Well, I mean, I'm no psychologist but isn't this more about you than the Romans, who – let's be honest – probably don't care much any more?'

'Of course they care! They want to go home. They've waited all these years in the cold soil of Loner's Wood.'

Bart – or Bartolomeo Buffone to give him his birth name – had been brought to England, aged five, by his mother, when she divorced her Italian husband. But Bart hadn't wanted to come to England with his mother; he'd wanted to stay in Italy with his father. And over the years, Bart had grown more Italian rather than less. When he heard about the Roman burial site, the gathering of bones far from home, something stirred – it became 'this obsession', in his words. Tamsin thought him quite mad . . . though even as she judged him, there were echoes inside her, something about being a stranger in your own home. Where was home for Tamsin?

265

'Perhaps it's time to stop thinking about everyone else's well-being, Bart – and ponder your own.' Bart nodded. 'That, I think, is what the abbot would say, at least. I'm not designed for conversations like this.'

'So you won't charge me?'

'Not if you let sleeping Romans lie. Perhaps they wanted to be here – perhaps they were happy migrants who fell in love with this sceptred isle?'

The determined figure of Mrs Docherty was now firmly in the doorway.

'When are you lot going to be out?' she asked, curtly. 'I mean, no offence, but I need to clean this room before I go, and I'm off at two. It won't clean itself over the summer!'

'We're all leaving now,' said Tamsin, collecting her stuff and the others followed suit. It was time to go.

*

'Cutting was her mother's name,' said Benedict, as he walked with Peter towards Matron's Landing. 'She chose her mother's name. I was always a disappointment to her – she blamed me for the end of the marriage, of course. She said I pushed her mother away. But I didn't push anyone – she floated away like a balloon with no string, like a boat unmoored. She lost interest in me – well, who wouldn't? And I lost interest in her . . . we waved goodbye to each other from some distance.'

'I'm sorry for all this,' said Peter. The successful pursuit of a murderer leaves various victims in its wake, not all of them criminal. 'It must be the most difficult of times.'

'It's a horrible relief, if I'm honest. I think that describes it. A lanced boil – yet such regret, from which there's no recovery, Abbot – I don't think so.'

They'd reached the wardrobe on Matron's Landing. Benedict paused here. This was as far as he wanted company.

'And the affair?' said Peter.

'Oh, I think you spotted the affair, Abbot . . . eventually.'

'An affair not with a person but with an idea – the idea of excess.' Benedict nodded.

'She was quite captivated.'

'As you said, it's ideas that really wield the knife.'

'She said I drew too many lines in the sand, walled her in with my dos and don'ts. I don't remember that particularly, but it was how she felt . . . and so the growing urge to smash the walls, to stamp on those lines, to obliterate every boundary. And I saw her, you see.'

'How do you mean, *you saw her?*'

'It was Monday night. I was going for my night walk, when I came across her in the common room.'

He remembered it well. He'd been walking past the common room at midnight when he heard a noise inside. Curious, he'd looked in and had seen Cressida at the sink.

'What are you doing?' he asked his daughter in the half-light.

'Why does it matter to you? Washing up?'

'Washing up in the common room at midnight? Don't you have a sink at home – or is this charity work?' It was then he saw the phone in her hand. 'Washing phones?'

'I suggest you carry on keeping yourself to yourself, Father. This is just something that had to be done. Good night.'

She'd walked right past him, out of the common room and down the corridor, making her way home, via the side door and the bins. It was not a well-policed route . . .

'A dangerous doctor,' said Peter.

'A very good doctor, as you know. But she began to celebrate excess like some frustrated teenager. It was there when we spoke, I heard it . . . and it led her by the snout . . . to this . . . such anger. The sins of the fathers, eh,' said Benedict as he stepped inside the wardrobe and closed the door behind him.

Peter listened to his footsteps on the stairs . . . they sounded weary.

The common room

had been thoroughly cleaned for the first time since Easter. The whirlwind that was Mrs Docherty had been ruthless in her purge of dust, spillage and stain. And Tamsin and Peter were allowed to sit in the corner only so long as they didn't add to it.

There were no half-measures with Mrs Docherty. You cannot *half*-clean a room, this was her take on the matter, just as you can't *half*-wash up. Sometimes Mr Docherty left the saucepans to 'soak' – as if that was washing up! 'You've washed up, Mr Docherty, when the saucepans are cleaned, dried and in the cupboard!'

'And they never wash their cups!' she muttered to herself and the world. Mrs Docherty offered a running commentary on the appalling housekeeping habits of the staff as she cleaned. 'Whatever they teach the children, it isn't about washing cups. Or if they do wash them, they're happy to leave the stain on the inside! As if someone else wants their stain! A cup has an outside and an inside and both need washing!'

'I couldn't agree more,' said Tamsin. A stained cup should never be offered to a guest.

So the cups had been washed, the sink cleaned, the tables dusted and sprayed, the floor energetically vacuumed and all magazines and newspapers thrown in a large plastic bag. And just when they thought she was finished, she discovered the fridge.

'Now that is *disgusting!*'

Ten minutes – and much elbow grease – later, Mrs Docherty surveyed her work, and she was pleased.

'And none of those staff in here to ruin it for eight weeks!' she declared, hands on triumphant hips.

It was now two and Mr Docherty was picking her up. He'd wanted to stop on the way back for a cup of tea on the seafront, but she'd told him they didn't have time for that malarkey. 'He's all for stopping, Mr Docherty. He could stop for England, that one!' They were off to their caravan in Dorset the next day ...

Tamsin and Peter were now alone in Stormhaven Towers. The common room, such a theatre of emotion these past few days, seemed at peace, easy with the sunlight and the smell of coffee, furniture polish and bleach. The abbot was packed and ready to leave but Tamsin had said, 'Perhaps a quick catch-up?' There was awkwardness between them, the air full of the unresolved.

'Can I give you a lift?' asked Tamsin.

'That's kind. It would be helpful if you could take my bag and leave it by the door.'

'But not you.'

'Not me, no.'

'So what are you doing?'

'I need to walk before I can rest. I need to return to Loner's Wood, for a start ... and all that happened there.'

'And you need to go alone?'

'Of course.' He didn't mean it to sound quite so definite. 'And then I'll walk back via Stormhaven Head – it would be good to speak with Jamie ... and with Jennifer at Tide Mills.' He paused. 'Their ghosts must pass through me, but they haven't passed through yet.'

'No,' said Tamsin, with no understanding of his words. This was not her world or her way.

'And then perhaps some fish and chips on the way home,' said Peter, 'that will be good. We didn't have fish and chips in the desert. It's one of the happier aspects of my move to Stormhaven.'

A silence fell between them. Peter's words had merely been postponing it.

'I'm sorry,' said Tamsin.

'Sorry for what?'

'Not my finest hour. Though ...'

'Tamsin, you must do what you must do – until you stop doing it.' Tamsin's eyebrows were raised.

'What's that supposed to mean?'

'It means what it means.'

'Which is nothing.'

'But for now, I've had an adventure which I wouldn't have had but for you. Shall we leave it there for the present?'

Though Tamsin couldn't leave it there.

'So why did you think it was Cressida so early in the investigation? You said you knew.'

'It was Penny's phone. Why would the killer want to put the phone back in circulation, given that they had rendered it unusable? They could have got rid of it in a hundred different ways. So why didn't they? Why did they leave it in the common room? The only reason I could think of at the time was to point the finger of suspicion at one of those using the common room. Cressida was the only suspect who wasn't – she was living at home at the time.'

'Tenuous.'

'But strangely solid in the moment.' It was a reprimand. 'And then of course there was the overgrown garden we both witnessed.'

'When?'

'The initial interview. Seemed out of character for such an ordered person. And then Mr Thomas told me Dr Cutting was too snooty to have him work in her garden . . . but Gerry, his predecessor, had spent a lot of time there.'

'The one who died.'

'Of course – he'd found the aconite growing beneath the sycamore tree in the corner. It's quite a distinctive flower.'

'You mean she killed him?'

'I don't know. It could have been an accident, they do occur. Perhaps he didn't know what it was. But she certainly didn't want another gardener there. Given the choice of a well-kept garden or her precious aconite plants – well, that was easy, for one so intrigued by poison.'

They were leaving the common room as they spoke. Peter gave one last glance around before he closed the door. They walked to her car in silence. He opened the rear door and placed his bag on the back seat.

'We'll speak soon,' she said, getting into the car.

'We will,' said Peter.

And then she drove away from the flint walls of Stormhaven Towers.

Peter stood for a moment, watched her leave and then followed the car on foot, a solitary figure in habit and trainers. On reaching the school gate, beneath the gaze of the stone seagulls, another car pulled up alongside him, heading out into the world. He didn't recognize the young female driver. But he did know the two figures in the back.

'Can we give you a lift?' asked Holly, sitting alongside Crispin. 'My friend is driving us to her place for the night and then we're going travelling.'

'Travelling? Where to?' asked the abbot.

'We don't know,' said Holly.

'Then you won't be a needing a map.'

'We're rubbish with maps!'

'Speak for yourself,' said Crispin.

Peter smiled.

'Maps can be overrated. But I don't need a lift, thanks,' he said. 'I have a little journey of my own – on foot.'

'You're quite fit for an old man,' said Crispin.

'That's so gay,' said Holly.

Peter didn't quite know what to say.

'So go well, the two of you – I think you will. Trust the path and you'll be fine. It's a good world – though it does have its moments.'

'Goodbye then, Abbot!' said Holly. 'You're a really good drunk!'

'Cheers, Abbot!' said Crispin gruffly, as the car pulled out of the gates and away from the school, disappearing slowly down the lane . . . though Peter stayed awhile, by the side of the road, across from the grand school gates where Terence had . . .

'It was never God you had to worry about,' said Peter. 'It never is.'

He then set off towards Loner's Wood . . .